WEST TO
COMANCHE COUNTY

WEST TO
COMANCHE COUNTY

DOUG BOWMAN

A TOM DOHERTY ASSOCIATES BOOK
NEW YORK

WEST TO COMANCHE COUNTY

Copyright © 2000 by Doug Bowman

This book is printed on acid-free paper.

A Forge Book
Published by Tom Doherty Associates, LLC
175 Fifth Avenue
New York, NY 10010

www.tor.com

Forge® is a registered trademark of Tom Doherty Associates, LLC.

Library of Congress Cataloging-in-Publication Data

Bowman, Doug.
    West to Comanche County / Doug Bowman.
      p. cm.
    "A Tom Doherty Associates book."
    ISBN 0-312-86545-7
    1. Texas—Fiction. I. Title.

    PS3552.O875712 W47 2000
    813'.54—dc21   00-026471

First Edition: July 2000

Printed in the United States of America

0 9 8 7 6 5 4 3 2 1

For my Texas friends of long standing:
Jerry Dykes and Jess Hudson.

—Author

WEST TO
COMANCHE COUNTY

I

"I can't think of a single reason to keep putting it off, Ellie," Kirb Renfro was saying to his wife of six months. "The grass has long since turned green, and it'll last for another five or six months. That's a lot longer than it'll take us to get to Texas."

"I wouldn't know," Ellie said coolly. "I've never been to Texas."

"Neither have I!" her husband said, raising his voice. "I sure would like to go out there though, even if it is pretty plain that you wouldn't!"

Kirby Floyd Renfro and Ellie Mae Clemons had had one disagreement after another during their courtship, but this was the closest they had come to an argument since their marriage. Ellie gave a final stir to the cornmeal and water that she had been mixing in a clay bowl, then reached for a skillet. "Now, let's don't fight about this, Kirb," she said softly. "It's just that Texas is so far away, and I don't know anybody out there." She poured the bowl of corn-bread mix into the skillet and shoved it into the hot oven, then seated herself on her husband's lap. She pressed her lips against his ear. "If you've got your heart set on living in Texas, then I guess, by gosh, that's where we ought to be."

He kissed her and placed her back on her feet, then walked to the window and stood looking down the slope at his livestock. "The mules have eaten just about everything within reach of their picket ropes," he said. "I can't see the horse from here, but I imagine it's the same with him." He lifted his coat and his hat from a peg on the wall, then opened the squeaky door. "I'll go down and move 'em to new grass before it starts raining again." He stepped into the yard and headed down the slope.

Kirb Renfro appeared to be taller than his six-foot, two-inch stature, for at a 170 pounds, he had not yet filled out his big-boned, broad-shouldered frame. "You're due to start putting some meat on them bones any old time now," his uncle had said to him only last week. "Before it's over, you're gonna be the biggest Renfro by name."

Kirb smiled. "I don't guess there's anything wrong with that," he said. With coal black hair and eyes the color of a bright summer sky, he was a handsome young man who had almost been able to take his pick of the girls in the area. He had chosen Ellie Mae Clemons the first time he ever saw her, when she was only twelve years old. He informed her that same week that he intended to marry her someday, then kept his distance as she slowly developed into the most beautiful girl in Tipton County.

She not only had the prettiest face but was the most shapely, and Kirb Renfro was not the only young man who noticed. He was the only one she ever seriously considered, however; and when he formally asked her to be his wife, she eagerly accepted his proposal. Standing a foot shorter than her husband, with green eyes and light brown hair, today Ellie weighed about a hundred pounds and was still the most beautiful woman in the county.

Kirb and Ellie had both been raised in western Tennessee, and neither had ever been more than thirty miles from home. He had been too young for the fight during the Civil War, but his father had vainly devoted more than three years of his life to the Confederate cause.

Ellie's father had also been a soldier of the South and had died during the Battle of Nashville. She had been raised by her maternal grandmother, whose only daughter had died giving birth to Ellie. Lady Kerrington, as the grandmother was affectionately known by most folks in the area, had insisted that she be given custody of her granddaughter; and Ellie's father, Jed Clemons, having no earthly idea about how to care for an infant, had consented. The grandmother had wanted to adopt the girl after Jed Clemons was killed, but Ellie, who was twelve years old at the time, had refused to give up her dead father's name.

Kirb Renfro's father and mother had perished together last summer when the family home burned down with the couple inside. Kirb, who had been staying the night at the home of a man he was working for at the time, had taken their deaths especially hard, saying that if he had been sleeping at home, where he belonged, the smoke would have awakened him in time to save his parents' lives.

As time went on he gradually began to feel less guilt concerning the tragedy. He remembered hearing his father say many times that the heart pine lumber with which the house had been constructed was as "dry as a powder house" and would go up in a flash if fire and matches were not handled carefully. And his father's prediction had obviously been correct, for neighbors said that the dwelling was reduced to ashes in less than an hour.

After his uncle offered him the use of the cabin in

which he now lived, Kirb had married Ellie last fall, and the two had been living on the money he had inherited from his parents. The large wagon, the team of young mules, the farm equipment, the well-trained saddle horse, and the gun collection that had been left him were worth much more than the bank account contained, however.

The guns had not burned only because they were in a cabinet at the uncle's house. Kirb himself had taken them there a week before the fire so that they could be viewed by a prospective buyer. The buyer had made an offer shortly after the fire, but Kirb had refused to sell. He had changed his mind now, however. He would sell all of the farm equipment and most of the guns. He would keep a Henry rifle, a shotgun, and one of the Colt revolvers, and would sell the rest to the highest bidder. A neighbor had already looked the farm equipment over and had offered an acceptable price.

After Kirb had moved all three of his animals to new grass, he returned to the cabin. "We'll keep the mules, the wagon, the horse, and three guns," he said to Ellie. "Everything else is for sale." He looked around the cabin for a moment, then added, "We'll take all of our clothing and our bedding and, according to Uncle George, traveling folks ought to have a Dutch oven. While I'm on my rounds I'll be on the lookout for one of them." He took a seat at the table to await the hot buttered corn bread that he knew Ellie would soon be serving. "It depends on how long it takes me to sell all that stuff, but I'd bet we'll be on our way in about a week."

Ten days later, a covered wagon with a saddle horse tethered to the tailgate crossed the Mississippi River by ferry. With a Henry rifle, a ten-gauge shotgun, and a forty-four-caliber Colt revolver close to hand, Kirb and Ellie Renfro, he twenty years old and she eighteen, were finally on their way to Texas. The date was April 20, 1870.

After crossing the river into Arkansas, Renfro guided the mules onto what passed for a road and headed southwest. According to his map he would enter Texas at its northeast corner. And though he would have to use many different roads to get there, the map indicated that all were wide enough to accommodate wagon traffic. He expected to reach the Texas line in about twenty-one days.

George Renfro had offered plenty of suggestions, once he became fully convinced that his young nephew was pulling up stakes and heading west. Kirb had bolted a spare wheel on the side of the wagon as soon as his uncle mentioned it, then loaded a jack and an extra axle in the wagon bed. Then, continuing to heed his uncle's advice, he began to eliminate one article after another from the list of things he had originally intended to carry.

"The most important things are the mules, Kirb," Uncle George had said. "If you overload 'em, you won't ever get nowhere close to Texas. Every pound makes a difference. Don't carry a single thing you can do without, and you and Ellie oughta both get down and walk whenever you come to a real steep hill." He spat a mouthful of tobacco juice on a nearby rock, adding, "It's pretty easy to overwork a team before you realize it, son, so pay close attention to your animals. If you wear 'em completely out, it might take 'em a month or more to recuperate. Sometimes they never do."

The young couple respected George Renfro's judgment very highly, for both knew that the man had been to the other side of the mountain a few times. They continued to discard things till they were down to the bare necessities, and when they finally headed west their wagon was far from overloaded.

Aside from their bedrolls and a minimum amount of

clothing, they carried cooking and eating utensils and a two-months' supply of food. A medium-sized cardboard box held Ellie's toilet articles and Kirb's shaving gear, and a small barrel of water was attached to the side of the wagon. Uncle George had looked the load over and given his approval just before the wagon pulled out of the cabin yard.

And though the elder Renfro cautioned his nephew about the many dangers he might encounter while traveling, the warning was hardly necessary, for the young man had grown up during a violent period. Though neither Kirb nor Ellie had seen the violence firsthand, both had heard stories of defenseless people being waylaid and killed for their meager belongings.

Though Kirb Renfro was young and relatively inexperienced, he was hardly defenseless, for all three of his weapons were in excellent condition and he had an ample supply of ammunition. He had been introduced to guns at the age of eight and had been allowed to prowl the woods loaded for bear by the time he was ten. Consequently, he had become adept with both the long and the short gun by the time he reached his teens, and the years since had only served to sharpen his eye and quicken his reflexes.

During his growing years Kirb had been known as an excellent scrapper, and none of his schoolmates could recall ever seeing him lose a fight. It was not that he had ever had any encouragement or training regarding fisticuffs, but simply that he was exceptionally good at doing what came naturally. Though his many opponents had usually given other excuses to the teachers who sometimes broke up the scuffles, most of Kirb's fights with the boys had come about because he was liked by the girls. He had not had to fight a single time during the last year of his schooling, however, for by then the would-be bullies had all begun to give him a wide berth.

Kirb Renfro had never drawn a gun on another man but had no doubt that he would do so if it became necessary. He had long since decided that he would do whatever he had to do in order to protect himself and his beloved Ellie, and the small arsenal lying under his seat was within easy reach. The twelve-shot Henry rifle was ready for action, and both barrels of the shotgun were loaded with double-aught buckshot.

There were five shells in the cylinder of his six-shot Colt revolver, and the mere act of cocking the hammer would spin a round into the firing chamber. As he drove the wagon farther into Arkansas and began to meet more people, some in wagons or on horseback but most on foot, Kirb laid the Colt on the seat between himself and his wife, then covered it with an old shirt. He might never need it, he was hopefully thinking, but if he did, it was right under his hand.

At noon, they halted at a roadside spring and washed down ham and biscuits with the cold, sweet water. They allowed the animals to graze for an hour, then took to the road again. Although the area had received more than the normal amount of rain for the month of April, none had fallen during the past few days. The road was dry, but not dusty. As they topped a long hill, Kirb reached for the brake pole in order to keep the coasting wagon from forcing the mules into a run as they headed down the other side. "We couldn't have hoped for better traveling weather," he said, pointing to the cloudless sky.

"It's beautiful," Ellie said softly. "I've just been sitting here looking at the flowers. The way the violets and daffodils grow along both sides of the road looks just like they were planted there on purpose."

"Maybe they were," Kirb offered, suddenly knowing exactly what his highly religious mother would have said. "For all we know they might have been lined up along those ditches just so we'd have something pretty to look at."

"Maybe so," Ellie said. She was quiet for a few moments, then changed the subject. "We can keep traveling as late in the day as you want to. I won't need more than half an hour to make a pot of coffee and heat up some of those beans and cornmeal hoecakes I cooked yesterday. Fact is, if you can stand hoecakes and molasses for breakfast, we won't have to do any real cooking for a week."

He reached for her hand and brushed it with his lips. "I can stand anything you can, honey, and I'll eat whatever you dish up."

The sun was still an hour high, when they forded a shallow creek and pulled off the road. The ashes of several campfires scattered around the trunk of a large oak marked the area as a popular campground, and Kirb suspected that he would very soon have company if he selected this particular site. He passed up the tree and guided his team farther up the creek. He drove into the clearing for a hundred yards or so, then circled the wagon and brought it to a halt facing the road.

He set the brake and jumped to the ground, then walked around the wagon to assist his wife. "I'll rustle up some deadwood and get a fire going before I do anything else," he said. He pointed to the open field behind the wagon. "Look at all that green grass. These mules are liable to get fat and sassy between now and daylight." He jerked his thumb toward his black saddle horse. "Midnight's gonna appreciate it too."

By the time he returned with an armload of fuel, Ellie had unloaded everything she needed from the wagon. Kirb raked a small area clear of dead grass and anything else that might burn, then kindled a fire between two flat rocks. Then, as his wife began to prepare a meal, he unhitched and unharnessed the mules and led them to water.

Half an hour later, all three of his animals were picketed on long ropes. Moving them to new grass at least once before he went to sleep would be a simple matter, for there was not a cloud in the sky and the moon was already beginning to rise above the horizon. The big bright ball was a welcome sight, for its glow would provide plenty of light for him to keep an eye on his livestock once the sun disappeared.

When he returned to the fire, he was handed a tin plate and a hot cup of coffee. "When you get done eating your beans, I'll put some of that strawberry jam on your plate," Ellie said. "Seems like it oughtta go good on a hoecake while you're sipping an extra cup of coffee."

Kirb nodded and took a seat on the ground, crossing his legs. "I've eaten jam on a hoecake before, little one. It was good then, and it's gonna be good now." He sat waiting till Ellie filled her own plate and joined him, then he began to eat like there was no tomorrow.

Even as the Renfros ate their supper, two westbound covered wagons rolled around the curve and forded the creek. Drawn by teams of large draft horses, with a man and a woman sitting on the seat of each, the big vehicles pulled off the road and stopped under the big oak. As the men began to unhitch and unharness their animals, and the women started to scour the area for firewood, Kirb decided that the people were most likely harmless. From all appearances they were nothing more or less than two middle-aged men and their wives headed west with the hope of improving their lot.

Kirb watched as the men led their horses to water, then staked them out on good grass a hundred yards west of his own animals. The women had succeeded in finding fuel and were now busy preparing a meal. Kirb had just extinguished his own campfire and poured his third cup of coffee, when he saw one of the men walking in his direction. Renfro pulled the shirt hiding the Colt revolver a little closer to his hand.

Appearing to be about forty years old and wearing a battered felt hat and a shaggy, walrus mustache, the man stopped ten feet short of Kirb's fire. "Howdy, folks," he said with a high-pitched voice, "my name's Sam Allred. Y'all goin' to Little Rock?"

Renfro shook his head. "Farther west," he said.

"Farther west," Allred repeated. "All the way to Texas, I'll bet. I'll tell you one thing: If me an' th' wife were anywhere near as young as you two, we'd have been in Texas a long time ago." He pointed toward his own campfire. "That's my brother and his wife travelin' with us.

"One of our uncles has done right well over in Little Rock, and he's been after us for the past two years to come and join him. Last week we finally got up nerve enough to pull up stakes and go." He stood fidgiting for a moment, then spun on his heel and headed for his wagon. "I'm gonna eat supper and crawl into my bed-roll," he said over his shoulder. "You folks be careful now."

Once the man was out of earshot, Ellie turned to her husband. "What did you think of Mr. Allred?" she asked.

"I'm not sure," Kirb answered, "but it could be that he just wanted to look us over and see what kind of people he's sharing a campground with. He's probably as leery of strangers as I am."

Ellie squeezed his arm and got to her feet, then pulled a canvas tarp over the leftover food and cooking utensils. "All we'll have to do in the morning is reheat the hoecakes and coffee. There's a jar of molasses right here in this box under the tarp."

Kirb nodded, then motioned to the plates, spoons, and cups they had just used. "I'll walk down and wash those things up so I won't have to do it before breakfast," he said. He gathered up the utensils and headed for the creek with long strides.

Once the dishwashing chore was done, he walked out into the clearing and moved each of his animals to new grass. Then he returned to the campsite and boosted Ellie up into the wagon, climbing in behind her. All was quiet for the next hour, then Kirb jumped to the ground and spread his bedroll under the wagon. With his Henry and his Colt lying close to hand, he dozed off quickly.

2

★

The moon had long since disappeared when Kirb opened his eyes again, and although the night was as dark as pitch, he felt that he had slept long enough. He lay on his bedroll listening to the silence for several minutes, then spoke barely above a whisper, "Are you awake, Ellie?"

"Yes," she answered softly. "I've been awake for a long time."

He struck a match on the rim of a wheel, then looked at his watch. Seeing that it was already past four o'clock, he snuffed the match and crawled out from under the wagon. He lit the lantern and set it beside the small pile of firewood, then walked to the far side of the wagon to relieve himself. When he saw Ellie open the rear flap and dash the contents of her chamber pot to the ground, he knew that she too was up for the day.

He had already kindled a fire under half a pot of left-over coffee, when his wife joined him a few minutes later.

"It looks like it's breaking day back yonder in the east," she said. "I'll walk down to the creek and wash up while that fire burns down a little more; then I'll heat up some hoecakes for breakfast." She picked up the lantern and headed down the slope.

Kirb watched the glow of the lantern all the way to the creek; then he sat staring into the cook fire, thinking. He had no idea how far into Texas he would go before he decided to stop. Nor had he given much thought to what he would do when he got there, but he had read many times that there was always a job waiting in Texas for any able-bodied man who was willing to work. Kirb Renfro was not only willing to work, but he actually enjoyed what most men called backbreaking labor: physically exhausting toil that made him eat like a horse and sleep like a baby.

He already had a good team and wagon, and what he thought was enough money to buy a piece of land of his own. He expected to have enough left over to buy the plows and other tools he would need, as well as a shiny tin roof for the log home he had promised to build for his beautiful Ellie.

"Don't you go worrying about nothing, now," Uncle George had cautioned Kirb a few days ago. "Onliest damn thing that'll get you is a trip to the sickbed.

"From what I hear, Texas was built by young men like you, and I dare say that you're just as strong and just as smart as any of 'em. I reckon it's couples like you and Ellie that Texas needs most, folks who are still young enough and strong enough to raise a big family of Texans. You two just go on out there and see what happens. If you talk to a lot of people and keep your eyes and ears open, I'll guarantee you that something good's gonna fall right into your lap." Kirb Renfro had listened well and hung onto every word. Just as his uncle had suggested, he would be talking to a lot of people. And he would definitely be keeping his eyes and ears open.

Ellie returned from the creek and blew out the lantern. "I can fry up a few slices of bacon if you want me to," she said. "That fire looks to be just about right, now."

Kirb shook his head. "Hoecakes and molasses'll be good enough, honey." He poured two cups half full of coffee and handed one to Ellie. "The bacon'll keep for another day."

They had eaten their breakfast and were sipping the last of the coffee when Ellie offered an idea. "If you'd take your saddle and that sack of grain out of the wagon at night, there'd be enough room in there for you to sleep with me."

Kirb sat biting his lower lip for a few moments and was slow to answer. "I'd certainly like to, honey," he said finally, "but I don't think it's a very good idea. If somebody wanted to harm us, they could already be in the wagon with us before I knew they were anywhere around. Of course, I might not know it even with me sleeping outside, but I believe I stand a better chance that way."

Ellie squeezed his arm. "I'm sorry, Kirb," she said. "I don't know why all that never crossed my mind."

He dashed his coffee grounds aside and dropped the cup in the box then began to kick dirt over the fire. "There's already enough daylight for me to hitch up the team," he said. "The sun's gonna pop over that hill yonder before you know it, and I'd like to be on the road by then." He pointed to the wagons parked under the big oak, where there was as yet no sign of life. "Looks like Mr. Allred's bunch ain't figuring on rushing off this morning."

Ellie shook her head. "They don't have near as far to go as we do, so I guess they're not in a hurry." She motioned to the assortment of things on the ground. "Don't concern yourself with any of that stuff. I can wash up the utensils and load everything back in the wagon while you bring in Midnight and the mules."

As he walked into the meadow, the abundance of lush, green grass brought a smile to his lips. He would certainly not have to feed any grain as long as he could find this kind of graze, he was thinking. If the mules were allowed to spend ten or twelve hours a day on grass like this, they could pull the wagon to Texas with no problems whatsoever and probably even gain weight on the trip.

He watered all of the animals and tethered the horse to the rear of the wagon then harnessed and hitched up the mules. He took one last look around the campsite to make sure they were not forgetting anything, then climbed up on the wagon, where Ellie had already taken her seat. "Ready?" he asked.

"Ready," she answered.

Still having seen no sign of life among the Allreds since the night before, Kirb guided his team around their campsite. Once he was on the south side of their wagons he could see that Sam Allred was very much alive. Squatting on his heels while kindling a cook fire, the man waved as the Renfros pulled onto the road. The couple returned the greeting and continued on their way. Their wagon was soon out of sight.

They traveled steadily all morning. Today, as the day before, they had not walked up any of the hills, for none had been particularly steep, and the mules had at no time appeared to be in a strain.

They halted at a roadside spring shortly before noon. Kirb unhooked the trace chains and hung them on the hames, then, leaving the mules' harnesses intact, led them into the meadow and put them on their ropes. After picketing the horse on good grass, he returned to the wagon.

Ellie had built her own cook fire and was now busy making a pot of coffee and heating up more hoecakes and beans.

A short time later, the couple sat in the cool breeze enjoying a hot meal. "I've been hoping we'd come to a store or a trading post," Kirb said around a mouthful of food. He swallowed, then continued. "I reckon we can spare the price of some chicken eggs and some cheese, and maybe a little something to nibble on as we ride along."

Ellie smiled. "You mean something like candy or cookies?"

He nodded. "Whatever you want."

They allowed their animals to graze for a little over an hour, then were back on the road again. Though the mules were willing workers, Kirb allowed them to take their time, even used the brake to keep the wagon from pushing them into a trot each time they reached a downgrade.

They met no other traffic after leaving the spring, and at midafternoon came to a small settlement that a roadside sign identified as MOODY'S CROSSROADS. After traveling another hundred yards and coming to a halt in front of a general store, neither of them was surprised to read that a man named Moody was the proprietor of the establishment. Kirb climbed down and tied the mules to the hitching rail, then helped his wife to the ground. "Just take a look at what they've got, honey. If you see something you want, all you have to do is say so. We've got money."

Made of rough lumber and having a rusty tin roof, the store appeared to be the oldest building in the community. It had a small front porch almost at ground level and a flimsy wooden awning that sagged at one corner. A tall, silver-haired woman, who had no doubt heard their wagon pull in, was standing in the doorway. She took a few steps backward as they approached, allowing them to enter. "Good afternoon," she said softly, then turned on a broad, commercial smile. "Is there something I can do for you?"

His first glance about the room convinced Renfro that the establishment was well stocked, and the second told him that the lady would probably have about anything a man might need. The walls, left, right, and rear, exhibited hundreds of small articles, and clothing, shoes, and bolts of cloth occupied one of the aisles. Another contained mostly hardware, and the two center aisles were devoted to household goods and groceries. Renfro returned the lady's smile. "I don't suppose we know exactly what we want yet," he said. "Can we just look around while we decide?"

"Absolutely," the lady said. "I ain't in no hurry. I'll still be here after dark for that matter, 'cause I do an awful lot of my trading after the sun goes down. People have to work all day, so I just light the lamps and do business with 'em at night."

She moved behind the counter and remained there for quite some time, rejoining the Renfros only after she was asked to do so. "I'm thinking about buying some of this canned fish," Kirb said, holding a tin of sardines in his hand. "How in the world do you open 'em?"

"With one of these," the lady answered, handing him a one-piece can opener. "You just puncture the edge of the can with that sharp point, then slice through the tin with that little blade."

Kirb stood looking the small implement over, turning it from side to side. "Well, I'll be doggone," he said finally, then pointed to the shelf. "Give us two cans of beef, two cans of the pork, two cans of the fish, and two pounds of that Bologna sausage back yonder."

The lady began to box up his order. "How about beans and potatoes?" she asked. "You got plenty of those?"

Kirb nodded. "Yes, ma'am," he said, "all we need for now. I reckon we will take three dozen eggs, though, and about two pounds of that cheddar cheese." He turned to Ellie. "I'll leave the choosing of the sweet stuff to you."

She smiled and wrinkled her nose, then headed for the front of the store, where a large rack displayed cookies, candy, and chewing gum. After making her choices, she stood waiting to point out her selections to the store-keeper.

The Renfros stayed in the store for the large part of an hour, and although they had spent almost three dollars, neither had any regrets. Ellie was looking forward to a plate of scrambled eggs and Bologna sausage in the morning, and Kirb couldn't wait to try out his can opener.

The road led into a heavily forested area, and twice during the afternoon the Renfros got down and walked up steep hills to lessen the strain on the team. After crossing a shallow stream about an hour before sunset, Kirb found a relatively level place and pulled off among the hardwoods. He set the brake and jumped to the ground. "No use trying to go any farther this day," he said. "It'll be dark by the time I take out these animals and feed 'em." He made a sweep toward the forest with his arm. "I'll have to put the nose bags on 'em, 'cause there sure ain't nothing growing out there for 'em to eat. Too much shade."

Ellie climbed to the ground unassisted. "I'll hunt up some fuel and build a fire," she said. "I might even have some supper stirred up by the time you get done taking care of Midnight and the mules."

Kirb opened the tailgate and reached inside the small cardboard box the storekeeper had provided. "Let me open a can of these sardines for you; then I'll go on about my business." He punctured the top of the can with the sharp point, then registered surprise at how easily the blade sliced through the tin. "How about that?" he said, dropping the opener back in the box and handing the open can to his wife. "Ain't that something?"

Ellie answered the question with a broad smile.

Kirb hung a nose bag half full of shelled corn on the horse's head, then tied the animal to a low-hanging limb a few yards away. When he had unhitched and unharnessed the mules, he put on their nose bags and tied them a little closer to the wagon. "I'll take 'em all to water after they get done eating," he said to Ellie; "then I'm gonna leave 'em standing right where they are for the rest of the night. No use putting 'em on pickets 'cause there ain't no grass out there. Ain't gonna be none till after we get out of this thick timber."

"Maybe we'll get out of it tomorrow," Ellie said. Pulling the coffeepot off the fire, she changed the subject. "This stuff's ready to drink, and I've done fixed you a plate."

Moments later, he seated himself cross-legged beside the fire and accepted the plate, which contained a generous helping of beans, several slices of cheese, and the entire can of sardines. "Hey," he said quickly, "you gave me all of the fish. Take some of it yourself."

She shook her head, and joined him on the ground. "I'd never be able to get past the smell," she said. "I'm having beans, Bologna sausage, and cheese."

They ate their supper quietly, then both drank an extra cup of coffee. A few minutes before dark, Kirb took the nose bags off the animals and led them to the creek for water. When he returned to the fire, he kicked dirt over the coals, then reseated himself. He pointed off into the trees. "We could just take our bedrolls out there in the woods and sleep together," he said. "We wouldn't have to go no more than twenty yards to be out of sight, and I could still keep an eye on the wagon and the livestock."

She giggled. "You gonna keep the boogers off of me?"

He nodded. "Absolutely. We need to get out there before it gets too dark to find a good place, too. The moon'll be up in a little while; then we can see without being seen."

Just as darkness settled in, they headed into the woods with their bedrolls. Kirb carried the double-barreled shotgun in the crook of his arm, and the Colt revolver was tucked behind his waistband. He found what he was looking for in less than two minutes: a level spot between two clumps of leafy bushes. He broke off the few branches that hampered his view of the wagon and the livestock, then spread the bedrolls side by side. He undressed Ellie, then himself, then pulled her to him tightly. He ran his hands over her curvaceous body and kissed her hungrily several times, then slowly lowered her to the bedrolls.

They were still making love like only young couples can when the moon came up more than an hour later. Finally, with both their passion and their energy spent, they moved apart and covered themselves with the blanket. Ellie was asleep almost instantly, and Kirb was not far behind. He took one last look at the wagon and the livestock, then slept soundly.

3

★

Daybreak found Kirb and Ellie sitting beside their camp-fire eating Bologna sausage and scrambled eggs, while their animals stood nearby crunching shelled corn. Kirb poured himself a second cup of coffee, then washed down a mouthful of food, saying, "I ain't gonna say nothing bad about hoecakes and molasses, honey, 'cause I know lots of families have been raised on 'em. What I am saying is that this sausage and eggs goes down a whole lot easier. I don't believe anybody else could have fixed 'em any bet-ter'n you did either."

Ellie smiled. "The sausage was already cooked, and there sure ain't nothing hard about scrambling a skilletful of eggs. I'm glad you like it though 'cause you earned a good breakfast." She set her cup on the ground, then squeezed his arm. "Last night was the best it's ever been for me, big fellow."

Kirb smiled, then chuckled softly. "I'd like to repeat it some time, but I might have a problem remembering exactly what I did." He dashed his coffee grounds over his shoulder, then leaned forward and pecked her on the cheek. "I'll hitch up the team while you break camp; then we'll be on our way again." He got to his feet and kicked dirt over the fire. He watered the animals at the creek, then led one of the mules to its harness, which lay on the ground beside the wagon tongue.

Half an hour later, the wagon was once again rolling west. There had been no other traffic going in either direction this morning, and Ellie mentioned the fact. "Maybe people in this part of the country just don't move around as much as folks in Tennessee do," she said.

"I read about a month ago that Arkansas is a whole lot bigger'n Tennessee," Kirb said, "but they ain't got even half as many people. Maybe that's the reason there ain't much traffic on this road."

Kirb had just finished speaking when a buggy traveling in the opposite direction came over the hill. Two hundred yards away and being drawn by what appeared to be a matching pair of roans, the vehicle was moving at a fast trot. Kirb pulled his own wagon as close to the ditch as he dared, then brought the mules to a halt.

The buggy continued on down the hill at the same pace, with the driver making no effort whatsoever to slow the vehicle down. Finally, the Renfros would have been eye to eye with the man had it not been for the fact that he kept his eyes on the road. Dressed in bib overalls, flannel shirt and straw hat, and appearing to weigh at least three hundred pounds, the driver completely ignored the couple and passed so close to their wagon that Ellie shrieked and covered her eyes with her hand.

Kirb had not covered his own eyes and knew that the only reason the wheels of the two vehichles had not collided was because their hubs were of different heights. Never once acknowledging the presence of their wagon, the beefy man had continued to whip his team, burying the Renfros in a cloud of dust. "I oughtta shoot that stupid son of a bitch off of that damned buggy seat!" Kirb said loudly. "Inconsiderate bastard!"

"No, you shouldn't!" Ellie said just as loudly. "And please don't talk that way." She was quiet till the wagon was moving again, then added, "You were right about that man being inconsiderate though. Scared the daylights out of me."

Kirb kept his eyes on the road ahead. "Stupid son of a bitch!" he repeated.

Two more days of travel brought them to the L'Anguille River, which they forded an hour before sunset. Though the most suitable campsite on the west bank was already occupied by two oversized covered wagons, Kirb nonetheless pulled his team off the road, for the animals had put in a long, hard day. He walked around the wagon and helped Ellie to the ground, then stood for a few moments sizing up the people with whom he would be sharing the campground.

Two middle-aged men and two boys who appeared to be in their teens were seated beneath the canopy of a nearby oak, while two women labored at the cook fire. Even as Kirb watched, one of the men got to his feet and walked over to meet him.

While the man was more than two inches shorter than Renfro, he had a very muscular build and probably weighed at least twenty pounds more. He had large, brown eyes, and a full shock of brown hair tinged with gray covered his hatless head. "Hope our presence don't bother you young folks none," he said, with the reverberation of his deep voice sounding somewhat like an echo. "Me and the boys can push one of our wagons out of the way to give you a little more room if you need it."

Kirb shook his head. "That won't be necessary," he

said. "We've got as much room as we need."

The man offered a handshake. "My name's Gaylord Browning," he said, "and I just left Memphis three days ago." He pointed to the others. "That's my brother, Dossy, under the tree there, and the women are our wives." He chuckled, then pointed again. "Me and my brother each claim one of them boys."

Kirb grasped Browning's hand and returned the firm grip. "I'm Kirb Renfro," he said, "and this is my wife, Ellie. We're from Tipton County, Tennessee."

Browning released Kirb's hand and bowed slightly to Ellie. "You're from Tipton County?" he asked. "Lord, I was born and raised there. I was already grown and married when I moved to Shelby County." He stood smiling for a moment, then continued, "You folks came along at just the right time, and there ain't no use in the world in you having to mess around with a cook fire tonight. We've got more'n enough food for everybody, and I believe it's about time to eat." He turned and called to one of the women. "Dig out some more plates and cups, Bess! We're gonna have company for supper!"

The Renfros stood looking at each other for a few moments. "What do you think, Ellie?" Kirb asked finally.

She shrugged. "We'll eat with them if you want to," she answered. "I wasn't exactly looking forward to hunting up deadwood and cooking supper anyway."

Kirb nodded to Browning. "Sounds like we're gonna accept your invitation, sir, and we certainly appreciate it."

"No thanks necessary," Browning said, "and there ain't no reason for you to call me sir. Gaylord will be fine."

"Yes, sir," Kirb said.

When one of the women called out that supper was being served, Kirb said to Ellie, "Go on up and get yourself a plate of food. I'll be along after I take care of the animals."

"No," Ellie said quickly. "I'll help you with the chores; then we'll eat supper together."

Kirb nodded to his wife, then spoke to Browning. "We'll join you at the fire after a while," he said.

Browning smiled. "Take all the time you need," he said. "The wife'll warm something up for you whenever you're ready to eat. You're the first man I've met in a long time who's willing to let his own supper get cold while he's feeding his livestock, and I reckon that's worth remembering. Yes, sir, I admire you a right smart for that." He turned and headed for the cook fire.

Ellie untied the horse from the rear of the wagon, then stood waiting while Kirb unhitched and unharnessed the mules. That done, they led the three animals to water, then picketed them a hundred yards across the meadow. There would be no need for their nose bags tonight; they were out of the heavy timber now, and green grass was plentiful.

As Kirb pushed the last picket pin into the earth, he pointed to Browning's horses a short distance away. "Some mighty good-looking horseflesh out there," he said. "Eight of those big draft horses, and I reckon the three smaller ones would be saddlers." He stood shaking his head for a moment, his eyes glued to the powerful animals yearningly. "I'll bet a steep hill don't slow the Brownings down one bit. Not with them using four-horse hitches of animals that size."

Ellie put one of her hands over his eyes playfully, pulling on his arm with the other. "Quit looking at them," she said. "Your day is coming. You've already got a good start in life, and you're not even half as old as Mr. Browning. One of these days you'll be able to buy a whole herd of strong horses like those."

He smiled and allowed her to lead him toward the Brownings' campfire. "I sure like the sound of that," he said.

When the couple reached the fire, Gaylord Browning got to his feet and spoke to the others. "Listen up, everybody, while I introduce you to these nice folks. This good-looking young fellow's name is Kirb Renfro, and his pretty little wife's name is Ellie. They're from Tipton County." Then he nodded toward one of the women at the fire. "That's my wife, Bess, and the lady beside her is her sister, Carrie."

He motioned to the man sitting with his back leaning against a wagon wheel. "That's my brother, Dossy, and he's married to Carrie. You see, me and him married sisters, so that makes them two boys over there double first cousins. Their names are Bert and Bart, and they're both fifteen years old. Bert belongs to Bess and me. That's him sitting on the end of that log."

Once everyone had been introduced by name, the Brownings took turns shaking hands with the Renfros. Dossy, who was somewhat shorter and appeared to be a few years younger than Gaylord, was also of a muscular build and had the same brown eyes and salt-and-pepper hair as his brother. He shook Kirb's hand, then nodded to Ellie. "It's nice to meet you both," he said, with a deep voice that apparently ran in the family. "Fact is, it's always a pleasure to meet anybody from Tipton County."

His wife, Carrie, was next, and she neither nodded nor shook hands. Making eye contact with both of the Renfros, she simply said, "Nice to meet you," and moved on. Appearing to be about forty years old, she was almost as tall as her husband and had the same brown hair that was in the process of turning gray.

Bess, who was still standing at the fire, waved her ladle at the couple. "I reckon you folks would rather have food than a handshake, so I'll wait and bring you something to eat when I come." She was a little shorter than her sister, and the deep wrinkles on her face and the milky white color of her hair suggested that she was several years older. She offered a broad smile, then turned back to the fire and the business at hand.

The boys, both brown haired and bearing a strong resemblance to each other, stood about five-foot-seven, and each had the beginnings of a dark mustache on his upper lip. Bert, then Bart, shook hands with Kirb and smiled at Ellie then reseated themselves on the log.

A short time later, Kirb and Ellie sat side by side eating smoked ham, fried potatoes, brown beans, and corn bread, washing it all down with strong coffee. Just as they thought they were done eating, the lady named Bess delivered a plate containing a thick slice of pound cake to each of them. "I don't know where I'm gonna put this, dear lady," Kirb said, "but it looks entirely too good to pass up."

Bess nodded. "Seems like it turned out pretty good," she said, then walked back to the fire.

When the Renfros had finished eating and deposited their utensils in the dishpan, Gaylord poured himself a cup of coffee and sat down beside Kirb. "So," he began, then took a sip and wiped his mouth with the heel of his hand, "just where is it that you folks are headed to?"

Kirb emptied his own cup and dashed the grounds aside. "It's probably gonna sound silly to a man like you, Mr. Browning, but the truth of the matter is that we don't know where we're going. I've heard and read about Texas for most of my life and always thought I'd like to live there.

"I didn't see no use in hanging around Tipton County after Ma and Pa died, so right after I married Ellie I started on her about us heading west. She finally agreed to it, so here we are. I reckon we'll just keep moving till we get to a place we like or maybe find someplace that likes us. It'll have to be in Texas though. I want to live somewhere in Texas."

"That's where we're headed," Browning said. "Ain't none of us ever been there either, but it's beginning to look like we might spend the rest of our lives there. Our uncle, who owned a ranch in Comanche County, died right after the first of the year; and his lawyer says he left everything to us. The lawyer was the executor of Uncle Wash's will, and he started sending us papers of one kind or another way back in February.

"Now we didn't just up and sign no buncha stuff. We had our own lawyer read it all. He told us that Walt Rubin, the Texas lawyer, was doing everything above-board and by the book, and he advised us to go along with it. Now Rubin says he's ready to turn the ranch over to us once and for all, so he can get on with something else. Said he'd even send us some traveling money if we needed it."

Kirb sat staring between his knees for a while. "A ranch, huh?" he asked finally. "A big ranch? One with cattle on it?"

Browning nodded. "According to all the stuff Rubin has sent us, it consists of twenty-seven sections and runs about eighteen-hundred head of longhorns."

Renfro emitted an audible sigh. "Twenty-seven sections," he repeated softly, almost as if talking to himself. "Nearly two thousand head of cattle." He shook his head slowly, then added, "I'll bet it takes a whole slew of men to ride herd on that many cows."

Browning shook his head. "Evidently it don't take as many as us easterners might have thought. According to the lawyer, there are only ten men living on the ranch, and that includes the cook and the foreman, a man named

Bo Ransom. Rubin says Ransom knows the ranch better than any man alive and might even have names for half of the cows. Rubin also says I'd be smart to keep the foreman, no matter what I decide to do about the other hands." He absentmindedly flipped a small stone at the trunk of the large oak, missing by a wide margin. "Ransom was handpicked by Uncle Wash a long time ago, so one of the first things I done was send him word not to go packing his bags."

"Sounds like a wise decision to me," Kirb said. He bent over and retied his shoelace, then added, "Yes, sir, since you probably don't know any more about cattle ranching than most Tennesseans do, I'd say hanging on to your uncle's foreman was smart."

"It was the only thing that made sense to me," Browning said. "Of course, I've owned a few cows in my time, but I've heard that a fellow has to forget most of what he knows about cattle when he starts dealing with longhorns. That's what a man at the courthouse in Memphis told me, and he claims to have lived in Texas for a long time."

Kirb was quiet for a while. "I wouldn't know," he said finally. "I don't reckon I've ever even seen a longhorn."

Nothing else of importance was said during the next several minutes, and the conversation eventually died on its own. First the Renfros, then the Brownings, headed for their bedrolls and slept the night away.

When Kirb crawled out from under his wagon an hour before daybreak next morning, he saw that the Browning campfire had already been rekindled. A closer inspection showed Gaylord sitting in the glow with a coffee cup in his hand. Kirb walked into the darkness to relieve himself, then joined the older man at the fire. "Good morning," Browning said, making an obvious effort to speak softer than usual.

Kirb returned the greeting, then Browning continued

to talk, pointing to a wooden box. "Get a cup outta there and pour yourself some coffee."

Kirb did as he was told, then took a seat on the ground. "Did you get a good night's sleep?" he asked.

Browning nodded. "As good as I ever do," he said. "The older I get, the less sleep I seem to need. About five or six hours nowadays, and both of my eyes pop wide open."

"I've heard other men with a few years on 'em say that," Kirb said. "Women, too, for that matter."

Browning sat quietly for a while, then walked to the fire and refilled his cup. That done, he seated himself directly in front of Kirb, then began to speak even softer. "I spent most of the early part of the night thinking about you two young folks," he said. "You say you don't know where you want to live, so I'd suggest that you keep going till you get to Comanche County. Of course, you don't know me very well, but my word is my bond, and I certainly ain't gonna let no good-looking couple from Tipton County starve.

"You've probably thought about and maybe even planned on having a big place of your own, but a fellow has to crawl before he can walk. Now, I've never even talked to my foreman in person, but if I ask him to hunt up a job for you on the Lazy Bee, I have no doubt that he'll find one. Would you accept a job as a ranch hand?"

Kirb nodded, then chuckled. "I couldn't find work of any kind back home, so accepting a job on a cattle ranch would be an easy thing for me to do. The hard part might be getting Mr. Ransom to accept me 'cause, like I said before, I don't think I've ever even seen a longhorn."

"We won't worry about that 'cause there was a time when Mr. Ransom had never seen one either. You can learn on the job, just like the foreman himself probably had to do." He sat biting his lower lip for a moment, then added, "I don't know what kind of housing setup the ranch has, but we'll build a place for you and Ellie to live if we need to." He finished off his coffee. "How does all that sound to you, Kirb?"

"It sounds good," Kirb answered. "It sounds like I might finally be headed to a particular place for a particular reason. There ain't no way in the world that I can get there when you do though." He pointed out across the dark meadow toward Browning's picketed livestock. "Those big horses of yours'll walk nearly twice as fast as my mules do."

"I already thought about that," Browning said. "I can't hold the horses down below their natural gait 'cause it would ruin 'em, and if you try to speed up your mules, you'll wear 'em out pretty quick.

"What I intend to do is just keep moving till I get to Comanche County, and you can come on at your own pace. When you get to the town of Comanche, just hunt up my attorney, Walt Rubin. I'll make sure he knows who you are and tell him to be expecting you. I understand that his office is right in the center of town, so you can't miss it. You think you can find the town all right?"

"Yes, sir," Kirb answered. "I've already seen it on my map."

Browning nodded, and lowered his voice even more. "You folks got enough traveling money?"

"Yes, sir. We left home with a decent stake."

The encampment came alive a short time later, and the Browning women insisted that the Renfros join them for breakfast. The meal was eaten in relative silence, and the fact that Renfro would soon be working on Browning's Lazy Bee Ranch was not mentioned again by either party.

It was only after the Renfro wagon was on the road, with the Browning vehicles ahead and already out of sight, that Kirb informed his wife that he had accepted a job as a ranch hand. He slowly and deliberately described his earlier conversation with Gaylord Browning.

"Do you know anything about that kind of work?" Ellie asked after a while.

"Nope. But Mr. Browning says I don't have to. He says I can learn on the job just like everybody else does."

She squeezed his arm. "You can learn anything, Kirb."

4

The Renfros traveled uneventfully for the next ten days; then the rain came. It began with a sudden cloudburst at midmorning, then gradually settled down to a slow drizzle that continued throughout the remainder of the day. When the day was gone Kirb parked close to a medium-sized oak, then stretched a tarpaulin between the wagon and the tree. Because they had been carrying a small amount of deadwood in the wagon, they made coffee and heated up their food without difficulty. At bedtime, Kirb put the grain sack and his saddle under the tarp, then slept in the wagon with Ellie.

When he awakened next morning to the sound of rain on the canvas, he knew that traveling was about to become a little more difficult. He raised the flap and poked his hand outside, then spoke to Ellie. "It's still coming down," he said. "Don't look like it's gonna let up anytime soon either."

He slipped on his pants and shoes, then raised himself

up to his knees. "I'm about as hungry as a wolf, honey, so I'm gonna hunt up some kindling. I'll take the ax and try to find a pine log that's been on the ground for a while. Heart pine burns fairly well even when it's wet."

He put on his coat and hat, then stepped to the ground. "I'll try to find a good one and snake it back to camp with one of the mules before I chop it up, then we'll put a bunch of it in the wagon so we won't have to go through this again. I don't believe the weather's gonna change much within the next few days, and I can think of a whole lot of things I'd rather be doing than hunting kindling in the rain." Moments later, he leaned his ax against the wagon, then headed for the grazing mules with a bridle in his hand.

His idea of carrying a pile of kindling in the wagon proved to be a good one, for the rain fell continually for the next three days and nights. And although traveling at such a time was something less than hazardous, the mud nonetheless created numerous problems. Having to pull the wagon over a berm each time it slid out of the main rut put a considerable strain on the mules, and more than once one of the animals lost its footing and fell to its knees on the slippery surface.

On the morning of the third day the team balked at a shallow, fast-moving creek. Even after Kirb measured the stream with a pole and assured himself that it was no more than two feet deep, he was still unable to get the mules to budge. It was only after he decided to wade the water and lead the animals by their bridles, that they leaned into their collars and pulled the wagon across. He climbed back up to his wet seat, then spoke to Ellie, who had been sitting behind him under the canvas all morning. "It's gonna get worse, honey," he said. "You can just count on that."

"I know," she said. "Maybe we should just stop somewhere and wait it out."

"I expect that'll be our only choice before it's over. We'll keep moving for now, but I believe we're gonna have to stop eventually."

And they did have to stop. The rain ceased and the sun came out early next morning, but the damage had been done. When they topped a hill within seeing distance of the Ouachita River just before noon, Kirb knew immediately that they would go no farther this day. "Look at that, Ellie," he said, pointing down the slope. "That river's liable to be out of its banks before sundown. See all those wagons parked on both sides waiting to cross? The folks on the west bank are gonna be all right, but that water's gonna be all over the ones on this side before the night's over. They'd better get their asses back up this hill a-ways."

Ellie squeezed his arm. "Don't talk that way, Kirb."

He drove the mules off the road and brought them to a halt in a level area, then jumped to the ground and helped his wife down. He pointed down the hill toward the river again. "Yep, those people had better get out of that damn hole while they can." He unhooked trace chains from singletrees, then began to unharness the team.

Ellie walked to the rear of the wagon and untied Midnight. She led the animal to the front of the vehicle and retied it to a wheel, then opened the tailgate and removed the things she would need for preparing a meal. With a handful of pine kindling and an armload of dry oak, she had a cook fire going between two smooth rocks in short order. She emptied all three of their canteens into the coffeepot and added a handful of grounds, then set it aside. She would wait for the fire to burn down some, then set the pot on the rocks above the hot coals. The coffee would be ready to drink a short time later.

Once he had unhitched and unharnessed his animals, Kirb had to lead them no more than thirty yards to good graze. The level area around his campsite obviously held moisture well and was consequently blanketed with lush, green grass. He picketed all three of his animals on forty-foot ropes, then followed the smoke back to his wife's cook fire.

"That coffee's done," Ellie said, as he seated himself on the ground. "I took it off the fire to keep it from getting too bitter to drink. The cups are in that box over there."

Kirb shook his head. "I reckon I'll just wait till you get dinner done. I've about decided that drinking coffee right before a meal interferes with my appetite a little bit."

"It probably does," Ellie said, turning a hoecake in the skillet with a spatula. "I've known for a long time that it cuts down on the amount of food I eat."

They were soon eating ham, beans, and cornmeal hoecakes. Even as Kirb seated himself, he noticed a man leave one of the wagons down below and begin to walk up the slope. The couple continued eating quietly, and Kirb was on his second plate of beans by the time the man reached their fire. "Howdy," Kirb said, pointing to the blackened pot. "Plenty of ham and beans there if you're hungry. That coffee's still hot too."

The man shook his head. "No, thank you," he said. "I done my eating more'n an hour ago." Slender, and of medium height, the man had blond hair and a ruddy complexion and appeared to be about thirty years old. His red flannel shirt, straw hat, and brogans had seen better days, and short suspenders held his pants up to an indeterminate waistline that was apparently located somewhere near his armpits. "I just walked up here to see what kind of ideas you might have," he said. He squatted on his heels and pointed down the hill. "What're we gonna do about all that doggone water?"

Kirb continued to chew a mouthful of food while he pondered the question, trying to decide whether or not it actually deserved an answer. He took a sip of coffee, then set the cup on the ground. "Do you think there's anything we can do about it?" he asked.

The man straightened up to his full height. "I don't know," he said, "but I'm in a hurry. I've gotta get across that river."

Kirb walked to the fire and filled his plate for the third time. He broke off half a hoecake, then reseated himself. "The only way I know to answer your question, mister, is to tell you that all I intend to do is sit down and wait. I thought I was in a hurry too till I saw all that water down there. One look at that, and I changed my mind. I don't reckon I could ever get in enough of a hurry to tackle that river."

The man stood staring down the hill quietly for a few moments. "Well, I can't just sit around here and wait," he said finally. "I'm getting married the day after tomorrow. The wedding's set to take place twenty miles west of here, so I've got to cross that river. I've got a mighty strong team, and my wagon's empty. I believe it'll float long enough to reach the west bank, and I aim to give it a try. If I don't do it today, I'll certainly be crossing it in the morning." He turned and headed back down the hill.

"I believe you'd be smart to wait a few days!" Kirb called after him.

The man walked on and never looked back.

"Do you believe his wagon'll float across that river?" Ellie asked after the man was out of earshot. "Do you believe a strong team can pull it across?"

"Nope."

"Do you think he's gonna lose his wagon then? Maybe his team too?"

"Yep. He'll be lucky if he saves himself."

She got to her feet quickly. "Well, there must be something we can do. He's trying to get to his own wedding."

Kirb shook his head. "He ain't gonna be marrying nobody unless he gets his ass back up here and waits for that water to run off, but there ain't no way to save a man from his own ignorance, Ellie. If he's made up his mind to buck that current, I reckon he'll do it, and I certainly can't stop him. You heard me advise him against it, and that's all I can do. Anyway, it might be better if he drowns before he gets married. If he's stupid enough to fight that river right now, I believe he'll eventually figure out some way to make his wife a widow."

"You make it sound so . . . so cold. So heartless."

Kirb dropped his empty cup in the box. "I don't mean to sound that way, honey, but life itself is cold and heartless; and the cost of even a small mistake can sometimes be mighty high. People live or die by the decisions they make, and I believe that's why the good Lord gave 'em a brain to reason with.

"Now the fellow who just left here ain't using his noggin. That woman he's rushing off to marry knows it's been raining, and she knows the river's up. She'll wait for him till next week and be just as willing to marry him then as she is now." He kicked dirt over the fire to save the fuel for another time. "It reminds me of something I've heard Uncle George say more'n once: He says that nobody on earth is truly in a hurry. He says we're all headed for the same place, and not a damn one of us has any control over when we get there."

Ellie managed a faint smile. "Uncle George said that?"

"Every chance he got."

She got to her feet. "I reckon it sounds like something he'd say." She walked to the wagon and returned with two wooden buckets. "Maybe you should go down to the river and get some water," she said. "It's gonna be muddy, but most of the dirt'll settle to the bottom of the buckets by suppertime."

Kirb accepted the buckets, then headed down the hill at a brisk pace. A few minutes later he knelt on the riverbank and filled the receptacles with the murky liquid, then straightened up to take stock of his surroundings. He could see that the five wagons on the west bank were far enough up the hill to be safe from the rising water, but the four vehicles on the east side were all parked on treacherous terrain.

As he eyed the small herd of mules and horses grazing a short distance away, he once again began to wonder why the travelers did not hitch up their wagons and move back up the hill. Looking into the strong current and swirling eddies of the swollen stream also made him think of the man he had talked with earlier. Would the man really attempt to cross the river? Surely not, Kirb decided quickly. The man had seemed to think that the lightness of his empty wagon would make the crossing easier, but Renfro thought the opposite was true. He believed that an empty wagon would remain up in the current instead of settling to the bottom, creating an insurmountable amount of drag on even the strongest of draft teams.

Hoping the man would rethink the situation and put his wedding off for a few days, Kirb waved to a family standing beside one of the wagons, then picked up his buckets and walked back to his campsite. He spent the next hour going over his map and trying to determine the distance between his current location and his destination. After finally deciding that he was not even halfway there, he put the map back in the wagon and made another pot of coffee.

As the afternoon wore on, Kirb and Ellie sat beside the expired campfire discussing the home they intended to build and the little Renfros they hoped to have someday.

They had expressed their mutual desire for children long before they were married, and now that they had been sleeping together for almost a year and doing nothing to prevent a pregnancy, Kirb was becoming concerned. "You still think it's gonna happen?" he asked.

She squeezed his arm. "Of course, it will. Sometimes it takes years, but if people just go on about their business and quit worrying about it, it nearly always happens. And once you get the first one, it seems like they just keep coming."

"Well, then, ma'am," he said, chuckling. "I'd like to order up two boys, if you don't mind. With them pulling a big crosscut saw and their old man swinging an ax, a lot of timber could be harvested in a day."

"What if they happen to be girls?"

He laughed. "I'll get a smaller saw."

An hour before sunset Kirb rekindled the cook fire, then moved out of his wife's way. It was then that he noticed the people beside the river hitching up their teams. "It looks like they're gonna move their wagons, Ellie," he said. "I reckon they might be a little bit smarter'n I thought."

"They probably intended to move 'em all along," Ellie said, as she mixed a panful of flour dough to make fritters. "It could be that you just don't give people enough credit."

Kirb thought on his wife's words for a while, then admitted to himself that she might be right. Had he drifted into the habit of worrying too much about other people's business? Maybe he should just concentrate on looking out for Ellie and himself and limit his opinions to matters directly concerning them. He nodded at his thoughts, then spoke over his she shoulder. "Thank you, honey," he said.

Ellie staightened up from the fire. "Thank me for what?"

"Thank you for reminding me that I don't know everything."

"Just trying to help," she said, then went back to work.

Kirb sat watching as the men drove the wagons up the hill in his direction. When they were about a hundred yards from the river and had gained at least a dozen feet in elevation, they pulled off the road on the north side and parked in a straight line facing the river. The drivers jumped to the ground and chocked the wheels, then began to unhitch their teams.

Once their draft animals were staked out, all four of the men walked back down the hill and brought up their saddle horses. After picketing them in the vicinity of Kirb's mules, the men passed in close proximity to his campsite on the way back to their wagons. With the exception of the man who was concerned about getting to his wedding, they all appeared to be in their late forties or early fifties, all of which reminded Renfro of what his wife had said earlier. Nope, these were not the type of men who could be expected to go to sleep on a riverbank with high water threatening. Kirb waved as they walked by. Though none spoke or even slowed his pace, every man returned the greeting.

The Renfros finished eating their supper just as darkness closed in, then extinguished their fire. "Did you see any children with that bunch down there?" Ellie asked, pointing to a cook fire a hundred yards below.

"No," Kirb answered, "and I doubt that we're gonna see any. You heard that one man say he ain't married yet, and the other three look old enough for their children to be grown now. I got a pretty good look at one of the women, and I'd say she's about as old as the men." He peeled a small splinter off a stick of firewood and began to pick his teeth. "I ain't gonna be asking none of 'em about it, but I'll bet they'd already raised their families when they decided life might be better someplace else."

"Most likely," Ellie agreed. She dragged the tarp over the cooking and eating utensils, then said, "I'll wash these things up early in the morning; then you can walk down to the river and get me some more water."

Kirb chuckled, then got to his feet. "I don't believe it'll be quite as far to the river in the morning as it was today," he said. He walked to the rear of the wagon and raised the canvas flap, then put his arm around Ellie's waist. "Do you think we oughtta go to work on one of those babies we've been talking about?"

"Uh-huh," she answered.

He lifted her into the wagon, then climbed in behind her. The flap fell soon afterward and did not rise again for almost two hours, at which time Kirb jumped to the ground and spread his bedroll under the wagon. He retrieved his Colt and his shotgun from their place of concealment near the front of the vehicle then crawled into his bedroll. He went to sleep quickly.

He was up about midnight to relieve himself, then slept like a log for the remainder of the night. The sun was almost an hour high, when Ellie shook his shoulder. "Wake up, Kirb," she said softly. "I think something's happened down at the river."

Kirb was soon standing beside his wife looking down the hill. He could see several people beside the road where it entered the river and hear them calling to someone on the opposite bank. "I think I can guess what happened," he said to Ellie, "but I'll walk down there and see." He headed down the hill at a fast pace.

Surprised that the river had not completely jumped its banks, he arrived to find three men and two women standing on the east side. The oldest of the men nodded a greeting to him, then pointed to the west bank. "That's Cudahay across the river," he said, "and he's damn lucky to be there.

Poor fool lost his wagon and both of his horses, but the current washed him up on the other side when he got to that sharp bend down yonder. Like I say, he's damn lucky."

"I believe you're right," Kirb said. "Did the current carry the team and wagon on around the bend?"

"No," the man said, pointing to a spot about forty feet below the ford. "The wagon's lying on its side right yonder. See where the water kind of separates in a vee down there? If you look close you can see a little bit of a rear wheel."

"I see it," Kirb said. "I reckon the fellow can at least salvage the harnesses after the water goes down. Might even get the wagon too."

"Maybe," the man agreed. He stood shaking his head for a moment, then continued, "I tell you, I'm fifty-four years old, and I ain't never seen nobody quite like that man. Wouldn't listen to a damn thing none of us said. My wife even told him he couldn't make it, but he seemed to think the whole world was gonna come to a halt if he didn't get married tomorrow." He pointed to the turbulent water again, then asked, "What do you think, young fellow? Wouldn't the average six-year-old boy take one look at that and back off?"

Kirb stifled a chuckle. "Yes, sir," he answered, "I believe he would." He was quiet for a moment, then asked, "Is Mr. Cudahay gonna walk on to his wedding then?"

"Said he was," the man answered. "That's what he was shouting about just before you got here." He pointed across the river. "I believe that's him walking up the hill right now. See him?"

"I see him," Kirb answered. He watched the man out of sight, then yawned and stretched his long arms above his head. "I reckon I'll be getting on back to my camp now," he said. "I haven't even had my first cup of coffee yet, and my wife's probably gonna send me right back down here to get two buckets of water."

5

★

The Renfros were back on the road six days later. Although a few of the wagons had crossed the river the day before with no apparent difficulty, Kirb noted that each of the vehicles was drawn by a team of exceptionally large animals. Standing on the bank watching, he decided that he himself would wait one more day, for he knew that his mules were nowhere near as strong as the big draft horses. The drivers of four other wagons, two on each side of the river, had also decided to wait another day. Like Renfro, their animals were quite ordinary in size.

Next morning, even after seeing all four of the vehicles crossed the river with no problems, Kirb walked down to inspect the ford. Gauging the depth by an assortment of objects that he had mentally marked the afternoon before, he knew that the water level had dropped at least another six inches. He could see more than half of Cudahay's wagon now, and the bloated carcass of one of the horses as well.

He walked back up the hill and announced that he was about to hitch up the team, then headed for the meadow with bridles across his shoulder. Happy with her husband's decision, Ellie was on her feet quickly, gathering up things and loading them into the wagon.

Although Kirb had expected to have to lead the mules across the river while Ellie whipped their behinds with the reins, such was not the case. The animals actually seemed glad to be on the move and took to the water with little coaxing. "By, God, I'm glad that's over with," Kirb said as the dripping vehicle rolled up the west bank.

"Me, too," Ellie said. "I hope I never see that river again."

"You probably won't see this one again," Kirb said, "but according to the map, the Red River's less than three days ahead. Uncle George says it can get mighty rough too."

"Maybe it hasn't been raining so much there," Ellie said. "Maybe we'll get lucky."

"Let's hope so," Kirb said, slapping the mules with the reins.

They did get lucky at the Red River. Arriving there at noon three days later, they forded easily, then halted on the west bank to warm up their dinner and make a pot of coffee. A middle-aged man who was passing on horseback stopped by, and though he declined their offer of food, he very quickly produced his own cup and helped them empty the coffeepot.

The man introduced himself as a farmer named Jeff Penrod, then asked about their trip. He listened to Kirb's tale of woe concerning the Ouachita River, then pointed down the slope. "This is the lowest I've ever seen the Red at this time of the year," he said. "Sometimes she stays out of her banks for weeks at a time during April and May, and I've seen wagons and saddle horses backed up for more'n a quarter of a mile on both sides of the river."

Kirb sat shaking his head. "I sure hope we don't ever have to sit around and wait for another one to run off," he said.

"I don't reckon that'll happen anytime soon," Penrod said. "You'll probably camp on the Sulphur tonight, and it ain't gonna be no problem. You'll be in Texas before noon tomorrow, and you ain't gonna have no big water to worry about for another week. I reckon the Sabine is the next river of any size, and I've been told that they'll ferry your wagon across for fifty cents if the water's too high to ford."

"Fifty cents for the wagon?" Kirb asked. "How much for us? How much for my saddle horse?"

"Fifty cents for the team and wagon," Penrod said. "You and your wife can just keep your seats and ride free. I believe that fellow said they charge a quarter a head for extra livestock."

"Seventy-five cents, then," Kirb said. "That's awful high, but it beats sitting around waiting for a flood to run off."

"I should say so," Penrod said, getting to his feet. He dropped his cup back into his saddlebag, then mounted his gray mare. "I appreciate the coffee and the conversation, folks, and I wish you the best of luck on your journey." He kicked the animal in the ribs and headed toward the river at a trot.

They spent the night on the west bank of the Sulphur River then crossed the state line early next morning. Kirb brought the team to a halt and jumped to the ground when he reached the crude sign welcoming them to Texas. He stood for a few moments patting the sign. "I feel like kissing it," he said. "Getting here ain't been nowhere near as easy as I thought it would be, but we finally made it.

It's still a long way to Comanche County, but at least we're in Texas."

Ellie sat watching quietly. "Well?" she asked, after a while.

"Well, what?"

"Are you gonna kiss the sign?"

He pressed his lips against the faded paint, then climbed back in the wagon. He slapped the mules on their rumps, then said jokingly, "I'm surprised that you'd let me kiss anything other than you."

She wrinkled her nose. "Signs don't feel," she said.

They continued to travel in a southwesterly direction day after day. The Sabine River, which they had been dreading ever since talking with the man named Penrod, was actually running below normal, and they forded it with ease. Ten days after crossing the state line, they camped at a boxed-up spring a quarter-mile east of Hillsboro.

Even as Kirb kindled a cook fire, a horseman headed in the opposite direction pulled off the road and watered his animal from the spring's runoff. The two men talked for a few moments; then the rider continued on his way. And although he had not introduced himself and had declined an invitation to wait around for a cup of hot coffee, he left the Renfros with the information that four more days of steady traveling would see them in Comanche. They stood by the fire waving as he disappeared, comfortable with the knowledge that their long journey would be over before the week was out. "I'm looking forward to having a place to call home again," Ellie said, squeezing his arm. "I'm tired of traveling."

"I'm worn out too," he said. He patted her hand, then went about his chores. He filled the coffeepot from the spring, then set it beside the fire. "I'll let you put in the grounds, honey. Our coffee tastes a lot better when you do the measuring. Besides, I've got to water the livestock and put 'em on their picket ropes." He accomplished the job in less than half an hour and was back at the cook fire just as the coffee began to boil. "Right on time," he said, pulling the pot off the coals. He filled a cup for Ellie and another for himself, then took a seat on the ground, stretching his long legs out before him.

Ellie seated herself beside him. "It won't take more'n five minutes to warm up supper," she said. "I don't reckon it'll be dark for about two hours yet, but you just let me know when you start getting hungry."

"No hurry," he said. "The reason I stopped so early is 'cause we hit the road at daybreak this morning. The mules are tired, and they need the rest."

The terrain was relatively level for miles around in all directions, and after sitting quietly for a while, Ellie pointed toward the settlement a short distance to the west. "It looks like Hillsboro's a lot bigger than most of the towns we've seen lately. I can see twelve buildings from where I'm sitting."

Kirb nodded. "We'll get a better look in the morning 'cause I think the road runs right through the middle of it. I believe the town's been around for a good while, and there ain't no question about there being a lot of people in the area. Every field we've seen for the last twenty-five miles has done been plowed and planted, and it took more'n a few men to do all that."

"Of course it did," Ellie agreed. Getting to her feet, she changed the subject. "I'll go ahead and warm up some supper."

As she went about preparing the meal, Kirb continued to look toward the settlement. "I think we should try to find some more of that good cheddar cheese and Bologna sausage as we go through town tomorrow," he said. "It could be that sombody'll even have some of that rock candy you like so well."

Ellie chuckled. "Rock candy that I like?" she asked. "I'd almost swear that I saw somebody else eating most of the last two bags we bought."

Kirb was quiet for a long time, then said, "I guess maybe I did like it a little bit too."

When they had eaten supper, they bathed themselves as well as they could in the spring's runoff. After heating a pan of water, Kirb hung his mirror on a willow limb and shaved his face. "What a handsome man I married," Ellie said, handing him a towel.

He dried his face and kissed the top of her head, then kicked dirt over the fire. Then they sat side by side watching the sun go into the ground a few miles to the west. As darkness closed in and the townspeople began to light their lamps, Ellie began to count the buildings again: "One, two, three . . ."

The night passed without incident, and after an early breakfast next morning, the Renfros rolled into Hillsboro shortly after sunup. The first building they came to after passing the livery stable was a general store. Surprised to learn that it was open for business so early in the day, Kirb pulled in and climbed down from his seat. He tied the team to the hitching rail, then helped his wife to the ground. "I just saw a man come outta that store," he said, "so it must be open."

Ellie took his arm and followed him across the board-walk and through the doorway. A middle-aged man standing behind the counter offered a broad smile. "Good morning, folks," he said.

The couple nodded a greeting in unison. "I didn't really expect to find a store open at this time of day," Kirb said.

The man chuckled. "I don't reckon I've got much choice," he said. "People around here go to work early, and there ain't none of 'em ashamed to go pounding on that front door at daybreak. Somebody's always needing chewing or smoking tobacco or maybe something to put in their lunch. Everybody knows I live in the back room, and I don't recall ever trying to sleep late without somebody getting me outta bed for something they forgot to buy the day before."

Kirb smiled. "I guess you go to bed early at night then."

The man nodded. "It's the only remedy I've ever found." He moved in front of the counter. "Is there something I can get for you?"

"We'd like to buy two pounds of cheddar cheese and about that much Bologna sausage," Kirb said. He winked at Ellie, then added, "And my wife has a strong liking for rock candy."

"I've got all that," the storekeeper said. He walked to the rear of the building and the Renfros followed. He sliced, weighed, and wrapped the cheese and sausage, then led them back to the front. "The candy's behind the counter," he said. "If you buy one bag for a dime, you can get a second one for a nickel more."

"Two bags then," Kirb said. It was then that he noticed a large pound cake on a small table behind the counter. "Is that cake for sale?" he asked.

The man nodded. "My sister made it three days ago. She thought it outta bring twenty-two or twenty-three cents, but I told her right from the start that she'd never get that much for it. You want it for seventeen cents?"

Kirb looked at his wife, who smiled, then nodded.

"Yes, sir," he said. "We'll buy it at that price."

They rode out of the settlement twenty minutes later and followed the road due west. Kirb expected to reach the Brazos River at least two hours before sunset and had already made up his mind to spend the night there. Once they left the Brazos, they would have only one more river to cross before their journey ended. When they reached the Leon River three days from now, they would be less than ten miles from the town of Comanche and would already be in the county of the same name. The thought gave him a warm feeling. He kissed his wife's forehead, then gave the mules a whack across the rump.

6

★

The town of Comanche had been established as a trading
center for surrounding ranches in 1858 and aptly named
by an old settler from Belton, Texas. Chosen as the seat
when the county of the same name was partitioned in
1859, severe Indian raids inhibited the settlement's early
growth, and a host of knowing men went on record as
saying it's chances of survival were slim.

And there came a time two years after its inception
that the men's predictions appeared to be right on the
mark: On a moonlit night in May 1861, a braying mule
awakened the people of the town after most of their horses
had been stolen by Indians. Citizens spent the rest of the
night molding bullets, and a posse, under the command
of Capt. James Cunningham, set out at dawn.

Consisting of seventeen men and boys and a large
pack of hounds, the posse caught up with the raiders on
Brown's Creek, about thirty-five miles southwest of the

town. Nineteen Comanches died on the spot. The white men's only casualty was a slight wound to Captain Cunningham, and the posse returned home to a hero's welcome.

As a result of the Brown's Creek fight, Comanches suddenly became scarce in the county that bore their name, and there was wide agreement among the whites that the Cunningham posse's relentless pursuit of the red raiders had been the key to the town's survival. At any rate, when word got around that a row could be plowed or a cow tended without having to fight Indians, farmers and ranchers invaded the area in large numbers, and prosperity was seen at every turn.

Kirb Renfro drove his wagon into Comanche on the last day of June. He and Ellie had camped on the west bank of the Leon River last night and had made the two-hour drive this morning on the best road they had seen in weeks. Kirb pulled up at the first hitching rail he saw, then looked at his watch. "It's twenty minutes past ten," he said to Ellie. "Mr. Browning said the lawyer's office was right in the middle of town, and I reckon he oughtta be open by now. Do you mind just sitting here till I see if I can find him?"

Ellie smiled. "That's what I had in mind," she said.

He jumped down and tied the team, then stepped up on the boardwalk and turned left. He knew that the walk would be a short one, for he could see all over town. He passed a hardware store and a sweet-scented bakeshop, then read the sign on the door of the next building: W.C. RUBIN, ATTORNEY & LAND CONSULTANT. Kirb twisted the knob and pushed, then stepped into the office.

A dark-complected man who appeared to be in his late forties sat behind a large oaken desk. He got to his feet quickly, then walked to the front of the room with his

right hand extended. His lips broke into a broad smile.
"You look like your name oughtta be Kirb Renfro," he
said. "Welcome to Comanche."

Kirb nodded, then took the man's hand. "And I
reckon you'd be Mr. Rubin."

The man smiled again. "My friends call me Walt," he
said. "Just old Walt." He pointed to a chair, and Kirb
seated himself.

"Gaylord Browning told me you'd be coming along,"
Rubin said, returning to his seat behind the desk. "He
seemed to think you'd get here about a week earlier'n you
did though"

"We had to wait for some high water to run off," Kirb
said.

Rubin nodded. "That's the very reason spring never
has been my favorite time to travel. Any little creek is
liable to become a river in March, April, or May."

"We managed to get across a lot of creeks that were
running mighty high," Kirb said, "but the Ouachita River
held us up for a week."

Rubin nodded, and changed the subject. "Mr. Browning said you had your wife with you. Where's she at?"

"She's out there in the wagon," Kirb answered, "and
I imagine that hot sun's beginning to bear down on her."

"Of course it is," Rubin said, "and I think you oughtta
get her out of it." He motioned toward the street. "Bring
her in here; I've got plenty of chairs."

Kirb was through the doorway quickly and several
long strides brought him back to his wagon. He held his
arms up toward Ellie to help her down. "I've been talking
with Mr. Rubin, and he thinks you should come in outta
this hot sun."

Ellie smiled. "I like Mr. Rubin," she said, leaning into
her husband's arms and jumping to the ground.

The attorney was standing just inside the office door

when Kirb reentered with Ellie hanging onto his arm. "I'll say one thing for Mr. Gaylord Browning," Rubin said, after closing the door. "There sure ain't nothing wrong with his eyes. He told me that Kirb Renfro's wife was the prettiest woman he'd ever seen, and I reckon, by gosh, that makes two of us." He pointed to the extra chair he had placed in front of the desk while Kirb had gone to the wagon. "Have a seat, little lady, and welcome to Comanche."

When the Renfros had seated themselves, Rubin returned to his own chair. "Mr. Browning told me that you had already agreed to a job on the Lazy Bee Ranch," he began, looking Kirb straight in the eye. "But when I mentioned the fact that I could offer you a chance at a place of your own, he decided that you and I oughtta have a talk.

"Now, Mr. Browning says he took a strong liking to both of you young folks when he first met you on the road, and the fact that you were practically neighbors back in Tennessee didn't hurt none. He says the job at the Lazy Bee is always open to you, but he doubts that you'll ever be happy till you've got a place of your own. Is that true?"

Kirb sat fidgiting in his chair for a moment. "I reckon it is," he said finally. "I've always wanted my own land."

The lawyer pulled out a desk drawer. "What I've got in mind is the old Nelson place," he said, opening a folder. "It's a two-section piece of property, and you might appreciate the fact that it borders the Lazy Bee Ranch on the north."

Kirb sat looking between his knees and shaking his head. "Two sections?" he asked after a while. "Over twelve hundred acres? Ellie and I are just starting out, Mr. Rubin, and we ain't got nothing close to what it would take to buy a place like that."

The lawyer chuckled. "You're wrong, Kirb. You've got it, all right, and I can see it through that shirt you're wearing." He reached across the desk and squeezed the bicep of Kirb's right arm. "Yes, sir, I can feel exactly what it'll take to buy the Nelson place. I'm talking about muscle, young man, muscle and determination."

Kirb looked at Ellie, then back at the floor. "Payments on a place like that would be sky-high," he said.

Rubin nodded. "I suppose they might be sky-high for some folks, but not for you. You'd have the money to meet 'em. There are more ways to make a living on two sections of land than you can shake a stick at, Kirb. Why, just fifty acres of hay would bring in enough money to meet your yearly note and then some. Fence in a good-sized plot along the river and plant it in hay, and I'll guarantee you that the ranchers'll buy it when cold weather comes. The Lazy Bee might even buy all you've got."

Kirb sat staring at the wall behind the lawyer. "I know how to farm, and I might end up growing hay, but I believe I'd try something else first."

Rubin shrugged. "Like I said, there are a bunch of ways to make a living on a piece of property that size." He shuffled his papers. "Honey Hathaway owns the place. Her pa, Correy Nelson, acquired it right after statehood and left it to her when he died. She's hung on to it all these years, most likely expecting her son to eventually do something with it. He got himself killed in a gunfight this past New Year's Eve, though, so now she's decided to sell.

"Honey's past seventy years old, and she ain't got no use in the world for that place. That don't mean she's gonna give it away, but I'll guarantee you that the price is right."

Kirb folded his arms and looked the man in the eye. "Just how right is the price?" he asked.

"Twelve hundred dollars," Rubin answered. "Less

than a dollar an acre. Your payments will be about a hundred and twenty dollars a year on a twelve-year loan, and you can take possession anytime you like. There's already a cabin on the place, but it ain't much. I'm sure you'd want to build something else to live in. That two-stall barn, shed, and pole corral are all in pretty good shape though.

"There's a spring in the front yard that puts out sweet water year-round, and the runoff goes right through the corral. You never would have to haul or tote water down to your animals 'cause they'd always have it running right under their noses."

"What about a down payment?" Kirb asked. "Are you saying she don't want no money up front?"

Rubin nodded. "I'm saying she'll allow any man over twenty-one years old and in good health to buy that place on credit. You are over twenty-one, right?"

When Renfro did not answer the question, Rubin picked up a pencil. "Kirby Renfro," he mumbled, beginning to scribble on a writing pad, "age twenty-three."

Kirb sat quietly for a while. Finally, he put his arm around Ellie's shoulder and spoke to the lawyer again. "How much would the payments be if a man paid three hundred dollars down, Mr. Rubin?"

"Three hundred?" Rubin asked, a broad smile suddenly appearing on his face. "Why, that would make a sizable difference. Me and her ain't never talked about it from that angle, but I'd say offhand that you could save some real money if you put three hundred up front. A down payment that big would reduce the amount of your yearly notes and shorten the duration of the loan both." He closed the folder and put it back in the drawer. "You want me to talk with Honey and see what she's willing to do?"

"Yes, sir," Kirb answered, getting to his feet. "I'm not

saying I'll buy it even if she does offer me a better deal,
but I can promise you that I'll take a look at it. For all I
know now, it might be exactly what Ellie and I need." He
squeezed her shoulder again. "If you'll direct us to the
Lazy Bee, we'll be going now. I reckon we're both anxious
to see the Brownings again, and it could be that Mr. Gaylord'll want to help me look the Nelson place over."

"I'm sure he will, son. He told me himself that he was
concerned about you and your wife getting off to a good
start. If you'll come back to this office two days from now,
I'll have the final word from Honey Hathaway. You can
bring Mr. Browning with you if you want to, and the three
of us'll ride over the property together."

Rubin rounded the desk and pumped Kirb's right hand
a few times, then led the way through the doorway. Standing on the boardwalk, he pointed east. "Turn left down
there at the livery stable, then follow the road on around
the hill. The Lazy Bee borders the Leon River on the east,
and it's located about ten miles northeast of town.

"The old Nelson place also borders the river, and
you'll drive across part of it before you get to the Lazy
Bee. There's a little road that turns off to the west and
goes up to the cabin, but it ain't been used much over the
past several years. You'll miss it if you don't keep your
eyes open. You can't miss the road to the Lazy Bee
though. There's a big sign with an arrow pointing to ranch
headquarters."

Kirb nodded. "Thank you, Mr. Rubin . . . uh, Walt.
I'll keep thinking about the Nelson place." He took Ellie's
hand and led her down the street to the wagon.

They followed the lawyer's directions and had been
traveling for about an hour, when Kirb pulled up at a
roadside spring and motioned toward the rear of the
wagon with his thumb. "I've got enough pine kindling left
back there to make a coffee fire," he said. "I believe be-

tween the two of us we can finish off the rest of that pound cake, too."

Ellie smiled. "I'll build the fire while you water the animals."

Kirb unhitched the mules and watered them from the spring's runoff, then put them back in the traces. By the time he had watered and retied the horse to the tailgate, Ellie had a fire going under the coffeepot. She handed him a cup, then set out the cake, two-thirds of which had already been eaten. As they waited for the coffee to boil, Kirb sat staring at the cake. "The lady who baked that thing knew what she was doing," he said finally. "I don't think I ever tasted anything that good before."

When she said nothing, he continued. "Maybe you could learn to make 'em, honey. I'll bet either one of those Browning women could tell you how to do it."

Ellie had heard enough. "I've been knowing how to make a pound cake since I was ten years old, Kirb. Heck, you could make one yourself if you wanted to 'cause the name of it tells you how to make it. You put a pound of flour, a pound of sugar and a pound of butter in a bowl, then stir in some milk or water till you've got a batter. Then you pour it into a baking pan and put it in a hot oven. When the moisture cooks out of it and it turns brown, you've got yourself a pound cake."

"Well, I'll be damned," he said. "Now that you've told me how simple it is to make, it might not taste as good to me."

"Don't use that word, Kirb."

They drank half a pot of coffee and ate the remainder of the cake, then took to the road again. When it reached the river two hours later, it made an abrupt turn to the northwest, then ran parallel with the stream. They had ridden alongside the murky water for about twenty minutes when they came to a narrow road leading off to the west. Even from his sitting position Kirb could see that, due to the fact that there was no ditch on either side, erosion had taken its toll on the road. Tall weeds and small bushes grew in the center, and bunches of thick grass littered what had once been wagon ruts. He brought the team to a halt and pointed. "If we lived on the old Nelson place, I reckon that would be the road home."

"Yep," Ellie said. "According to Mr. Rubin, that would have to be it."

Kirb stared for a while longer, then urged the team on down the road. "If that place belonged to me, I'd do something about that road before I even moved in." He drove on for a short time, then added, "On second thought, I don't believe I'd do anything to it. I'd build a new one. I'd hitch a team to a slip scraper and dig two ditches about twenty-five feet apart all the way from the river to the house, then dump the exess dirt between in 'em and smooth it out. That way I'd have good drainage, and I'd be using the dirt I took out of the ditches to build up the road."

Ellie nodded. "I can understand that," she said. "Sounds like an awful lot of work though."

"Sure it would be a lot of work," Kirb said, "but the mules would be doing most of it. I'll bet I could do the whole job in less than a month, and I'll bet you Mr. Browning's got a slip scraper at the Lazy Bee."

Ellie shrugged. "Maybe so," she said. "I don't think I've ever seen one of those things. What do they look like."

Kirb spent a few minutes explaining to her that a slip scraper was a large steel scoop with a sharp blade on the front and wooden handles on the back. As a team pulled it forward, a man walked behind it holding onto the handles, raising or lowering them in order to determine the biting angle. First he would raise the handles to send the blade into the ground, then gradually lower them as the scoop filled up. Regardless of how much dirt was in it at any given time, the weight was always on the ground, never on man or animals.

When the scoop was full, the man dropped the handles to the ground and drove the team to wherever he wanted to dump the dirt. Once there, he simply unhooked the doubletree from the front of the scoop and hooked it to a metal ring on the back. The team had to move forward for only two or three steps to dump the dirt. It could be smoothed out later with shovels, or even the same slip scraper. "I don't expect you to understand all of that," he said when he had finished his description, "but that's what a slip scraper is, and that's what it does."

"I had no trouble at all understanding what you said, Kirb. You're very good at explaining things."

"Why, thank you, my dear," he said with a chuckle. He pointed up the road to the sign and the arrow Rubin had told them about. "There's the turnoff to the Lazy Bee up ahead. Our journey's almost over."

Kirb turned west at the sign, then headed for Lazy Bee headquarters. Passing one cluster of grazing longhorns after another, he traveled for about an hour, then rounded a long curve and brought the team to a halt. "There it is," he said, pointing up the slope to a large cluster of buildings.

"Looks like some of those pictures I've seen from other countries," Ellie said.

"It hasn't been too long since this was another country," he said. "I've read that a lot of Texans act like it still is."

He sat looking awhile longer. On the east side of the road a short distance up the slope was a large, unpainted barn. Just below it, with a tin-roofed shed attached to either side, was a smaller building that was no doubt used for storing saddles, harnesses, horse feed, and a wide assortment of other things. Adjoining the back side of the barn was a pole corral, and Kirb could see at least a dozen horses there.

The long, narrow building on the opposite side of the road, with a dogtrot on its north end and three hitching rails out front, would be the bunkhouse, he was thinking, and the large addition north of the dogtrot was most likely where the cook lived, worked, and fed the crew.

The main house, at the top of the slope and a good forty yards above the other buildings, was a large, single-story affair with a shingle roof. It appeared to have at least ten rooms, and a front porch that ran the width of the building. A bonneted woman who looked tall enough to be Carrie Browning was working in the front yard at the moment.

Kirb urged his team on up the slope. Noticing as he passed the corral that the enclosure had been built around a spring, he decided that whoever laid the place out had been using his head. Nobody would ever have to bring those animals a drink, and cleaning out a spring a few times a year was much easier than hauling a hundred gallons of water every day.

As the wagon reached the hitching rail at the edge of the yard, Carrie Browning straightened up from her digging and lifted the bonnet from her eyes. "Land sakes!" she said loudly, dropping her hoe to the ground. She walked to the wagon. "I reckon everybody but Gaylord gave up on you two a long time ago. Not him, though; he kept saying that mules are slow walkers, and that you might've even had some sort of breakdown. He told us last night that you'd probably be here today, and I'll be doggoned if you ain't."

"Yes, ma'am," Kirb said, jumping to the ground. "We would have been here sooner, but high water held us up for a week."

He tied the team to the rail, then walked to the other side of the wagon to see that Carrie had already helped his wife to the ground. The two women stood embracing each other. "I know the trip's been mighty hard on you, girl," Carrie was saying, "but it's over now and you're among friends." She made a sweeping motion with her arm. "You two are gonna love this place just like we do. We all fell in love with it before we even got the wagons unloaded. Especially the boys. The only times I ever see that'n of mine nowadays is when he's hungry."

Ellie dropped her arms to her sides. "We both like the ranch a lot," she said. "We saw more cattle on the way in than we could count."

"They're everywhere you look," Carrie said. "As soon as the boys settle down, I'm gonna have 'em fence in this yard with stout poles. I intend to have some flowers, but I can't do it with the cows eating up everything I plant. I wore three of 'em out with a stick and chased 'em off the hill yesterday, but they'll be back. Just as sure as something green pops outta the ground, they'll be back."

"It wouldn't be hard to fence 'em outta the yard," Kirb said. He pointed back the way he had come. "I noticed a good stand of saplings on the east side of the river that would do the trick."

Carrie nodded. "Of course you did. But I'll bet that boy of mine didn't see 'em. He's exactly like his pa, a flower or a pretty yard wouldn't cross his mind in a million years."

Kirb was trying to think of something else to say when Bess Browning called to them from the porch. "You young-uns come on to the house and get some cool lemonade!"

When they reached the porch, Bess hugged Ellie just as Carrie had done. "I've been worried about you two, but I can see that I was worrying about nothing. You both look good; healthy as a horse." She pointed to a table and chairs on the west end of the porch. "Have a seat over there while I make a trip to the kitchen. I'll be back in a jiffy."

She returned shortly with a tray of oatmeal cookies and two tall glasses of lemonade. "There's plenty more of these cookies," she said as she set the tray on the table. "If you run out, just holler." She turned back toward the door, adding, "I've got to look after my fire. I've got a beef brisket in the oven."

Once her sister was gone, Carrie also excused herself. "I reckon I'll go on with my digging," she said. "You folks just sit there and rest yourselves." She was soon back in the yard swinging the hoe.

Munching the cookies and sipping the lemonade, the Renfros were quiet for several minutes. Now at a higher elevation they had a better view, and Kirb was surveying the area with his eyes. To the south the slope played out after about five hundred yards, then the terrain was fairly level for as far as the eye could see. The view to the west was even more impressive. Consisting of long, rolling slopes, the area was treeless except for an occasional cluster of junipers or cedars. And though he could not see into the shallow valleys, he could see cattle grazing on every hillside, some of them so far away that they appeared to be the size of ants. "I sure never saw nothing like this before, Ellie," he said finally. "What do you think?"

"The same as you," she answered. "It's beautiful."

It was then that they saw the Browning brothers walk out of the cookshack. Though Dossy headed toward the barn, Gaylord, seeing the wagon at the hitching rail and the Renfros sitting on the porch, turned his footsteps toward the house. "I knew you'd be along," he said as he neared the porch. He climbed the steps and held his right hand out for a shake. Kirb got to his feet and grasped the hand.

"I told 'em all that you wouldn't let nothing stop you," Browning continued, pumping Kirb's arm. "I could tell that by the way you talked and acted."

"High water on the Ouachita River held us up for a week," Kirb said. "Other than that, I reckon I'm a little surprised at how trouble-free our trip was."

Gaylord released Kirb's hand. "We never had no problems neither," he said. "We kept on the move every day for the first three weeks; then the women began to complain about us traveling on Sunday. Once they got their hackles up about us working seven days a week, we started setting up camp on Saturday afternoon and staying right there till early Monday morning. All we done on Sundays was thank the Lord for the good week we'd just had, then ask him to give us another one."

"I didn't expect you to have no problems," Kirb said. "You've got well-built wagons and some mighty good horses."

Browning nodded. "I reckon that helps," he said, then seated himself across the table.

At that moment, Bess Browning called Ellie's name from the doorway. "You want to come in and let me show you about the house?" she asked.

Ellie nodded. "Yes, ma'am." She got to her feet and walked across the porch, then disappeared inside the house.

Neither Kirb nor Browning spoke for a while, then Gaylord crossed his legs and leaned his chair against the wall. "I reckon you talked with Walt Rubin in town," he said finally. "He told me he was gonna offer to help you get some land of your own. Did he mention it to you?"

"Yes, sir," Kirb answered. "He talked about a two-section piece of property he called the old Nelson place. The east section borders the west bank of the river, and both sections border the Lazy Bee. He says a lady named

Honey Hathaway owns it, and that she'll treat me right if I want to buy it. I drove across the east end of it coming out here, but I couldn't tell much about it. What I could see of it looked just like the Lazy Bee though."

Gaylord nodded. "Rubin told me a little bit about it, but my foreman, Bo Ransom, told me more. I reckon he knows every foot of it 'cause he rides over it several times a year. He says a lot of my cows spend about as much time down there as they do at home, and that he never has tried to discourage 'em from doing that. He says the grass is just lying there for the taking, and that since nobody's ever complained about it, he don't see no reason not to fatten Lazy Bee steers on it."

Kirb chuckled. "Sounds right to me."

Browning was quiet for a moment, then continued. "Bo says about the only difference between the Lazy Bee and the old Nelson place is the size of 'em, and that Uncle Wash talked about buying that property before he got so sick. Ransom even went so far as to say I oughtta buy it myself. I told him I'd hold off and see what you do. I'll give you first crack at it if you decide you want it."

"I don't know enough about it to make a decision," Kirb said. "I don't know what Mrs. Hathaway's bottom dollar is, what kind of terms she'll give me, or how much my yearly notes would be. Besides, I'd first have to figure out some way to make enough money to pay for it. Mr. Rubin mentioned growing hay, but I didn't much like the sound of that."

"Rubin didn't go into the terms with me either," Gaylord said. "But I imagine he's the one you'll have to go through if you decide to buy. Making up your mind might be a little easier if you ride down there and prowl around on the property for a coupla days. I don't reckon nobody'd mind."

Kirb nodded his head. "Mr. Rubin pretty well invited

me to do that. He said if I'd come back to his office the day after tomorrow, he'd have the final word from Mrs. Hathaway. Fact is, he suggested that I bring you with me; said the three of us'd ride over the place together."

"Of course he wants me along," Browning chuckled. "He's a salesman, and I never met one yet who wouldn't rather talk with two prospective buyers than one. I'll be happy to ride over there with you, but you just pay attention to what Rubin says, see if you don't think a lot of his words are meant for my ears instead of yours."

Kirb sat quietly for a moment, then smiled. "Ain't no doubt in my mind, Mr. Browning. Especially with him figuring you've got the ready money and knowing that I ain't."

Browning sat thoughtful for a while, then said, "Even if you did have the money, you'd be foolish to pay cash for the land, Kirb. You should buy it with the smallest down payment you possibly can, and I'll tell you why. It's true that they'll charge you eight, maybe ten percent interest on the unpaid balance, but just keep listening to me. Let's say you're thinking about paying an extra hundred down in order to avoid that eight or ten percent. You'd be better off to go ahead and pay the interest and spend that hundred on brood cows.

"A hundred dollars'll buy six or seven breeders, and every one of 'em'll drop a calf before the end of the year. The calves'll be worth five bucks apiece when they hit the ground, and their mammies'll raise 'em for you for nothing. Now, let's look down the road about four years. In four years you'll pay somewhere between thirty and forty dollars in interest on that hundred, but in the meantime the six or seven cows you bought with it have turned into twenty-five or thirty head. A fellow don't need no whole lot of education to figure out which way to go in a situation like that. You know what I mean?"

Kirb chuckled loudly. "Yes, sir," he said. "I know exactly what you mean."

"Very well, then," Browning said, getting to his feet. "We'll go to Rubin's office the day after tomorrow, then ride over the property. Remember what I told you though. If you decide you want it, you'd be smart to buy it as cheap as you can with the lowest down payment possible. Drive a hard bargain and use your credit, Kirb. Hang on to your cash till you get a chance to put it to work for you." He stood quietly for a moment, then pointed down the slope. "You can park your wagon down there beside mine and turn your animals into the corral. Then we'll hunt up the ranch foreman so you can meet him."

"Yes, sir," Kirb said. "I'd like that."

Half an hour later, with the harnesses stored in the wagon and his animals scampering around inside the corral, Kirb followed Browning past the crib to an open-sided structure that joined the small building on its south side.

"Where you at, Bo?" Gaylord asked, stepping underneath the shed.

"I'm over here," a deep voice answered. A six-footer who appeared to weigh about two hundred pounds got to his feet and walked around the buggy he had been working on. Dark-haired with a black mustache, he looked to be about thirty-five years old. Wiping his hairy hands and forearms on a feed sack, he spoke again. "Right rear wheel on that buggy was about to run dry," he said. He made a final effort to clean the grease from his hands, then tossed the sack into the corner.

"I've got somebody here that I'd like you to meet," Gaylord said.

The foreman smiled broadly. "You must be the young man from Tennessee that I've heard so much about," he said, offering Kirb a handshake. "Welcome to the Lazy Bee."

Browning was quick to make the introductions, pointing to each man as he called his name. "Bo Ransom, meet
Kirb Renfro."

They shook hands, each man matching the other's firm
grip. "Gaylord says you might go to work for us," Ransom said, his smile constant. "I reckon we can always use
a stout-looking young ox like you."

Browning spoke quickly. "I think Kirb's sorta got his
heart set on a place of his own, Bo. Walt Rubin advised
him to look the old Nelson place over."

Ransom nodded, then spoke directly to Renfro. "Well,
if you've some money to spare or maybe want to stretch
your credit a little, I'd advise you to do the same thing.
Two creeks and three good springs on that property, and
it borders the river on the east. The grass down there's
just as good as ours too.

"That's what I was thinking," Kirb said. "I really
couldn't see any difference in the terrain." He was quiet
for a moment, then asked, "Have you looked inside the
cabin or noticed what kind of shape the outbuildings are
in?"

Ransom nodded. "The only outbuilding down there is
a little two-stall barn, but I believe it's in pretty good
shape. I turned my horse in the corral one night about a
year ago and pitched my bedroll inside the cabin. I built
a coffee fire in the fireplace next morning, and to the best
of my memory the chimney drew very well. I don't know
whether the roof leaks or not, but it's made outta cypress
shingles, so I'd almost bet that it don't. The cabin's got
two big rooms and a solid foundation, and it's built outta
foot-thick logs. It's liable to start leaning a little bit over
the years, but I figure it'll be a lifetime before it falls."

"I could live just fine in a two-room cabin," Kirb said.
"That's all my wife and I had back home. We ain't even
got enough stuff to furnish one room now."

"People don't need houses nowhere near as big as a lot of 'em think they do," Gaylord said. "How much can you do in a house anyway? Usually you just eat and sleep, then get the hell outta there. Ain't nobody in the world who really needs a special room for every little thing, and everybody gets along just fine when they ain't got it. Two rooms is just what you and Ellie need, Kirb. Of course, your situation would change if the babies start coming, but adding a room or two onto a log cabin is one of the easiest jobs I know of."

"Nothing to it," Ransom agreed. "No more'n a coupla days' work for a man and a few of his friends."

"I could add a room by myself," Kirb said.

"Sure you could," Browning said, patting Renfro on the back. "Of course, there ain't nothing to be gained by talking about enlarging the cabin till after you own it. Even if you buy it, the decision about whether to add a room or two is still a long way down the road." He cleared his throat and spat between his boots, then pointed to the cookshack. "Let's go see if the cook's got the coffeepot on."

"I'll be right behind you," Kirb said. He nodded to Ransom, then followed Browning across the road.

8

★

Browning and Renfro rode off the hill shortly after sunup two days later, Gaylord aboard a tall roan and Kirb riding the big black gelding named Midnight. They were on their way to visit Walt Rubin at his office, then have a look at the old Nelson place.

Kirb twisted his body in the saddle and lifted his hat to Ellie, who stood on the front porch waving good-bye. Even as he headed for the corral to get his horse this morning, Ellie had whispered into his ear that she hoped he could make a deal for the property. Although the Brownings had accepted her into their home, fed her royally, and even provided her and her husband with a bedroom that had a lock on the door, she nonetheless longed for a place to call her own.

Kirb was just as eager to have his own home, but was not at all sure it should be the old Nelson place. There were probably millions of acres for sale in Texas, and cash money was in short supply. Therefore, he felt that he had enough to buy a good piece of property. And he had made up his mind to do it. If the Nelson place failed to meet his expectations, or if Rubin did not offer him payments that were low enough, he would simply settle for a smaller tract of land and buy it for cash. He waved his hat to Ellie one last time, then rode out of sight, determined to keep his eyes and ears open throughout the day.

"I'll tell you what, Kirb," Browning said, after they had ridden about a mile. "As far as us looking at the Nelson place is concerned, I can't see no reason why we'd need Rubin for that." He pointed east. "If we leave the road and turn south about a mile before we get to the river, I think we'll run right into that homestead. That's all you really need to look at anyhow, 'cause the property looks just like this." He waved his arm in a sweeping motion to indicate the entire area.

"Makes sense to me," Kirb said. "I'll follow you whenever you decide to leave the road."

An hour later, they watered their horses at the spring in the front yard of the cabin then tied them to a rickety hitching rail a short distance away. "Mr. Ransom was probably right about that roof," Kirb said, pointing. "I don't believe it'll leak either."

"I'll leave all that predicting stuff to you and him," Browning said. "I've been fooled more'n once after a good rain."

Noticing that the hinges were on the outside of the door, Kirb made a mental note to move them inside if he bought the place, then stepped inside the cabin. Browning followed, then both men stood leaning against the wall. "Mighty big rooms," Gaylord said. "Good hardwood floor. Women like them."

"Men too," Kirb said. He stood measuring the building with his eyes. "From the way Mr. Rubin talked, I was expecting to see a little cabin, but this thing looks to be about twenty-four by forty-eight feet. Take an awful lot of wood to heat it in the winter, but I've got a good ax." He motioned toward the back room. "If Ellie ever had a baby, I could just build a partition back there. It's big enough to make two bedrooms without crowding anybody." He pointed to the ceiling. "The flue's already up there. A stove and a few joints of pipe, and Ellie'd be in business for cooking."

Browning was smiling now. "Sounds to me like you've already sold yourself on it," he said.

Kirb chuckled. "I'm weakening. Let's taste that spring water and take a look at the barn."

Moments later, they knelt beside the spring and dipped water with cupped hands. They drank, then both nodded. The water tasted good, they agreed, and it was sweet.

A quick tour of the barn also left Kirb pleased. Though built of smaller logs than the cabin, it appeared to be newer, and the mud that had been used to chink the cracks had stayed put over the years. It had a fair-sized hayloft, a separate room for storing grain, tools, and harnesses, and the roof was also made of cypress shingles. "I'd need at least one more stable," Kirb said, "but I could add that on either side of the barn if I wanted to." He was quiet for a few moments, then added, "On second thought, I believe I'd just let these two stables be the south side of the building. I'd leave a hall on the back side wide enough to drive a wagon through, then add two more stables on the north side of that. Wouldn't take more'n five or six posts and a coupla dozen poles to run the corral on around past the hall."

"Nope," Browning said. He chuckled, then pointed to their horses. "I can see that you've already made up your mind, Kirb. I reckon the only thing left to do is ride on into town and buy the place."

"Well, I wouldn't say that," Kirb said, leading the way toward the hitching rail. "I am kinda anxious to hear what Mr. Rubin's got to say though."

They mounted and rode off the property, picking up the main road about two miles to the southeast. Less than two hours later, they dismounted in front of the lawyer's office. Walt Rubin stood in the doorway watching them as they tied their animals to the rail. "Good morning, fellows!" he called loudly. "Come on in here; I've been expecting you!"

The two men stepped up on the boardwalk and covered the short distance to the doorway with long strides. "Come on in here," Rubin repeated, taking a few steps backward to allow his visitors to enter. He pointed to cushioned chairs neatly arranged on the near side of his desk. "Have a seat and make yourselves at home." Both Browning and Renfro nodded, then sat down.

Rubin walked behind the desk and seated himself in his swivel chair, then continued. "I've had a long talk with Honey Hathaway," he said, his eyes darting back and forth between the two men, "and today I can answer any questions either of you might have about the old Nelson place." He reached for a drawer, then stopped his hand in midair, appearing to have suddenly changed his mind. "Don't reckon you'd want any answers till after you've seen the place though." He got to his feet quickly. "If you'll follow me down to the livery stable to get my horse, we'll ride out and take a look at it."

Both Browning and Renfro shook their heads, but it was Kirb who spoke. "That won't be necessary, Mr. Rubin," he said. "Mr. Browning and I rode across it this morning, even went inside the cabin and checked out the barn. I also talked with the Lazy Bee foreman about it. He knows the place well."

"You talked with Mr. Ransom about it?" Rubin asked quickly. "What did he have to say?"

Kirb ignored the question. "I haven't decided whether I want to buy the old Nelson place or not, Mr. Rubin. I won't be able to make up my mind till I've heard the lady's bottom dollar and how high the yearly notes are gonna be."

This time Rubin did pull out the drawer. "It's gonna be hard for you to say no to this deal," he said with a broad smile, his eyes continuing to dart from one man to the other. "Mrs. Hathaway is an old woman by anybody's standards. She has no use whatsoever for that property and is in fact, tired of fooling with it. She's instructed me to make it easy for somebody else to own it." He laid a writing pad on the desk where both men could see the figures. "Read it for yourselves, men.

"You can see right off that I've cut the price to the bare bones, and there ain't no way in the world that I can shave off another dollar. Mrs. Hathaway says she'll donate the land to the county if nobody wants it on these terms." He nudged the pad a little closer to his prospects, then got to his feet, tapping the columns of figures with a forefinger. "Take all the time you need to study the deal," he said. "I'm gonna step outside a minute. The air's a little cooler out there."

Rubin had hardly taken up a leaning position against a post, when Browning appeared in the doorway, saying, "Both of us can read good enough, Walt, but we can't make heads or tails outta all those figures you've got on that pad. All Kirb wants you to do is sit down and tell him what kind of deal you're offering him on that property. Neither one of us can make anything outta that stack of figures, but we can understand plain old English pretty well."

"Oh, sure," Rubin said, heading for the door. He

walked past Browning and reclaimed his seat behind the desk. "I'm sorry, men, but I gave you those figures because I thought you'd probably want to look 'em over. I do that with everybody, so they can plainly see that I'm not hiding anything." He returned the writing pad to the drawer and closed it. "There's nothing complicated about the transaction, so I won't need those figures to explain it.

"Mrs. Hathaway and I went over the deal several times, and with a minimum of help from me, she laid out the terms herself. Twelve hundred dollars is her rock-bottom price, but a responsible party can buy it on time without paying any interest whatsoever. In other words, if he pays a hundred twenty dollars down and a hundred twenty dollars a year for the next nine years, he'll own the old Nelson place, lock, stock, and barrel. Mrs. Hathaway'll take care of my commission, so he'll owe me nothing." He smiled broadly, then spoke directly to Renfro. "It's all up to you now, young man. There's no point in me trying to talk you up or you trying to talk me down. The lady's terms might as well be carved in granite."

Both Browning and Renfro sat quietly for a few moments, then Gaylord pulled a watch from his vest pocket. "It's already dinnertime," he said, glancing at the face of the timepiece. "If you'll let us discuss it over a plate of beef and beans, we'll meet you back here in one hour. I think my young friend'll have an answer for you by then." He turned to Renfro. "Is that right, Kirb?"

"Yes, sir," Kirb answered. "That's right."

"That'll be fine," Rubin said. "I eat dinner at home every day, but that's just a short walk from here. I'll see you fellows again at one o'clock." The three men got to their feet, then stepped out on the boardwalk and quickly parted. Rubin crossed the street and disappeared between two buildings, while Browning and Renfro walked to the restaurant on the corner.

They selected a table just inside the front door, and true to his word, Gaylord ordered beef and beans when the waiter appeared. "Well, let's see," the young man said, taking a stub of pencil from behind his ear. "There's a lot of beef in the stew, so I could bring you a bowl of stew and a bowl of beans."

"That'll be fine," Browning said.

The waiter then turned his attention to Renfro, who said, "Just bring me a bowl of stew. I've been eating beans every day for nearly three months."

Within minutes they were eating a tasty meal and washing it down with good coffee. "Mrs. Hathaway ain't gonna come down no more on that property, Kirb," Gaylord said after a few bites.

"That's the way it sounded to me," Renfro agreed.

Browning washed a mouthful of stew down, then laid his spoon in the bowl. "A man couldn't expect to buy it any cheaper, 'cause it's actually worth more than she's asking for it. You got the hundred and twenty for the down payment?"

"Yes, sir."

Browning nodded "This could turn out to be a good deal for you and me both, Kirb. If you buy the Nelson place you could still work for the Lazy Bee, and I'd advise you to do that. With Bo Ransom limiting your work assignments to the southeastern portion of the ranch, you could eat at least two meals a day in your own cabin and sleep there every night.

"Now, unless you start needing cash money awful bad, you'd be wise to take part of your pay in brood cows. If you acquire a breeder every month, you'll have at least a hundred head of cattle in three years. I reckon that's about as many as two sections of land'll support.

"Three years'll pass before you know it, Kirb, and if you take my advice I have no doubt that you'll someday be glad you did. Just forfeit ten dollars of your pay every month, then rope one of the brood cows and put your brand on her. Once you've got your brand on her, just turn her loose. Your cows'll graze my land and mine'll graze yours, and I think we can count on my bulls to keep calves in the bellies of all of 'em. Of course, you won't always know exactly how many cattle you own, but you'll get an accurate count at roundup time.

"Now, listen to this, Kirb; here's why you ain't got nothing to lose by buying the property: If you ever decide you don't want to keep it, I'll be glad to take it off your hands. I'll give you back every dollar you've paid into it, including your down payment, then buy every cow you've got."

Kirb exhaled loudly. "I couldn't let you do that, Mr. Browning. Why in the world should you be taking all the risks for something that's only gonna benefit me?"

Browning took a sip of coffee, then set the cup in the saucer noisily. "I don't see the risk," he said, "and I wouldn't necessarily be doing it for your benefit. There're more'n twelve hundred acres of good grazing land down there, and I reckon I could eventually find a use for the buildings."

Kirb finished his coffee. He sat staring into the empty cup for a while, then raised his head quickly. "I'm gonna buy that property," he said with conviction.

When Kirb repeated that statement in Walt Rubin's office half an hour later, the lawyer nodded. "Do you have the money on you for the down payment?" he asked.

Kirb laid six double eagles on the desk.

Rubin picked up the coins and placed them in his desk drawer. "That'll take care of the first year," he said. He opened a folder and began to fill in the blanks on several sheets of paper. When he was through, he shoved the papers across the desk to Renfro. "Take as much time as you need to read those, then sign your name on all the lines that I've marked with exes." He got to his feet and headed for the door. "I'll get Bill Harvey to come over from the hardware store and make it all legal. He's the local notary public."

Half an hour later, with the transaction completed and notorized, the three men stood in front of the lawyer's office. "It's been a pleasure doing business with you, Kirb," Rubin was saying as he shook Renfro's hand. "I guess you'll be giving the old Nelson place a new name, but I believe you're gonna be satisfied with it." Then he turned to Gaylord. "It was good to see you again too, Mr. Browning, and I hope you'll stop by from time to time. Whether we do any business or not, we should be able to find something or somebody to talk about." He disappeared inside his office quickly.

Browning and Renfro walked to the hitching rail. Kirb put his papers and the receipt for his money in his saddlebag, then slipped the knot in his horse's reins. "I'm gonna take your advice about working for the Lazy Bee, Mr. Browning, and I'll take part of my pay in cows too. I can't start right away though. The Nelson place needs a whole lot of work, and it'll probably take me the rest of the summer to get it done."

Browning nodded. "Of course it will," he said. "Take as much time as you need to fix up your own place, then let me know when you're ready to go to work. Ransom'll find a job for you."

Kirb stood holding his horse's reins, suddenly remembering some of the words spoken by his uncle. George Renfro had told his nephew that if he went to Texas and kept his eyes open, something good would fall right into his lap. Had Uncle George's prediction already come true? *Could be,* Kirb was thinking. He turned to Gaylord. "I appreciate everything you've done, Mr. Browning, and so does Ellie." He stood quietly for a moment, then pointed across the street to the Bank of Texas. "I've got more money in my pockets than I need to be carrying around, Mr. Browning. Maybe I should walk over there and make a deposit."

Gaylord chuckled. "There ain't no maybe to it, son. It's the only smart thing to do. You just go ahead, I'll hold your horse and wait for you outside the bank."

Renfro was in the bank for the large part of an hour, and when he came out he was smiling. "The banker's name is Mr. Witherspoon," he said, accepting his horse's reins from Gaylord, "and I think he took down my whole life history. I told him I'd bought the old Nelson place, and he said if I ever needed money he'd be glad to talk to me about it. He said he liked to do business with young men."

Gaylord chuckled. "Of course he does. He likes young customers for the same reason insurance companies do: They're apt to live longer." He untied his own animal. "I met Witherspoon the first day I was in town, and he seemed nice enough to me." He chuckled again. "Every banker I ever met was nice, and part of it might be because they don't have no other choice. Money's tight in most places, and there's an awful lot of competition for the working man's dollar." He stepped into a stirrup and threw his leg over the saddle. "I ain't belittling bankers now, 'cause God knows we need 'em. I'm glad you made a friend outta Witherspoon too, 'cause the day may come when he can help you over a rough spot."

Kirb mounted the black, and the two men rode down the street side by side. As they neared the livery stable and the road home, Gaylord pointed to the saloon on the corner. "You think we oughtta have us a cold beer before we tackle that hot ride, Kirb?"

"I'll leave that up to you," Renfro answered. "I'll drink one if you do."

They dismounted at the hitching rail and tied their animals. They stepped up on the boardwalk and Gaylord was just about to push his way through the bat-wing doors, when they suddenly opened from the inside, hitting him in the chest and almost knocking him down. A muscular redhead who was at least six feet tall and appeared to be about twenty-five years old now stood in the doorway. "Get outta my way, fellow," he said with a smirk. "You're lucky I didn't knock you on your ass."

When Browning appeared to be at a loss for something to say, the redhead turned his attention to Renfro. "Don't be standing there staring at me!" he said loudly. "I'll get you too!"

Kirb eased Gaylord out of the way with his elbow, then moved a step closer to his antagonist. "I believe you've got me mixed up with somebody else," he said. "You ain't gonna do a damn thing to me. Fact is, I might decide to whip your goddam ass for talking that way to Mr. Browning."

The man cursed loudly and charged instantly, almost knocking Renfro off his feet. Even as they locked arms and stumbled into the street, Kirb decided that his opponent was a very strong man, that he must keep the wrestling to a minimum and do his fighting with his fists. He emphasized that decision with a left, then a right to the jaw, with the last punch knocking the redhead between the feet of a horse standing at the hitching rail.

The man crawled on under the horse and got to his feet on the opposite side. He cursed the animal and punched it with his fist, then stepped around its rump. Renfro was waiting. He kept his left fist in the man's face constantly and knocked him to his knees twice with his right. Both times, the man was back on his feet quickly, seeming no worse for the wear.

Although Kirb was aware of the fact that a crowd had gathered to watch the fight, he was at no time distracted, and continued to concentrate on every move his opponent made. When the redhead's attempt at manhandling Kirb failed, he resorted to trading punches, which was another mistake. His eyes were now swollen almost shut, and his face was a bloody mess.

Nonetheless, the man still wanted to fight. Though now unsteady on his feet, he made one charge after another, and Renfro continued to hammer his face unmercifully. Renfro finally beat him to his knees again and was standing over him measuring him for a another right to the jaw when a hand grabbed his arm. "That's enough," a deep voice commanded.

Kirb turned to look into the eyes of a man as tall as himself and twice as old, who had a marshal's badge pinned to his shirt. "Whipping a man in a fistfight is one thing," the lawman said, "but beating him to death is something else."

Renfro nodded, then backed away and stood looking at the redhead. For all practical purposes the man was unconscious now, but he would not go down. He sat cross-legged in the dirt, staring down the street and seeing nothing.

Browning was beside Renfro now. "Let's go home, Kirb."

Renfro untied his horse and stepped into the saddle, then noticed that the marshal was standing beside his stirrup. "I ain't never seen a scrapper as good as you are before," the lawman said. "No, sir, never in my life." He waved his arm in a sweeping motion toward the crowd. "I'll betcha none of them ain't neither. I know for a fact that they ain't seen nobody put Pat Pollard down before 'cause it ain't never been done. You done it more'n once and made it look easy besides."

"A man does what he has to do," Kirb said, then turned his horse and headed down the street. He took the road to the Lazy Bee, and Browning caught up quickly.

"That's the first time I ever saw that man you fought with," he said, as he pulled alongside Renfro's black. "Never saw the marshal before either. Fact is, I probably don't know many more people around here than you do 'cause the only folks I've met are the ones I had to know in order to get established on the Lazy Bee. Rubin did mention the marshal to me once though; said his name was Frank Cotton. Judging from the way he talks, I'd say he came from our part of the country."

"I decided the same thing," Renfro agreed.

Nothing else was said by either man for several minutes; then Browning broke the silence. "I reckon I'm about like the marshal said he was, Kirb. I don't know that I've ever seen a man account for himself the way you did back there."

"It's like I told him," Kirb said, "a man does what he has to do."

Browning rode quietly for a mile or more. "I appreciate you taking up for me," he said finally. "I ain't likely to forget it either."

"That's exactly what I want you to do," Renfro said. "Start forgetting it right now." He kicked the black to a canter, and Browning was close on his heels.

9

★

The Renfros left the Lazy Bee next morning headed for their new homestead. When Kirb brought the wagon to a halt at the front door of the cabin two hours before noon, Ellie climbed down the front wheel to the ground. "Why, it's a whole lot bigger than the one we lived in back home," she said, then disappeared into the cabin. Kirb wrapped the reins around the brake pole, then followed.

Standing behind her with his arms around her middle, he said, "I'll fix it up anyway you want it, Ellie. Anytime you want something changed, all you gotta do is say so."

"I don't see anything I'd want to change yet," she said, wriggling out of his arms. She moved to the center of the room with palms up and arms outstretched, her eyes taking in the dimensions of the room. "It's so . . . big," she said. She stood quietly for a moment, then motioned to the north side of the room, adding, "That's the kitchen over there next to that wall. Look at all those shelves, and all those big nails to hang things on. I can see already that this is all we need, Kirb." Wrinkling her nose, she returned to him and put her arms around his waist. "I just wonder where we're gonna get enough stuff to furnish it."

"Furniture is going to be no problem, my dear," he said, making an effort to speak like a clown who had once visited his schoolroom. "Some of it Kirby Floyd Renfro will build and some of it he will buy, but it shall all be delivered to his beautiful wife's doorstep."

She hugged him tightly, then turned away. "I love you," she said, almost as if speaking to the north window.

"It's too late in the day to head for town now, but we'll go in tomorrow and get the first wagonload of stuff. You just pick out any cookstove you want at the hardware store, and we'll start with that. I'll get a turning plow and break up a spot for a garden so we can get that over with. Seems to me like the very first thing we oughtta do is get some vegetables in the ground; might already be too late in the year, for all I know.

"Anyway, it won't cost us nothing but a sack of fertilizer and a few packs of seed to find out. We'll buy some jars and sealing rubbers so you can put up whatever we manage to grow before the first frost gets here. We'll have plenty of time to fence in the garden after we plant it 'cause it'll be about two weeks before anything comes up. Gotta put up a fence 'cause Mr. Browning's cows'll eat up our plants as fast as they come outta the ground." Even as he spoke he had been pointing to three Lazy Bee cows grazing where his garden would eventually be.

He stepped through the doorway, then spoke to Ellie again. "I'm gonna put the livestock in the corral," he said. "When I get that done, I'll take the canvas and the ribs off the wagon so it'll be easier to load and unload." He unhooked the mules' trace chains and hung them on their hames, then retrieved his currycomb from under the wagon seat and led the animals toward the barn. Once he had cared for them, he would come back for Midnight.

Half an hour later, with the mules curried and tied to a post, Kirb unloaded a sack of shelled corn from the wagon and laid it across the back of his saddler. Then, with a nose bag under his arm, he led the big black to the corral. Within minutes, each of the mules was eating from a trough inside one of the stables, while the black stood in the pole enclosure with a bagful of grain hanging on its nose. Kirb headed back to the cabin. He would take the nose bag off the horse in half an hour, then allow all three of the animals to roam about the corral and drink from the spring's runoff.

Noticing smoke coming from the chimney as he walked into the yard, Kirb knew that Ellie had already unloaded a few things and gone about fixing dinner. He smiled, then reached into the wagon for his toolbox.

An hour later, having interrupted his work only long enough to take the nose bag off the horse and turn the mules loose in the corral, he laid the folded canvas and the ribs under the overhang on the east side of the barn where he intended to eventually build a shed. He had just returned to the wagon, when Ellie spoke to him from the doorway. "I've got some hot buttered hoecakes and cof-fee," she said. "I figured we'd better use up that butter Mrs. Browning gave us as quick as we can 'cause it won't keep long in this kind of weather."

"It ain't gonna get a chance to keep," Kirb said, pinch-ing her on the backside as he stepped into the building. "Just put it within reaching distance of me every meal, and it'll be gone long before it goes bad." He filled a cup from the coffeepot, then accepted the plateful of cornmeal hoecakes that Ellie had already buttered. He seated him-self well away from the heat of the fireplace, then began to wash the simple meal down with his wife's good coffee.

"I can't think of a single thing that would taste better than this right now, honey," he said.

"It's the only thing we had that I could fix quick," Ellie said. She pointed to the big iron pot on the fire. "I've got that thing about half full of beans and bacon, but they ain't nowhere near done yet. They'll be mighty good at suppertime though."

"Yep," Kirb said. He continued to wolf down the hoe-cakes for a while, then spoke again. "I don't know what in the world I'd do without you, Ellie. I mean, I'm so used to depending on you for every little thing that I'd be lost without you."

She chuckled. "I think you could find yourself pretty quick if you needed to."

When they were done eating, they unloaded the wagon and brought their things into the cabin. Everything except bedrolls and cooking and eating utensils was piled into a corner of the front room, for Ellie had said that she wanted to clean up the cabin before she concerned herself with putting things in their proper places. She had already put a broom and a mop on her list of things to buy when she got to town.

Just inside the door, Kirb laid his rifle and his shotgun on the short sections of forked limbs that had been nailed to the wall for that purpose. He buckled on his gun belt, then motioned to the dwindling pile of fuel beside the fireplace. "We're gonna need more wood pretty soon," he said. "I noticed a dead tree on the ground just below the barn, and I'm gonna chop up some of it and get it in the cabin before it gets wet." He stood in the doorway pointing. "Rain clouds have been floating around to west of us for the past two hours. If they ever get together, we'll find out real quick whether the roof leaks or not." He walked to the wagon and got his ax, then headed for the dead tree.

He chopped and carried wood for the next two hours, at which time he had a stack several feet high in the corner. "That's more wood than we're gonna need for the fireplace till cold weather," he said, "so I'll just save the rest of that tree. After I see how long the cookstove's firebox is, I'll cut the rest of the wood to fit it."

Ellie nodded, then cast her eyes to the rear of the cabin. "I've been fixing up our new bedroom," she said, pointing to the two bedrolls lying side by side near the wall. "Now you won't be lying under the wagon out of reach every night when I start dreaming about you."

Kirb hung his gun belt on the wall, then took Ellie in his arms. He stood kissing her and running his hands over her body for a few moments then led her across the floor. "Let's try out the new bedroom right now," he said.

Ellie giggled, and followed eagerly.

The Renfro wagon rolled into town at ten o'clock next morning. Wanting to buy and load up a cookstove and a plow before he even looked at anything else, Kirb brought the vehicle to a halt in front of Bill Harvey's hardware store. He tied the team and helped Ellie down; then the two stepped inside the establishment. Harvey himself was standing just inside the door. He tipped his hat to Ellie, then spoke to Kirb. "I'm very happy to see you again, Mr. Renfro. Did you get settled in on the old Nelson place all right?"

"We're there," Kirb answered, "but we ain't exactly settled yet. I brought my wife in to look at a cookstove."

Harvey nodded. "I've got three," he said. "A used one and two new ones. The new ones are prettier and cost more money, but the used one's the best stove. Nell Goodmire cooked on it for several years, and everybody claimed she was the best cook in the county. Her husband traded the stove to me after she ran off with a banjo player." He motioned toward the rear of the store. "They're all right back there, so you can look 'em over and take your pick." He led the way down the aisle and pointed out the stoves, all of which had their prices clearly marked.

Although Kirb was quick to notice the significant difference in the price of the old versus the new, he did not mention it to Ellie. "Look 'em over as long as you want to, honey," he said. "The one you choose is the one you get."

Ellie had also read the price tags. She opened and closed the oven door on the old stove a few times, then knelt to look inside. "Big oven," she said, "and the door fits tight." She lifted the eyes to reveal a long firebox, then turned to Kirb. "It wouldn't be very hard to get plenty of heat going in a box that big." She raised one of the eyes above the hot water tank. "Is that a three-gallon tank, Mr. Harvey?"

He nodded. "Yes, ma'am, I believe it is."

"How about these two eyelifters?" she asked, still holding one of them in her hand. "Are they part of the deal?"

"Yes, ma'am. They go right along with the stove."

She touched the price tag, which was tied to the stove with a string. "Twelve dollars and fifty cents," she read aloud. "I guess you're gonna throw in as many joints of stovepipe as we need, huh?"

"No, ma'am," Harvey said. "I paid ten dollars for the stove myself, and it's been sitting here for more'n three months. I'll have to have twelve-fifty, and I can't afford to throw in anything else."

Ellie turned to her husband. "Let's buy it, Kirb."

He nodded, then spoke to Harvey. "I don't mind paying for the pipe. I'll take six joints with me, and if I don't need that many I'll bring some of 'em back. The flue goes straight up through the roof, so I won't need but one elbow. I'll use it on top of the cabin to keep the rain out."

Harvey nodded and took the price tag off the stove. "Did you mean five joints of pipe and one elbow, or six joints?"

"I'm sure five joints'll be enough," Kirb answered. "I'll just use the elbow to cap it."

"Very well," Harvey said. He walked behind a counter and came back with the pipe. "Anything else?"

"A few more things," Kirb said. He took a list from his pocket, then pointed to the front of the store. "I want that turning plow up there, a sack of fertilizer, a hoe, some garden seed, a posthole digger, and two pounds of twenty-penny nails."

Harvey nodded, then headed for the back door. "I'm gonna get my sons to load the heavy stuff for you. I can't allow my customers to strain themselves." He disappeared through the doorway and returned a short time later with two barrel-chested young men at his heels. "Just show 'em how you want the stove and the plow to ride," he said to Renfro. "They'll do the lifting."

Kirb followed Harvey's suggestion, and the heavy items were in his wagon within minutes. He loaded the remainder of his merchandise himself, then paid the man and left the store.

The Renfros ate dinner at a small restaurant; then Kirb parked the wagon in front of a general store. He handed Ellie an eagle, then walked around the vehicle and helped her down. "This looks like a good place to get a broom and a mop," he said. "I'll wait right here for you. Buy anything else you see that you need, and if you get more'n you can carry, just holler."

She was in the store for no more than ten minutes. When she returned she laid a broom and a mop in the wagon, then shoved a brown paper bag under the seat. "I bought some soap and a few other things," she said. "I've got some big pans that I can bathe in till we get a wash-tub."

Kirb nodded. He scooted her up to her seat, then rounded the wagon and climbed to his own. Moments later, they took the road to their new home. They would be back in town many times within the next few weeks, for there were a myriad of other things they needed to buy.

10

★

As Kirb was plowing up the garden spot next morning, his wife was walking behind him smoothing out the ground with the hoe, raking up small mounds of earth for the six tomato plants Bess Browning had given her two days before. "I'm gonna put those plants in the ground this morning," Ellie had said as Kirb was hitching up the team. "I don't believe cows even like tomatoes."

"Set 'em out on the southeast corner of the garden," he said. "The cows won't eat 'em. Just build up some hills with the hoe, then pour a handful of fertilizer on each one. Don't put it right in the hole with the plants, now, 'cause it'll burn 'em up. You just mix it into the ground real good with the hoe, then pour your holes half full of water and set out your plants. Nothing to it."

Ellie smiled good-naturedly "I know," she said. "I've been doing it since I was ten."

Standing watching his wife walk to the cabin to get the plants and the water bucket, Kirb made up his mind right on the spot to stop talking to her like she was a child. She was a very intelligent woman, smart enough to ask questions about anything she did not understand. Besides, how many tomato plants had he actually planted during his lifetime? A few, but Ellie had probably planted more. He nodded at his thoughts as she disappeared inside the building. Yep, his pretty little partner had a fine mind of her own. From now on he would make it a point to be more considerate of her feelings and ask her opinion when there was an important decision to be made.

Ellie planted her tomatoes, and even after Kirb had finished the plowing and unhitched the mules, she continued to rake up dirt with the hoe and smooth out the rows for planting other things. "If you'll tell me how far apart you want the seeds," she said, "I can plant the garden while you go to the woods after a load of fence posts."

"All right," he said. "Be sure to plant the pole beans—" he suddenly stopped in midsentence and stood thinking for a while. "Didn't you say you'd done all this before?" he asked finally.

She smiled faintly, then nodded. "Yes," she said softly.

"Well, do it again," he said, then began to lead the team toward the wagon. "Do it the same way you've always done it," he added over his shoulder.

She turned her back and continued to lay off the rows.

Kirb hitched the mules to the wagon and laid his ax, a file, and his Henry rifle under the seat, then headed down the slope in a southwesterly direction. He could already see a stand of cedars a few hundred yards away that appeared to be about the right size. Though not nearly as easy to chop as many other species of wood, he had always used cedar posts when he could find them. Cedar was unbelievably durable and would very often be standing long after the fence builder had gone to his just reward.

Once he reached the big stand of evergreens, Kirb could easily see that there were many more posts here than he would ever need. More than he would ever want, for that matter. In fact, he might even spend a few days cutting and burning some of them next winter, for they were a constant drain on the earth's nutrients and moisture. The more trees, the less grass, the old adage went.

He worked right through the dinner hour and, after discovering that he was still not hungry, decided to make a day of it. The sun was no more than two hours' high, when he finally drove up the hill and began to scatter the posts at intervals around the perimeter of the garden. He would set the posts five ax handles apart, then use the same means of measurement to make sure he cut the poles the correct length. He had thrown off about half of his load when Ellie appeared beside the wagon. "I didn't have no way of knowing you were gonna be gone all day," she said. "I heated up beans and hoecakes for you about dinnertime, but I reckon they'll be just as good for supper."

"They'll be better," he said. "I wasn't hungry at noon, but I am now."

She turned toward the cabin. "I'll keep watch on you and try to have supper hot about the time you get done for the day."

He watched her till she reached the cabin. Preparing a meal would be much less drudgery for her now that she had a good cookstove, he was thinking. He had put up the stove immediately after they brought it from town, and Ellie had been delighted with it. She had popped a panful of popcorn on it after supper last night, then cooked a big platter of flapjacks on it this morning. "I can't wait to heat some water in that tank and take a good, hot bath," she had said at breakfast.

Even as Kirb went back to work he continued to think about the stove. He had seen smoke coming from the flue for most of the afternoon and had begun to wonder how much hot water his wife needed for a bath. Now, after thinking on it a while longer, he smiled. He threw off another post, then nodded at his thoughts. Ellie had been doing something to surprise him, he had decided. And what could she do to surprise him? She could bake him a pound cake. She had the flour, the sugar, and Mrs. Browning had seen to it that she had the butter. Yes, sir, he now knew what all the smoke had been about. As soon as he had eaten his fill of beans and bacon tonight, his little woman was going to surprise him with a pound cake.

After throwing off the remainder of the posts, he drove the wagon to the barn and unhitched the team. He spent the next half hour caring for his livestock, then called it a day and walked to the cabin. Ellie announced that supper was ready the moment he stepped through the doorway, and just as he had expected, the cake was presented after he had eaten two platefuls of beans. "I decided to bake this for you while I was heating my bathwater," Ellie said, taking the cake out of a box behind the stove. "I ate a pinch of it, and I think it turned out about right."

"Of course it did," he said. He got to his feet and hugged her with one arm, then stood by while she laid a thick slice of pound cake on his plate. "This sure is a surprise, honey," he said with a smile. "No telling what you'll hit me with next."

She laid a smaller slice on her own plate and refilled their cups with coffee, then joined her husband, who sat cross-legged on the floor. Neither of them spoke till they were done eating, then Kirb broke the silence. "This is the last supper we're gonna eat sitting on this floor," he said. "After we eat breakfast tomorrow morning, we'll go back to town and get a table and some chairs." He pointed over his shoulder with his thumb. "We'll buy a bed with a good cotton mattress and set it up back there too."

"That'll be so nice, Kirb. Can we really afford all that?"

"I don't reckon we can afford not to buy a few things for the cabin, honey. You ain't even got a table to work on, much less a place for us to sit down and eat. We need that bed too. Working people deserve a decent night's rest."

"I guess so," Ellie said, then changed the subject. "Three or four more hours in that garden, and I'll have all the seeds in the ground."

"That'll be good," he said. "I'll have the fence completed long before the plants come up. I want to pick up some half-gallon jars in town, so you can put up a lot of vegetables for next winter."

"I'll find the jars while you make a deal for the bed and the table," she said. She sat thoughtful for a moment, then added, "I've been thinking about something else, too. We ain't got many clothes, but I could keep those we've got smelling a lot better if I had a wash pot, a washtub, and a washboard set up out there beside the spring. I wouldn't have to tote the water so far on wash day, and maybe you could put me up a clothesline. And I'd need some clothespins too. They don't cost much, and you can buy 'em just about anywhere."

Kirb squeezed her hand. "You're gonna get all of those things," he said. "I'll even stop at that little lumberyard north of town and pick up some rough boards to build a bench for your washtub. I'll put up a clothesline for you too, but you'll have to remember to get the clothespins yourself."

"I've got a list made out," she said. "I'll add them to it."

"It's gonna take two trips to get all that stuff home,"

he said, "so let's count on going to town tomorrow and the next day both. Like I said, there ain't no hurry on that garden fence. It'll be at least ten days before there's anything out there big enough for a cow to notice."

The Renfros were as busy as ants for the next several days. By the end of the second week the cabin was adequately furnished and even had shades and curtains on the windows. Ellie's washing station had been set up beside the spring, and a clothesline ran from the southeast corner of the cabin to a post her husband had put in the ground.

The garden fence had been completed, and Kirb was now working at the barn. Since he owned three animals, two days ago he had begun the process of adding a third stable to the building. Once that was done he intended to build a shed for his wagon and other equipment, and the material for both was now piled on the ground a few yards away. He had met lumberyard owner Wilbur Hunt last week when he stopped off to get the boards for Ellie's bench and had inquired about the price of enough rough lumber to build the two structures.

"Aw, I reckon I could offer you a reasonable price on some rough stuff," the man had said. He stood scratching his bearded chin for a moment, then asked, "Why don't you just build the stable and the shed both outta tin? I reckon it's about as warm in the winter as wood is, and it'll turn water a hell of a lot better."

Kirb smiled, and shook his head. "I thought about that, Mr. Hunt, but not for long. I'm afraid tin would cost a lot more than I can afford to spend."

Hunt drenched a large rock with a stream of tobacco juice, then pointed across the field. "Won't cost you nothing if you don't mind getting your hands dirty," he said. "You see all that tin scattered around over yonder? It used to be the roof of a big storage building that burned down last year.

"It's dirty and smoky as hell, but otherwise it ain't hurt, and if a fellow took some pains to put his new nails in the same holes the old ones came out of, it might not even leak. I want to plant some turnip greens on that piece of ground, so if you'll haul that tin off and get it outta my way, you can have every sheet of it for nothing."

Kirb nodded. "I'll walk over and take a look at it," he said. He took a few steps, then came to an abrupt halt. "That don't mean that I'm all that particular, now, that I want to look it over before I decide whether I want it or not. I can promise you right now that I'll get it out of your way, and I certainly appreciate the gift. I was just gonna look at it to try to figure out how many trips it'll take."

Hunt nodded curtly, then turned his attention to something else.

Kirb had hauled the three wagonloads of tin home the very next day and had spent another day straightening and sorting it out. He not only now had enough material on the premises to build the barn and the shed, but he could build a springhouse and an outhouse as well. Once he had finished the buildings he would paint them red; then nobody would know that he had used secondhand material.

II

By the middle of September, Kirb had his place in much better shape. Once he saw that he had enough material on hand to do the job, he had built two stables instead of one. The springhouse was also up, and a new outhouse was located thirty yards down the hill. Once the building was done, he had spent two weeks working on the mile-long stretch of road, making it passable all the way to its conjunction with the main road near the river.

Following his wife's suggestion, he had named the place the Circle R Ranch and had already registered the brand. A few days ago he had ordered branding irons from the blacksmith shop in Comanche and had been told that he could pick them up next time he was in town.

Today he intended to ride to Lazy Bee headquarters, for he had decided that the time had come to discuss employment with Gaylord Browning. Renfro was not yet hurting for money, but with no income and so much outgo during the past several months, he was anxious to recuperate his expenditures. He was also eager to see his brand on the rump of a cow and had already decided to accept one every month as part of his pay. Although Gaylord had not said exactly how much would be deducted from Kirb's wages for each cow, he had hinted at ten dollars.

Even if the price turned out to be higher, Renfro would nonetheless make the trade. He had been doing a lot of figuring lately. Plain old arithmetic told him that if he continued to acquire a brood cow every month he would own more cattle than his property would support after only a few years, and that a large number of them would be marketable steers. Maybe he could acquire enough money to buy more land by sending the steers to Kansas with one of the Lazy Bee herds. Yes, sir, it was very possible that he would someday own thousands of cattle, and a spread twice the size of the Lazy Bee.

When Kirb showed his figures to Ellie, she nodded, then produced some of her own. "I did this more'n a month ago," she said, handing him a sheet of paper with columns of figures on both sides. "I didn't show it to you then 'cause I was afraid you'd think I was being pushy."

Kirb glanced at each side, then handed it back. "Hang on to this," he said. "I want to look it over closer when I've got more time."

Ellie refolded the paper and shoved it into her apron pocket. "According to these figures, even if half of your calves turned out to be bulls, you'd still own enough cattle to fill up this whole county in less than fifteen years."

Kirb had then grabbed Ellie and swept her off her feet, spinning her round and round. "We're gonna make it, honey," he said excitedly. "We're gonna make it big."

This morning after breakfast Kirb had told her of his decision to ride to the Lazy Bee, and the sun had been up about an hour when he led Midnight from the barn to the

cabin door, where Ellie stood waiting to say good-bye. He
lifted her off the ground and kissed her eyes, then dropped
her back to her feet. "I don't know how long this'll take,
honey, but I reckon you can find something to do in the
garden while I'm gone."

"I've got plenty to do out there," she said. "You just
go on and take care of your business. I'll be fine."

He kissed the top of her head, then stepped into the
saddle. The big horse responded instantly to a kick in the
ribs and carried him out of sight at a fast trot.

When he rode up the hill to the Lazy Bee ranch house
more than an hour later, he was not surprised to learn
that a fence now surrounded the front yard. And he knew
where the poles had come from, for although he had seen
neither of the Browning boys when he was on the east
bank of the river cutting saplings to fence in his garden,
he saw plenty of evidence that someone else had recently
harvested poles there.

He continued up the hill at a walk and, seeing no one
in the yard or elsewhere on the premises, was drawn to
the cookshack by the gray smoke rising from it's flue. He
tied the black to the hitching rail, then walked across the
breezeway and knocked on the jamb of the open door,
stepping inside as he did so. "Can I come in, Mr. Kelso?"
he asked.

"Of course, you can," the cook answered. "Been
awhile since I've seen you, young fellow."

"I bought a place of my own," Kirb said, "and I've
been mighty busy. It sure is nice to see you again. You got
a cup of coffee to spare?"

The cook pointed to a shelf that held at least a dozen
tin cups. "Just help yourself there," he said. "I made a
fresh pot about an hour ago."

Kirb filled a cup with coffee, then took a seat at the
table. He dumped a spoonful of sugar in the cup and

stirred, then spoke to the cook again. "I rode over to have a talk with Mr. Browning or Mr. Ransom. Do you happen to know where either of 'em is?"

"Ransom's out riding with the hands," Kelso answered, "and Dossy left for town in the buggy a little while ago. I'm surprised you didn't meet him on the road."

"I traveled cross-country," Kirb said. "Didn't use the road for more'n a mile." He sipped at his coffee, then added, "Anyway, Dossy's brother is the man I need to talk with. Seen him this morning?"

"Not yet," the cook answered, "but it won't be long. He comes in here and drinks a cup of coffee at nine o'clock every morning, and you can almost set your watch by him." He pointed to a clock on a shelf beside the stove. "It's five minutes to nine now, so he should be here anytime."

The cook had hardly finished speaking, when they heard Gaylord outside. "Whose black horse is this?" he shouted, then walked across the plank breezeway noisily. Framing himself in the doorway, he stood for a moment chuckling, then pointed. "Whose dark steed stands at yonder hitching rail?"

"The animal belongs to Robin Hood!" Renfro said loudly. "From Sherwood Forest!"

Browning crossed the room quickly and shook Kirb's hand. "Thought maybe you'd forgotten all about us up here," he said. "A few of us were talking about you yesterday, and Bo Ransom said the reason you hadn't come to see us was that you hadn't had the time. He said you were probably working ten or twelve hours a day fixing up your own place."

Kirb nodded. "Fourteen," he said.

Browning filled a cup, then seated himself on the op-

posite side of the table. "We've missed seeing you and
your little woman both," he said. "Tell me about the
things you've been doing to the old Nelson place."

"Lemme see," Kirb said, drumming his fingers on the
tabletop. "I plowed up and fenced in a garden spot for
Ellie, then did a few things around the cabin that made
her happy. I added two stables to the barn and built a
springhouse and an outhouse, then spent two weeks working on the road. I can get over it without tearing up my
wagon now."

"Good," Browning said. "Sounds like Bo Ransom was
right about you being busy." He sipped at his coffee.
"Ain't none of us been breaking our backs around here
lately, but all that'll change before long. The fall cow
hunt's coming up pretty soon, and it'll put every man on
the premises in the saddle. All except me and Dossy and
Mr. Kelso, that is. Me and Dossy are gonna be helping
Mr. Kelso keep the hands fed. Be a lotta extra mouths to
feed during the cow hunt."

Kirb refilled his cup, then returned to his seat.
"When's the cow hunt gonna get started?" he asked.

"About twelve or fifteen days from now, depending
on the weather. Bo says a two-week dry spell would be a
godsend; but if we don't get it, we'll go anyhow. If it starts
raining, every man in the bunch is gonna earn his pay."

Kirb nodded. "You said there'd be some extra mouths
to feed. How many more men are you gonna hire?"

"Ransom's got a free rein on that 'cause he's the only
one who knows exactly what he wants. He said if he could
get the same fellows he used last time he'd probably hire
six, but if not, he might have to sign on as many as ten.
Anyway, he's gonna take off next weekend and go hunting
men. He said he'd see who was available around Comanche first, but that he'd go all the way to Hamilton or Stephenville if he had to. He's mighty picky about who comes

on the Lazy Bee. I don't believe he'll hire just anybody."

Kirb nodded. "He's smart, and he seems like a good man."

"That's his reputation," Gaylord said, "and he never has said or done nothing to make me doubt it." He refilled his cup and reseated himself, then changed the subject. "I reckon you ain't out riding just to enjoy the morning air, Kirb. You got something you want to talk about?"

"Yes, sir," Renfro answered. "I've got all the building done down at my place and the cabin's in good enough shape to please my wife, so I thought we oughtta talk some more about me going to work for the Lazy Bee."

"Me and Bo already talked about it some," Browning said. "He says he's got a job for you that'll allow you to keep right on living in your own cabin. You can eat your meals at home and sleep in your own bed every night."

Renfro smiled broadly. "That's mighty good news, Mr. Browning. The idea that I might have to leave Ellie alone at night has been bothering me a whole lot." He stared over the older man's shoulder for a moment, then asked, "What kind of job was Mr. Ransom talking about?"

"He said he'd put you to work as a line rider on the southeastern portion of the ranch. I told him I thought we oughtta give you about five dollars extra every month since we won't be having to feed you, and he said that sounded right to him." He drained his coffee cup, then added, "Your pay'll be thirty-five dollars a month, so you'll have twenty-five a month coming after you pay for a brood cow. Once you've registered a brand and got an iron made up, somebody'll touch one of the proven breeders with it every month."

"I've already registered my brand, and that fat man at the blacksmith shop said I could pick up my irons next time I'm in town. I ordered three."

"Oh," Browning said. "I reckon, by gosh, you have been busy. What brand did you decide on?"

"Circle Ar," Kirb answered. "Ar for Renfro."

"Of course," Gaylord said. He got to his feet and dropped his cup in a pan of water, then stood leaning on the table. "I'm sure Bo can use you on the upcoming cow hunt; then after that's over you can get lined out on your regular job. I know it'll all be brand new to you, but while you're rounding up the cattle you're gonna be learning a whole lotta stuff that'll come in handy later on." He pointed toward the doorway. "Let's go back outside and get away from Mr. Kelso's hot stove."

They stepped onto the breezeway and turned toward the hitching rail just as a man walked around the corner of the bunkhouse and headed for the cookshack. Browning leaned against the wall and stood waiting for him. "Howdy, Laney," he said as the man drew near. "Found that ginseng yet?"

The man shook his head. "Not yet, but I know it's out there. I tell you, some days when th' wind's jist right, I c'n smell it like it wuz growin' right under my nose."

Browning nodded and one corner of his mouth broke into a smile. "Are you gonna remember us after you find it and get rich, Laney?"

"Gonna remember ever'body," the man answered. "I b'lieve there's enough ginsang growin' somewhere in this county to make a lotta people rich, and I've got it narrowed down to jist three places: the Lazy Bee, the old Nelson place, and that wooded land on the east side of the river. I ain't gonna stop lookin' till I find it neither; then ever'body I know's gonna be rich."

"Well, that's nice to hear, Laney. When you find it, just holler."

The man nodded, and pointed to the cookshack. "Mr. Kelso gives me some leftovers when he's got 'em, so I thought I'd stop by and check with 'im. I ain't et nothin' for two days now."

Browning moved aside to allow him to pass. "Go right in," he said. "Kelso's got some hot coffee too."

The man nodded, and disappeared into the cookshack. Carrying a small sack resembling a pillowcase over his shoulder, he stood about five-seven and weighed around a 140 pounds. With a ruddy complexion and several large moles on his face, and brown hair that was turning gray around his temples, he appeared to be about forty years old.

"That fellow's name is Laney Crosley," Browning said, "but everybody calls him 'the Ginseng Man.' I met him the second day I was here, but he didn't start promising to make me rich till after he'd seen me a few more times. I reckon he's a little bit soft in the head, but everybody says he's harmless. He probably walks several thousand miles a year hunting that damn ginseng, but I'll bet he wouldn't know what to do with it if he found it."

Kirb smiled. "I wouldn't either," he said. "Fact is, I don't even know what it is."

Browning chuckled. "I didn't know nothing about it myself till my wife, Bess, explained it to me. She says ginseng sometimes grows in the woods, but that it's mighty scarce, so scarce that she's never even seen none. She says it's a valuable plant though. The bushes don't grow very tall, and the roots are where the value is. They make medicine outta the roots."

Kirb stood thoughtful for a moment. "You think there's really any of that stuff around here?"

"Nope. Bo Ransom don't either. He says he don't even believe there's any in Texas."

"Do you really think that man walks several thousand miles a year hunting it?"

"Of course he does. People say he's in the woods all

the time except when the weather gets too cold. He prowls around on the Lazy Bee and the old Nelson place, your Circle Ar, about eight or nine months out of the year, and Ransom says he's even seen him crawling around on his knees on the east side of the river. Don't that sound like several thousand miles?"

"Yes, sir," Kirb said. "It certainly does." He stepped off the porch and untied his horse. "I reckon we've discussed about everything we need to for now," he said. "Ellie'll probably be expecting me back for dinner."

"You speaking of her reminds me of something," Browning said. He stepped off the porch and stood beside Renfro. "When the cow hunt begins, every man on these premises is gonna be sleeping out where the cattle live. Even me and Dossy and the cook are gonna be out there with 'em. Now, Bess and Carrie are both gonna stay here at the house, and I think your Ellie oughtta be up here with 'em. The hunt'll last two weeks or more, and you'll be out there with us day and night. I don't think your little woman oughtta have to sit in that cabin down yonder by herself."

"Neither do I," Kirb said. He put a foot in the stirrup and threw his leg over the saddle. "I'll take that up with her as soon as I get back home."

Browning nodded. "Good," he said. "If you'll ride back up here next Tuesday morning, Ransom'll probably be able to tell you everything you need to know. I reckon he'll have his crew lined up by then."

Renfro nodded, then turned his horse toward the road and kicked the animal in the ribs. He was off the premises quickly.

12

★

Monday morning at sunup, Renfro hitched the mules to the wagon. Today he and Ellie were going to town to buy groceries, grain for the animals, and pick up the Circle R branding irons at the blacksmith shop. "I remember you saying a few days ago that you needed soap," Kirb said, as he lifted his wife to her seat on the wagon. "Don't forget to buy some while you're in the general store."

"I've got a list," Ellie said.

Moments later, he whacked the mules on their rumps and headed east. He had named the stretch of road leading from his cabin to the river "Circle R Lane" and fully intended to put up a sign as soon as he had the time. Driving down the lane admiring his own recent handiwork, he was more than pleased to hear his wife say, "You did a good job on this road, Kirb. I reckon it's about as smooth as anybody could expect now."

Kirb nodded. "It's in pretty good shape, all right, even

if I do say so myself. I just hope the winter rains don't wash all this new dirt down the river."

She squeezed his arm. "I'll pray about it," she said.

When they reached the east end of town, Kirb pulled in at the blacksmith shop. He handed the reins to his wife, then jumped to the ground. "This shouldn't take but a minute. I'll be right back.

It did take only a minute, and when Kirb returned to the wagon he held up the branding irons. "This is the Circle Ar, little one. It's the mark that'll someday be on the backs of a thousand head of cattle. Maybe two or three thousand head."

Ellie put her hand on one of the irons and looked closely at the business end. "That sure sounds good," she said. "Mighty good. Maybe then you won't have to work so hard."

"I might not work at all if I ever get rich," he said. "I'm liable to be too busy taking my pretty wife to all those fancy places on the other side of the ocean."

She shook her head. "You'd never do that, Kirb. You're not the type to go gallivanting around the world."

"Maybe not, but I'd sure slack up on my working. I'd hire somebody to take the load off of you too."

"I don't have no load, Kirb. Taking care of you and that cabin ain't no load. Why, I'd probably go crazy if I had to just sit around doing nothing."

Without another word, Kirb backed the mules away from the hitching rail and headed up the street. A short time later, he tied the team in front of the general store and helped Ellie to the ground. He handed her an eagle. "Just take your time and be sure you get everything you need," he said. "I'm gonna take that joint of stovepipe back up to the hardware store. Mr. Harvey said he'd refund my money on whatever I didn't have to use."

Ellie dropped the coin into her handbag, then disappeared inside the building quickly. Kirb headed up the street to find Bill Harvey sitting on a bench outside his hardware store. "I see you had a joint of pipe left over," Harvey said. "If you'll give it to my daughter-in-law behind the counter, she'll refund your money."

"I'll do that in a minute," Kirb said. "Right now, I'm just trying to kill a little time." He seated himself on the bench beside Harvey. "My wife's in the general store buying groceries, and that's not one of my favorite things to do."

"Helping your wife stock up on groceries is one of the worst things you can do," Harvey said. "Hell, knowing beforehand exactly what you're gonna eat every meal takes all the fun out of it. I like being surprised when I walk to the table."

"Me, too," Kirb agreed.

Neither man spoke again for a while, then Harvey broke the silence. "I guess you and your wife are pretty well settled in on the old Nelson place by now," he said.

"We're calling it home. Of course, I changed the name of it; it's the Circle Ar Ranch, now."

Harvey nodded. "The Circle Ar," Harvey repeated. "That's a good name for a ranch, especially one owned by a man named Renfro."

The tongue of the hardware store owner suddenly became looser, and he talked almost nonstop for three-quarters of an hour. He had been in Comanche since its inception, he said. What he had not said was that he had borrowed money and bought up lots on both sides of the street right from the beginning and had sold most of them at a profit that many of the townsfolk considered obscene.

"A bunch of people said Comanche had about the same chance as a snowball in hell of becoming a permanent town. The naysayers told everybody who would listen that the Indians would eventually take it back and use the lumber for their campfires. A lot of folks believed 'em, too, and just kept on going. Not me, I dug in my heels and invested every dollar I could get my hands on.

"Now the Comanches did try to do just what the naysayers said. They stole every damn thing that wasn't nailed down and a lotta things that were. When it finally came down to us or them, we gave 'em a good ass whipping, and they ain't caused no trouble around here since. I don't know of anybody whose even seen one in ages."

Renfro looked at his watch, then got to his feet. "I'd better trade in this pipe, then get on back to my wagon. My wife's probably already waiting for me."

Kirb saw that his prediction was true long before he got to the wagon, for Ellie was sitting on the seat, her bonnet tied under her chin. He quickened his step and untied the team the moment he reached the hitching rail. He climbed aboard and was about to back away from the rail, when Ellie spoke. "I'm so glad you're back, Kirb," she said, staring at her feet. "I was getting . . . uneasy."

"Uneasy?" he asked. "You worried about me?"

"No," she said. "It's . . . it's just the way those men over there keep looking at me. I mean, it's . . . like they're completely undressing me with their eyes. Gives me a creepy feeling."

Kirb saw the men when he looked down the boardwalk to his right. Standing leaning against the wall in front of the saloon was the redhead, Pat Pollard, along with two other men about his age. At the moment they were laughing and talking among themselves, appearing to be totally unaware of anyone else's existence. "They don't even seem to know you're over here, honey. They're not looking at you."

"No," she said. "Not now."

He stared at the men for a moment. "Did they say something to you? What the hell did they say?

"They didn't say anything. Let's go home."

He spent a few moments rearranging Ellie's merchandise, then took another look at the men. All three were now staring at his wife hungrily. Kirb dropped the reins in Ellie's lap, then stood up in the wagon. "You men see something over here you want?" he asked loudly. "How about you, Pollard? You got something on your mind?"

Pollard shrugged, then all three men spun on their heels and stepped inside the saloon. Kirb stared at the batwing doors for a few moments. "I've already had it out with that redhead," he said finally. "He's the one I worked over for talking disrespectfully to Mr. Browning."

"He's the man you fought with here in Comanche? The one Mr. Browning said you beat the daylights out of?"

"I ain't got no way of knowing how much daylight he could see, but he didn't have much fight left in him." He jerked his thumb toward the saloon. "What he got then was a drop in the bucket compared to what he'll get if he ever insults my wife."

"He knows that now," she said. "He stopped staring at me as soon as he realized I was with you. Let's go home."

He backed the mules away from the hitching rail and turned them toward home. "I want to stop at that feed store on the way outta town and get a few sacks of grain," he said. "I'll probably have to take shelled corn again, 'cause they're just about always outta oats." He drove on for a few moments, then looked back at the watering hole on the corner. "I reckon there ain't no law against a man looking," he said, "but I still feel like I should've dragged Pat Pollard's ass outta that saloon and stomped the hell out of him."

She squeezed his arm. "Don't talk that way, Kirb."

It was midafternoon when they reached the cabin.

Kirb dropped off Ellie's groceries and received the promise of an early supper, then drove the wagon to the barn. He unharnessed the mules and turned them into the corral, then unloaded the four sacks of grain he had bought in town. He had been both surprised and pleased at the feed store, for Johnny Waters had indeed had a supply of oats on hand.

Kirb had built a grain bin out of scrap lumber, knowing all the while that it was hardly what he would need in the long run. Even though he had fitted the boards together as tightly as he possibly could, he knew that it was just a matter of time till the rats, then the grain-eating insects, found their way in.

A good tight box would discourage insects, but once a rat smelled grain, it would gnaw right through the wood, leaving an open door for every pest known to man. He knew that he would eventually have to replace the bin with one made of metal and had already resolved himself to the fact. The first time he saw a hole in the wood or found insects in the grain, he would go looking for one.

He put the grain sacks in the bin, then fed all three of his animals, leaving their stable doors open so they could return to the corral at will. Then he walked to the cabin, where Ellie was now standing in the doorway. He stood leaning against the wall. "One of these days when I ain't got nothing better to do, I think I'll build a porch right here and put a tin roof over it."

"It would be nice sitting out here in the evening," Ellie said. "There's usually a good breeze running across the slope late in the day, especially when the wind's outta the southwest."

Kirb nodded. He was quiet for a while, then said, "Yes, ma'am, I'm gonna build that porch. The only material I'll have to buy is the tin for the roof and the boards for the floor. I've already got the posts and poles down there by the barn, and I have enough nails left over from those other jobs."

Ellie nodded, then smiled sweetly. "You're a handy man with hammer and saw, Kirb. I reckon you could build just about anything you decided to." She pointed into the cabin. "I've got a pot on the stove, but it's gonna be at least an hour before it's ready. If you feel like it, you can chop up some more wood while you're waiting. I'll be outta cooking fuel after about one more meal."

He nodded and headed for the dead tree he had snaked up and sawed into blocks last week. Once there, he began to split the blocks into foot-and-a-half-length sticks for the stove's firebox. He worked for close to an hour, then buried one blade of the double-bitted ax in the oak chopping block and knelt to gather up an armload of fuel. He made one trip after another to the cabin and eventually had a stack half as tall as himself in the corner behind the stove. "That'll be enough for a while," Ellie said. "No use bringing in the whole tree."

He hung his hat on the wall and rolled his shirtsleeves up to his elbows, then stepped back outside, where a shelf along the wall supported a wash pan and a bucket of water. He washed his face and hands, then returned to the cabin to see that his favorite food was already on the table: a steaming pot of beef stew and a pan of hot biscuits. He chuckled softly, then pulled out a chair. "This reminds me of what Bill Harvey said this morning, honey. He said he liked to be surprised when he sits down at the table, and I reckon I do too." He motioned toward the pot. "You surprised me all right."

"I'm glad," Ellie said, then began to fill his bowl with the ladle. "I know how much you like beef stew, and when Mr. Hill said the beef had been butchered late yesterday afternoon, I bought two pounds."

He accepted the bowl, then kissed her hand. "I wish

I was as smart as you," he said. He broke off a biscuit and dusted black pepper into the bowl, then dug in.

Kirb enjoyed another good meal next morning, for Ellie had also bought fresh eggs and a smoked ham at Hill's general store. Once he was done eating, he put his Colt revolver and a box of shells in his saddlebag, then kissed his wife good-bye and headed for the corral. Today he would be riding up to the Lazy Bee again, as Gaylord Browning had suggested. He put a rope around the black's neck with his first throw, then led the animal to the shed to be saddled. Five minutes later, he mounted and headed over the hill at a canter.

He slowed the pace to a fast walk after the first mile, then gave the horse its head. By the time he had traveled another mile, he decided that Midnight knew exactly where he was going, for he was headed for the Lazy Bee corral as if guided by a compass. Kirb patted the big animal's neck, then wrapped the reins around the horn and leaned back in the saddle with his arms folded across his chest.

He reached the Lazy Bee an hour later. As he rode up the hill he could see two men sitting their saddles beside the cookshack, and a man he easily recognized as Bo Ransom standing on the ground talking to them. As Kirb drew closer, the riders suddenly turned their horses and galloped across the hillside, no doubt on their way to whatever job assignment they had been given. It was then that the foreman noticed Renfro, who was still about fifty yards away. Ransom motioned him on with a wave of his arm, then cupped his hands around his mouth. "Shake a leg, fellow! The coffee's getting cold!"

Kirb kicked his horse to a trot and dismounted at the hitching rail a moment later. Ransom walked over and offered a handshake. "Gaylord said you'd be here this morning, so I've been expecting you."

Kirb grasped the hand and returned its firm grip. "He told me to come up and talk to you today, so here I am."

Ransom nodded, then jerked his thumb toward the black. "Good-looking piece of horseflesh," he said. "Does he know anything about working cattle?"

Kirb shook his head. "Nothing at all. He was raised on a farm in Tennessee, and the only cattle he's ever been around were the neighbors' milch cows."

"Well, he wouldn't be any good for the kind of work you're gonna be doing next week. You can just leave him here in the corral. He'll be fed and taken care of. Gaylord said your wife was gonna stay with the Browning women till the cow hunt's over, so I reckon you'll be bringing your mules up here too, huh?"

"I'd planned on it," Kirb said. "Won't be nobody left down at my place to feed 'em."

"Just turn 'em in the corral," Ransom said. He walked around Midnight, then stood with his hand resting on the horse's hip. "I reckon this fellow's a little bit too big to make a good cow pony anyhow, but he sure is a looker. I bet he can move out too."

Kirb nodded. "He's a good horse."

Ransom nodded. "I can tell that much by looking. He'll catch onto the line riding pretty quick, so you can use him after you start your regular job. I'm gonna put you to riding the eastern half of the southern boundary and the southern half of the eastern boundary. You'll wear out two horses a day, so I'll give you another one to keep down at your place. You can switch mounts at noon every day and sleep in your own bed every night."

"Sounds mighty good," Renfro said.

Kirb followed the foreman to the cookshack. After asking permission from the cook, both men helped themselves to the coffeepot, then sat down at the table. Ransom blew air into his cup and took a sip, then continued to talk. "I know all this stuff coming up is gonna be brand new to you, Kirb, so I'm gonna put you with a man named Clay Summer. He's a good hand who knows exactly what he's doing, so I want you to stick to him like glue. He probably won't tell you every little thing, so keep your eye on him. Do what he does and learn from him." He took another sip of his coffee. "You understand what I mean?"

"Yes, sir," Kirb said. "I just hope I understand Mr. Summer."

Ransom laughed loudly. "I believe one of the worst mistakes you could make would be to start calling him mister. Hell, it ain't like I was putting you with somebody old enough to be your granddaddy." He chuckled again. "Clay ain't much older'n you are, it's just that he was raised in the saddle with a rope in his hand."

Renfro nodded. "I'll be paying attention. I'll watch what he does and listen to everything he says."

"Good. We'll start rounding up, cutting, and branding next Monday, so you need to bring your wife and your livestock on up here beforehand.

"I will," Kirb said. "I'll do it sometime Sunday afternoon."

Both men were on their feet now. "I can't think of anything else we need to talk about," Ransom said. "You got any questions?"

"No," Renfro answered. "I reckon the next thing is for me to see how much I can learn from Clay Summer." He dropped his cup in the dishpan, then headed for the door. "Thank you for the coffee, Mr. Kelso," he said, then headed for the hitching rail.

Ransom followed, then stood outside the cookshack leaning against the wall. He waved good-bye as Kirb threw his leg over the saddle. Renfro smiled broadly, then sent the big black down the hill at a canter.

13

★

The roundup, as the cow hunt was called by many of the cowhands, had been underway for more than a week and had gone smoothly. And although Renfro had spent only a short time with Clay Summer, he had learned much from him. Less than a year separated the two men in age, and they seemed to speak the same language in spite of the fact that they had been raised in different parts of the country.

A solidly built young man who would celebrate his twenty-second birthday on Christmas Eve, Summer had been raised in neighboring Hamilton County and had spent all of his teen years working on one ranch or another. Though he lacked formal education, he was loaded with common sense; and his prowess with a rope was unmatched by any man in the area. And though it was something that the young man never mentioned himself, others had told Kirb that Summer possessed phenomenal speed with a six-gun, and that his marksmanship was questioned by none.

Though he was at least three inches shorter than Renfro, the brown-haired, dark-complected Clay Summer probably weighed a few pounds more, for he was thick-chested and very muscular. And he was exceptionally strong. On more than one occasion Kirb had seen him pick up a three-hundred-pound calf and put it on the ground easily. "I believe my uncle would say that a fellow's back wouldn't last too many years picking up calves that heavy," Renfro had once said after seeing Summer throw a sizable animal to the ground.

"I'm sure your uncle would be right too," Summer agreed, "but there ain't no other way to get one of the little bastards down. You damn sure can't wish him to the ground, so back or no back, you've got to pick him up and slam him." He smiled and pointed after the calf that had just been branded and turned loose. "I'm hoping to be in some other line of work before my back goes out," he added.

"I've seen young men with bad backs," Kirb said. "Anyway, the only reason I mentioned it was 'cause Bo Ransom told me that he hired you for your rope not your muscles. That sounded to me like he expected you to just cut out the calves and rope 'em, then let somebody else put 'em down."

Summer shook his head. "I never did like to do that," he said. "It's a good way for the roper to save his back all right, but it's also a good way to build up resentment among the other hands. A good many of 'em already think us ropers've got it too easy; and just as soon as they find out that some of us make a few bucks more'n they do, they start avoiding us like we've got the plague."

The two men had been sitting side by side eating their noon meal, and Renfro had emptied his plate and his coffee cup. "A fellow who can put a rope anywhere he wants it is worth more money than a regular hand," he said, getting to his feet to carry his utensils back to the cook fire. "A man don't learn all that overnight, and I can't even imagine anybody getting better at it than you are."

As he had done every day for the past week, Renfro stayed close to Summer all afternoon, constantly aware of the bulging gun belt in the man's saddlebag. "You never know when you'll have to put a mean old cow down," Summer had said a few days ago. "Some of 'em'll try to kill you when you start dragging their calves to the fire, and the only way to stop 'em is to put a bullet between their eyes. I've had to do it more'n once."

Renfro accepted the explanation, but he also knew that Summer wore the gun belt around his middle when he was not working. In fact, Kirb had been in the yard the morning Clay arrived at the Lazy Bee to begin the cow hunt. He had been wearing the gun belt when he rode up the hill, and only after dismounting and tying his horse at the hitching rail, did he unbuckle it and place it in his saddlebag. "That's Clay Summer there," a man standing beside Kirb had said. "He's hell with that six-gun too."

Renfro wanted to hear more. "Does he try to lord it over other people just 'cause he's a good gunman?" he asked.

"No, no," the man answered. "I ain't never known him to run over nobody, but he sure don't take no shit. Duke Hathaway found that out last year, but it didn't do him no good. No, sir, by the time he figured out that he'd picked on the wrong man, he had a forty-four-caliber slug to chew on. About two seconds later, he was lying flat on his back in the middle of the street, dead as a doornail."

"Summer killed him?"

"Yep, put him down on a Saturday afternoon. Hath-away'd been drinking all day and insulting everybody he came across. Along about four o'clock in the afternoon he dashed a glass of whiskey in Summer's face and challenged him to a gunfight. That, my friend, was the biggest and the last mistake he ever made. I didn't see it with my own eyes, mind you, but my cousin did. He said Summer drew that Colt so quick that it was just a blur and drilled Hathaway right in the mouth."

Renfro stood quietly for a few moments. He was thinking of what Walt Rubin had told him the first day he was in Comanche. He turned back to his new-found friend. "You said the man Summer killed was named Duke Hathaway. Was he Honey Hathaway's son?"

"Absolutely," the man answered. "Honey Hathaway's a good woman who didn't deserve no good-for-nothing son of a bitch like him for a son, but of course she didn't have no choice in the matter. She knew he wasn't worth killing, and some folks say she'd already disowned him. She went to the funeral, all right, but I've heard it said that she sure didn't shed no tears."

Renfro and Summer continued to be inseparable. They not only worked as a team but ate their meals together and spread their bedrolls side by side at night. By the time the cow hunt was over, Kirb had learned much from the young roper, and the two had become fast friends. When the last calf had been branded, and Bo Ransom had announced his pleasure with the way things had gone, the men broke camp and headed back to Lazy Bee headquarters. Once there, they would receive their pay, and Kirb had already heard one of the men say that he intended to say drunk for a week.

Renfro and Summer arrived at the barn ahead of the others and turned their horses into the corral. "I'd like to see that Colt you say you've got, Kirb," Summer said. "I never pass up a chance to look over another fellow's hardware."

Renfro pointed. "It's in my saddlebag over there under the shed. I didn't take it on the cow hunt 'cause I didn't expect to need it." He led the way and took his saddlebag from a peg on the wall. A moment later, he handed the gun belt and the holstered Colt to Summer. "No shell in the chamber, but the cylinder's full."

Summer nodded and looked the belt and the holster over admiringly. "This ain't no store-bought outfit," he said finally. "And whoever made it knew what the hell he was doing."

"He was a neighbor of ours back in Tipton County, Tennessee," Kirb said.

Summer unholstered the Colt and stood inspecting the unblemished weapon. "Looks brand new," he said after a while, spinning it on his finger to test its balance. "It's exactly like mine and it's probably just as old, but it looks like it was manufactured yesterday." He gazed at Renfro for a moment, then shook his head as if he already knew the answer to his next question. "You wouldn't want to part with it, would you?"

"No," Kirb answered quickly. "It belonged to my pa. Him and Ma died in a fire last year."

"I'm sorry to hear about your folks," Summer said, "and I'm sure you intend to hang on to it till something kills you too." He held the revolver at arm's length and aimed it at an imaginary target. "Can you hit what you shoot at with it?"

Kirb nodded. "I don't miss many things," he said. "I reckon I had a good eye right from the start, but what I'd like to do is get fast with it, like everybody says you are."

Summer spun the weapon on his finger again, then shoved it back into the holster. He handed the outfit back to Renfro, saying, "If you can hit what you shoot at, you're already a better gunman than most men. And like everything else a man does, the speed comes with practice.

"The eye's the main thing though; and I'm a firm believer that if a man didn't come into the world with it, he ain't never gonna get it. Anybody who claims they can teach a man how to have good coordination between his hand and his eye is full of shit, Kirb. They can't do that no more than they can teach him how to grow taller. Nobody can teach you how to make a fast draw either, 'cause there ain't no secret to it. You just have to want it bad enough to keep working at it till the speed comes.

"Practice with an empty gun till you get so it don't take you all day to draw, then load up and start firing at a target after every pull." He backed up a few feet and provided a slow demonstration as he continued speaking. "Don't ever take your eye off your target. You cock the hammer with your thumb while you're pulling the gun from the holster. Then you just think where you want your shot to go and squeeze the trigger. Always shoot from the hip, 'cause if you're ever in a contest you ain't gonna have time to aim."

The other hands were arriving now, and all of the women were standing on the porch. "I'll try to remember the things you've taught me, Clay," Kirb said, offering a parting handshake. "You take care, and I hope to see you again."

Summer took the hand. "You hope to see me again? Hell, I know where you live now, and I might just stop off to see you one of these days."

"Anytime, old buddy," Kirb said. "My wife's usually got something in the pot." He turned his back and headed up the pathway to the house. Ellie ran down the steps and met him in the yard. She leaped into his arms and kissed him, then whispered into his ear. "I've thought of you just about every minute." She kissed him again. "Have you been thinking of me?"

"Not at all," he answered, sticking out his tongue and

tickling her ribs with his thumb. "I've had nothing but cows on my mind."

"You oughtta be ashamed," she said, as he dropped her to the ground. They walked up the steps holding hands, and Kirb nodded a greeting to the Browning women. "I've come to reclaim my wife," he said. "I appreciate you ladies looking out for her while I was gone."

"Well, you ain't leaving just yet," Bess Browning said with finality. "We've got a pork loin and two beef briskets in the oven, and there oughtta be enough men down there around the corral to eat it all. Why don't you go down and spread the word for us, Kirb. Tell 'em we're expecting every one of 'em to eat with us before they head off to wherever they're going."

"Yes, ma'am," Kirb said, then went down the steps two at a time.

The feast began an hour later. The dining room table and a dozen chairs had been moved onto the front porch, and the fact that there were more people than chairs presented no problem whatsoever. Men sat on the steps, the porch railing, or cross-legged on the floor, as the Browning women moved back and forth keeping the plates full. The ranch cook brought a chuckle from everybody's lips when Carrie refilled his plate. "Best meal I ever ate that I didn't cook myself," he said.

Several of the regular hands jumped on him in unison. "You never cooked a meal this good in your life, Kelso," one of them said.

The cook laughed loudly. "I just wanted to see if anybody was listening," he said.

The sun was still an hour high when the Renfros pulled into their own yard. Kirb helped Ellie to the ground, then unloaded the wagon. "I want to put most of this meat in the springhouse right away," she said, as she held up the package of broiled beef and pork that Bess

Browning had given her. "I believe there's at least four pounds of it here. I really didn't think I should accept it, but Mrs. Browning said that was nonsense, that it would just go to waste if I didn't take it home with me."

Kirb chuckled. "I can't imagine it going to waste with nearly twenty people up there to eat it, but it sure won't be hanging around here long enough to go bad." He climbed back to the seat and drove the wagon to the shed, his saddler trotting along behind.

Even as he was caring for his animals Kirb had seen smoke coming from the flue, and when he returned to the cabin Ellie had warmed-over beef, pork, and bread on the table, and a pot of hot coffee on the stove. "I didn't eat nowhere near as much of this stuff up at the Lazy Bee as I could have," he said. He pulled out a chair and seated himself. "I believe I can do it justice now though." He ate close to a pound of meat before coming up for air.

When they had finishing eating, he lit the lamp and turned the wick down low, then walked to the doorway with two chairs in his hands. "Let's sit outside till it gets too dark to see anything or the bugs eat us up," he said. "Whichever comes first."

Ellie put their supper dishes in a pan of water to soak, then followed him outside. They pushed the chairs together and sat holding hands till long after the sun had kissed the trees good night and crawled into the earth a few miles to the west. Then he tilted her head back and brushed her lips with his own. "I sure do love you, Ellie," he said.

"I know that, Kirb," she said. "I've known it since I was twelve years old." She squeezed his arm. "I love you the most though."

"I don't know so much about that," he said. He sat quietly for a moment, then pulled her to him, kissing her wetly and running his hands over her body. "I don't reckon there's but one way to settle it," he added, lifting her out of her chair. He carried her into the cabin and bolted the door, then headed for the bedroom.

"It might rain, Kirb," she said. "You just gonna leave the chairs outside?"

He did not answer and had her halfway undressed by the time he reached the bed.

14

★

Though icicles hung from the trees and the eaves of buildings for much of November and December, January brought springlike weather to the area. It was now two weeks into the new year, and most days Kirb Renfro worked in his shirtsleeves. He had been riding line for almost three months now and had found nothing to complain about. In fact, he had taken to the assignment immediately, for he loved prowling the great outdoors. And the job could hardly be described as backbreaking labor for it involved few chores that could not be performed from the back of a horse.

Renfro appreciated the isolation because it gave him a chance to practice his quick draw out of eyeshot of other humans. He had begun working on his speed the day after coming home from the cow hunt and often spent an hour or more slapping his leg before riding off to work in the morning. It was the same story after he cared for his animals in the evening. More than once he had stood in the stable drawing his Colt and pointing it at an imaginary target till his wife lost patience and allowed his supper to get cold.

He could see a marked improvement in his speed from week to week, and sometimes from day to day. Clay Summer had visited him in the middle of November and had taken the time to give him some more pointers. On a second visit a few days before Christmas, Summer had stood in the stable and watched Renfro go through the motions for several minutes. "There probably ain't many men around who can match your draw right now," he said, as Kirb unbuckled his gun belt. "You're getting it outta that holster mighty quick."

"Not quick enough," Renfro said. "I've got a lot more work to do."

Kirb had been practicing at least three hours a day since the first of the year, and the blisters that had appeared on his right hand at the beginning had long since turned to calluses. The Colt felt like an extension of his right arm at times, and since he began using live ammunition a month ago he had learned to twist his body so he faced his target head-on, giving him a straightaway shot as he cleared his holster. Shooting from the hip, he seldom missed his target, which was usually a chip of wood or a piece of bark out at the woodpile.

Renfro knew without being told that he had gotten much faster during the past month, and he was eager to hear what Clay Summer thought. He might hear that opinion very soon too, for Clay had promised to drop by the Circle R again about the middle of January. Today was the fifteenth of the month, so Kirb was expecting a visit from his friend anytime, now.

Clay Summer had put in a full day riding the boundary with Renfro on both of his prior visits and had even helped to chase several bunches of cattle back onto the

Lazy Bee range. He had also eaten several meals at the Renfro table and had never once forgotten to compliment the cook. When bedtime came around, however, despite Ellie's offer to make him a pallet beside the fireplace, he insisted on sleeping in the barn. "I've got a good bedroll and warm blankets," he said with finality, "and I'll sleep in the hayloft."

At midafternoon Kirb reached the spring marking the halfway point of the southern boundary, and the fresh tracks told him that his counterpart who rode the western portion had already been there and gone. Renfro had become acquainted with the man during the cow hunt, and one afternoon about three weeks ago they had happened to arrive at the spring at the same time. Neither man had been in a hurry, and they had dismounted and sat around talking for half an hour. Today, Kirb could read the hoofprints without even leaving his saddle. He watered his horse, then reversed his course and headed for home.

Even as he rode out of the cedars several hundred yards west of his cabin, he could see that he had company, for there was no mistaking Clay Summer's big piebald in the corral. He kicked the black to a canter and closed the distance quickly. As Kirb dismounted at the gate, Summer walked from the shed. "I tried to get here about the same time you did," he said. "I didn't miss it much; been here about fifteen minutes."

The men shook hands. "It's good to see you again, Clay," Kirb said. "Thank you for coming."

Summer smiled broadly. "I got tired of hanging around my brother's place over in Hamilton County. Anyway, I told you I'd be here in the middle of January, and I reckon this is about the middle. I always make it a point to keep an eye on my students, and besides, I like your wife's cooking. She offered me some coffee a few minutes ago, but it's always been my policy to stay out of a man's house when he's not at home."

Renfro spoke quickly. "You should've gone in and got yourself a cup, Clay. She might even have some cookies in there."

Summer shook his head. "Like I said, it would be going against my policy, and I ain't likely to ever do that."

Renfro shrugged, then pointed. "I see smoke coming from the flue, so I'd say supper ain't far off." He stripped the saddle and carried it under the shed, then led the black to the stable. Summer followed and stood by quietly while the animal was fed and curried. That done, Kirb poured oats in the remaining troughs for the braying mules and the whinnying Lazy Bee saddler, then led the way across the corral and through the gate.

Summer pointed under the shed, where his saddle and his bedroll lay. "I've got an appetizer over there in my saddlebag," he said. "You want a snort?"

Kirb chuckled. "I'm already hungry enough to eat a skunk, but I don't reckon a sip or two would hurt nothing." He followed Summer under the shed.

"I've had this stuff since the last time I was in Comanche, but my brother won't have nothing to do with it, and I don't like to drink by myself." He twisted the stopper out of the bottle of brown liquid. "You get first pull," he said, handing it to Renfro.

Kirb touched it to his lips and smacked them a few times, then raised the bottle and gulped down two swallows. He wiped his mouth on his sleeve, then smacked his lips again. "This ain't near as hard on a man's throat as some of the stuff I've drunk before," he said. "Goes down easy enough."

Summer nodded. "It's pretty weak liquor," he said. "I drank a quart of it right by myself one time, and it didn't hurt me none."

"It didn't make you drunk?"

Summer chuckled. "I ain't gonna say that. I don't reckon I'd know anyhow, 'cause a drunk man's the last one to know that he's drunk. He don't know it 'cause his head's just as drunk as his ass is, and he thinks he's standing as straight as a fence post."

Kirb laughed aloud. "I believe that," he said, reaching for the bottle.

Supper was served a few minutes later, then the two men moved chairs into the yard and talked till long after dark. When Summer finally headed for the barn and his bedroll, Kirb walked into the cabin to find his wife reading a book she had bought on her last trip to town. "I'm sorry if it seems like I've been ignoring you tonight, honey," he said. "I just figured you wouldn't want to listen to Clay and me jabber back and forth."

She smiled. "You figured right," she said. She bent the corner of a page to mark her place, then closed the book and pecked on it with a forefinger. "This is a story about two men and a woman who left Texas just before the war and rode all the way to Alaska on horseback. I think you'd enjoy reading it if you ever have time."

"All right," he said. "If I ever have time." He kissed her on the nose, then picked up the lamp and led the way to the bedroom. Three minutes later, he blew out the lamp and pulled her to him.

Sunup found Renfro and Summer back at the barn, their horses saddled and tied to the corral posts. "What time do you get back home for dinner every day?" Summer asked.

"I get done with the first half of my job at eleven o'clock," Renfro answered, "give or take a few minutes. Ellie always has dinner waiting for me, so I just eat and change horses, then head out along the southeastern boundary. Most times there ain't near as much to do in the afternoon, so I usually get back home about the same time I did yesterday."

Summer nodded. "Well, I'm gonna ride up to the Lazy Bee and visit with Bo Ransom for a while this morning, but I'll meet you back here at eleven o'clock. If you don't mind, I'll ride the boundary with you this afternoon, then spend one more night in your barn. You think you oughtta warn your wife that she'll have another hungry mouth for dinner and supper?"

Kirb shook his head. "Nope. She always cooks enough for an army anyway."

Summer was thoughtful for a while, then spoke again. "If you feel up to it, I'd like to watch you pull that six-gun a few times. I didn't mention it yesterday 'cause we were working on that bottle, and I make it a point to never mix alcohol with firearms."

Kirb pointed toward the corner stable. "I usually do my practicing in there. I ain't never done none of it in front of Ellie, and I don't reckon I ever will." He led the way, adding, "It might all be in my head, but it seems to me like I'm a little bit faster early in the morning than I am later in the day."

Summer shook his head. "It's not your imagination," he said. "A man really can draw faster early in the morning. His mind is clear and more alert after a good night's sleep, and his hand, his eye, and his reflexes are all quicker."

With Summer standing in the doorway of the stable looking on, Kirb jerked the Colt out of its holster more than a dozen times, pausing as if squeezing off a shot from the hip after each pull. "That's enough," Summer said. "Maybe I can watch you practice with live ammunition this afternoon."

"I always do that," Kirb said, stepping through the doorway. "I've been using live shells for over a month."

Summer nodded. "You've got plenty of speed," he said. "I'm anxious to see you do some target shooting."

"The big spring's a good place for that," Kirb said. "We'll probably get there about two o'clock this afternoon."

Summer smiled. "The big spring," he repeated, then headed for the gate.

Moments later, the two men mounted their horses and parted, with Summer heading northwest toward Lazy Bee headquarters and Renfro guiding his animal toward the east boundary.

Kirb's morning followed the same pattern as always. Every day he chased the same old cows back onto Lazy Bee property. He had learned to recognize many of them from a distance of a quarter mile and had even made up names for a few. The cattle also recognized him and usually skedaddled back to their home range long before he reached them.

One morning he had spent more than an hour working with three particular cows. He had whipped them with a coiled rope and chased them a mile onto Lazy Bee range, only to find them right back in the same location next morning. The fact that they had hightailed it onto their own range the moment he rode into view convinced him that they knew exactly where they belonged and reminded him of something he had heard one of the Lazy Bee riders say during the recent cow hunt. "Half of the problem with cows is that they don't know," the man had said, "and the other half is that they don't give a shit." Renfro thought the man had summed it up nicely.

He found the usual strays in the usual places this morning, and even after he reached the halfway point and reversed his direction, he had to chase many of the same cows he had chased on the way up. *Yes, sir,* he was thinking, as he whipped an old longhorn back onto the Lazy

Bee for the second time that day, *the man on the cow hunt knew exactly what he was talking about.*

Just before he came within sight of his cabin, Kirb looked at his watch to see that the time was ten minutes to eleven. As he topped the rise a few moments later, he could not only see the cabin, but saw Clay Summer riding down the hill from the northwest as well. He kicked his animal to a fast trot, and the two men met at the corral gate. "You're right on time," Kirb said, dismounting. "Everybody all right up at the Lazy Bee?"

Summer nodded. "I reckon they are," he answered. "They looked the same as always, and nobody was complaining."

Renfro stripped the saddle from his mount, then led it to a stable and poured a bucketful of oats in its trough. Summer fed his own animal in the adjoining stall. Unlike Kirb, who would be switching horses, Clay merely loosened the cinch and left his saddle intact, for he would be back aboard the piebald within the hour. Renfro saddled his black and tied it to a fence post, then led the way to the cabin. Ellie met him at the door with a kiss, then motioned to the table. "I timed that corn bread right, for a change," she said, "and I believe it's still hot." She poured a cup of coffee for each man, then moved across the room and sat down in the open doorway. "If either of you need anything else, just holler," she said. "I'm gonna get away from that hot stove for a few minutes. If I didn't know better, I'd think it was July instead of January."

"I've been working in my shirtsleeves all day," Kirb said around a mouthful of food. "This sudden switch to hot weather in the middle of January is hard on the horses too; a whole lot worse than July, where they've had a chance to get used to it gradually. The bay was already lathered by eight-thirty this morning."

The men ate half a pan of corn bread and two bowlfuls each of black-eyed peas and bacon, then pushed back their chairs. "Thank you for a good dinner, Ellie," Summer said, picking his hat up from the floor and getting to his feet. "First time I've had all the black-eyed peas I could eat in years. A few of the restaurants serve 'em once in a while, but most places don't give you much more'n you could put in your eye."

Ellie got to her feet and leaned against the door jamb, smiling. "I'm glad you liked them, Clay, and I'm happy to hear that you got enough."

Summer stepped through the doorway and headed for the barn, while Renfro tarried and took his wife in his arms. "I love you more with every day that passes, honey," he said. "I can't even imagine what I'd ever do without you." He kissed her eyes, then pulled her to him tightly.

She put her arms around his waist. "I love you the most," she said. She clung to him a little longer than usual, then added, "The day won't ever come when you don't have me, Kirb. At least, not till the good Lord calls one of us home."

He brushed her lips with his own, then headed for the barn.

As Renfro had predicted the day before, they arrived at the big spring at two o'clock. Both men dismounted and watered their horses, then Summer sat down on an uprooted tree. Holding onto his own horse's reins, he asked, "Your black gun-shy?"

"Sometimes he gets a little fidgety when he hears the first shot, but he settles down pretty quick after that. I don't take no chances on him deciding to leave the country though. I always tie him to a good stout limb before I do any shooting." He led the animal to the opposite side of the ditch and tied it to a willow sapling. Then he picked up a charred, four-inch chunk of wood from the ashes of

an old campfire. He threw it as high and as far as he could
with his left hand, then drew and fired with his right. He
missed his target. "I didn't expect to hit the damn thing
while it was in the air," he said, reholstering his Colt.

Summer chuckled. "I didn't expect you to hit it either," he said. "I wouldn't let that bother me none
though. Just remember, a man's a whole lot bigger'n that
block of wood, and he ain't gonna be flying."

"That's the way I had it figured," Kirb said. He spread
his legs slightly and made another quick draw, snapping
off a shot that sent the chunk of wood flying into the air.
It had barely touched the ground, when a second shot sent
it on its way again.

"Now that's what I've been talking about," Summer
said. He tied his horse to the log, then walked over to join
Renfro. Even as he came to a halt, he ripped his Colt from
its holster and fired. The block went for still another ride.
"I drew and fired from that position in order to demon-
strate the fact that you ain't gonna always have time to
plant your feet just right, Kirb." He holstered his weapon.
"I want to see you draw and hit that piece of wood from
one side, then the other.

"After that, I want you to turn around and face in the
opposite direction, then spin on you heel and hit the target
again. You don't spin around and draw now; you draw
while you're spinning. You should never use this maneu-
ver unless it's the only chance you've got, but it's a good
thing to know, and it could damn well save your life some
day."

Without a word, Renfro turned the left side of his
body toward the target, then drew and fired. The slug
kicked up dirt about an inch from the block. When he
turned his right side toward the target, he hit it dead center. Then he turned around and faced the opposite direction. "Count to three for me, Clay," he said.

Summer counted, and Renfro whirled. When he fired, the chunk took to the air again. "Aw, shit, Kirb," Summer said, "you've done that before."

Renfro nodded. "Yep." He stood in his tracks while he ejected the spent shells and reloaded, then added, "I practiced that one whole afternoon, about three weeks ago." He stepped across the ditch and untied the black, then mounted and turned the animal toward home. "Well, what do you think?" he asked, when Clay had ridden up beside him.

"I'm surprised at your speed and marksmanship both, Kirb, and I think every would-be gunfighter in Texas would be wise to walk around you. You're already better'n most gunmen ever get; and if you keep practicing, you'll keep right on improving."

"I don't intend to let up none," Kirb said. He kneed the black. "Let's go see what Ellie's got for supper."

When they reached the northwest corner of the Circle R, they turned south, for just as Gaylord Browning had suggested, Kirb had begun to look upon his own property as an extension of the Lazy Bee. They rode south for two miles, then turned east. When they were almost to the river they changed directions again, pointing their horses toward the Renfro cabin.

"I don't see no smoke coming from the flue," Kirb said as they rode into the clearing. "Maybe Ellie's decided to feed us cold leftovers."

"I sure wouldn't mind," Summer said. "Hot or cold, it's all the same to me."

They rode on to the corral and dismounted. When both men had stripped their saddles, Kirb stood for a while staring toward the open cabin door. Finally, he handed the black's reins to Summer. "I don't like the looks of this, Clay," he said, pointing up the hill. "Ellie always knows when I get home, and she's usually standing in the doorway waving." He headed up the hill in long strides, while Summer led the horses to the barn.

Clay poured a bucketful of oats for each animal and was about to begin the currying process, when he heard Renfro call his name at the top of his lungs. He stepped out of the stable and looked toward the cabin just as Kirb called out again. Summer dropped the currycomb and hurried up the hill, drawing his weapon as he ran. When he stepped through the doorway he froze in his tracks, for the scene before him seemed to turn the marrow in his bones to ice.

Renfro sat on the floor beside the bed whimpering, holding his wife's hand to his cheek. Ellie lay on the bed naked, and Summer had no doubt that she was dead. Not knowing what to do or say, he holstered his Colt and stood in his tracks for a long time. Kirb continued to cry with low, plaintive, broken sobs, sounding much like a lost puppy whining for its mother. Finally he turned to look at his friend standing in the doorway. "You see this, Clay?" he asked softly.

"Yes, Kirb," Summer answered. "I see it." Spotting an apron hanging on the back of a chair, he carried it to the bed and spread it over Ellie's genital area, then backed away and leaned against the wall. He stared at the dead woman for a long time, trying to imagine what the last few minutes of her life had been like. The fact that she had not taken off her own clothing was obvious, for it was scattered about the room with complete abandon. One article of underwear had caught on a nail that had been driven into the wall for hanging things.

The young woman's hair was matted with blood, the pillow was soaked, and one eye had almost been knocked out of its socket. Ellie Renfro had been beaten to death, and even from where Summer was standing, he could see the murder weapon lying in the corner. He picked up the stick of oak firewood to see that one end was splotched with blood and several strands of brown hair. He laid it down exactly where he had found it, then walked around the bed and put his hand on Renfro's shoulder. "I know there's not a single thing I can say or do to help your feelings, Kirb, but I want you to know that you have my sympathy."

Seeming not to hear, Renfro sat with Ellie's cold hand against his lips and continued to whimper. Summer tightened his grip on the young man's shoulder and shook him several times. When Renfro showed no reaction, Clay slapped his face. "Talk to me, Kirb!" he said. "Say something!"

With tears rolling down both cheeks, Kirb slowly raised his eyes to meet those of Summer. "Some . . . somebody . . . raped Ellie and killed her, Clay," he said haltingly, then buried his face in his hands and continued to sob uncontrollably.

Summer stood by for several minutes, then shook Renfro's shoulder again. "I know it's not gonna be easy, Kirb, but you've got to pull yourself together. There are certain things that have to be done at times like this, and there's nothing to be gained by waiting around." He placed his hands under Kirb's arms and lifted him to his feet. "Let me cover up your wife, then I want you to step outside the cabin. We've got some thinking to do."

As if in a trance, Kirb staggered to the door without a word. He looked back for only a moment, then stepped outside. Summer very quickly spread a quilt over the body, then walked into the yard with two chairs in his hands. He seated his distraught friend first, then himself. "I've got to ride to town and let Sheriff Miller know about this, Kirb," he said. "But first, I want you to promise me that you'll stay outta the cabin till I get back. You know what they always say: Don't touch nothing at a crime scene till after the authorities have gone over it with a fine-tooth comb." When Renfro said nothing, Summer asked, "Do you understand, Kirb?"

Renfro stared off into space for a long time. "I understand what you're saying, Clay," he said finally. His countenance had suddenly returned to normal, and he now seemed to be in control of his emotions.

In an effort to test his friend's faculties a little further, Summer asked, "Do you know why I'm gonna ride into town and talk with Sheriff Miller, Kirb?"

Renfro nodded. "So he can have a look inside that cabin. So he can try to figure out who killed Ellie."

"Good boy!" Summer said loudly, getting to his feet. He patted Renfro on the back several times. "I'm gonna saddle up and head out now, and I want you to stay outta that cabin till I get back. Take your bedroll down to the barn and spend the night there if you want to. I'll be back just as early tomorrow morning as I can make it." He headed for the barn and the big piebald at a trot. A few minutes later, he rode away from the shed and was off the premises quickly.

Renfro sat watching till his friend had disappeared from view, then got to his feet and headed for the barn to saddle his black. He had plenty of time to make it to Lazy Bee headquarters before the Brownings went to bed.

15

★

Rudolph Miller had come to Texas from Arkansas and had been a resident of Comanche since the town's inception in 1858. A six-footer with thinning brown hair and gray temples, the slender, dark-complected man was now serving his second term as sheriff of Comanche County. Though it was often said that he had more friends than any other man in the county, there was also another side to the good-natured, forty-five-year-old Miller, as the criminal element had quickly discovered. He had personally escorted several such men to the state penitentiary at Huntsville and had provided occupants for at least two graves at the local cemetery. He was faster than most men with a six-gun and deadly accurate.

It was only a few minutes after daybreak when the sheriff was awakened by a loud knock at his home on the outskirts of town. When he opened the door, he was standing face to face with Clay Summer, a young man he knew well. "There's been a murder out at the Circle Ar,

Dolph," Summer said, then backed away and leaned against a post.

Miller stepped onto the porch with his nightcap still on his head. "The old Nelson place?" he asked. He pointed to the porch swing, and both men seated themselves there. He called to his wife to bring his tobacco and did not speak again till after the lady had come and gone. He blew on a book of cigarette papers and selected one, then poured in a measure of tobacco and began to smooth it out with a forefinger. "The old Nelson place," he repeated. "Ain't that where that young man from Tennessee's been setting up his homestead?"

Summer nodded. "His name's Kirb Renfro, and it was his wife who was murdered."

Miller lit his cigarette and blew a cloud of smoke into the air. "Well, where's he at?" he asked. "It's usually the husband who does these things, you know."

"That's what I've always heard," Summer said, "but it sure didn't happen like that this time. He was with me when his wife was killed. She served us a good meal at dinnertime, then we went off riding line all afternoon. When we returned to his cabin about five o'clock, she was dead. She had obviously been raped before she was killed 'cause she was lying on the bed naked with her clothing and undergarments scattered all over the room.

"I wouldn't believe that Kirb had done anything to hurt his wife even if he hadn't been with me. Why, he loved that girl more'n anything on earth, and he hardly ever went for more'n an hour without telling somebody what a good woman he had and how good she treated him. I know that to be the gospel truth too, Dolph. I reckon you'd just have to have been around her for a little while to understand what I'm saying, but she was the sweetest little thing—"

"I've got the picture, Clay," Miller interrupted. He got

to his feet. "Soon as the old lady fixes us some breakfast, we'll take a ride out to the Nelson place." He jerked his thumb in the general direction of the livery stable. "I'll have to walk up to the livery and get me something to ride before I can go anywhere."

Less than an hour later, Sheriff Miller mounted one of the county-owned horses at the livery stable, and Summer climbed aboard the tall gray he had rented to replace his tired piebald. They left the stable at a fast trot, then took to the main road at a canter.

They reached the Circle R at midmorning. As they rode into the clearing, they could see clusters of people standing around outside the yard, among them two bonneted women who were now making their way toward the hitching rail to meet the riders. Both men recognized the ladies as the Browning sisters. "I hope it ain't gonna take you all day to do your looking, Sheriff," Bess Browning said. "Me and Carrie need to lay little Ellie out so they can bury her as soon as possible." She pointed to a canvas-covered vehicle parked nearby. "One of the men built a coffin this morning at daybreak and brought it down here in that wagon. Her husband wants her buried right over there in her garden. We finally got him to tell us that much.

"Whoever killed Kirb's wife has just about killed him too, and the quicker we get her in the ground, the easier it's gonna be on him." She motioned toward the cabin. "He's just been standing up there guarding that door all morning, won't even let nobody in the yard."

Both men had dismounted and tied their horses. Nodding toward the cabin, Miller spoke to Summer softly. "Is that Renfro in the yard?" he asked.

"Yep."

The lawman led the way, offering a handshake as he neared the distraught man. "I'm Comanche County sheriff

Rudolph Miller," he said, "and I'm terribly sorry that we had to meet under these circumstances."

Renfro accepted the hand limply and said nothing.

The sheriff stood quietly for a moment, then asked, "Do I have permission to go inside your cabin, Mr. Renfro?"

Kirb nodded, and moved away from the doorway.

Summer followed the lawman inside, for he thought the situation warranted a full explanation. The two men stood at the foot of the bed for a few moments; then Summer stepped forward and removed the quilt he had spread over the corpse the day before. "Now you're looking at exactly what we saw when we got here yesterday afternoon, Dolph." He pointed to the stick of stovewood lying in the corner. "You might want to take a closer look at that," he said. "I think you'll be able to see with one eye that it's most likely the murder weapon. I picked it up and looked it over yesterday 'cause I wondered what the hell a chunk of firewood was doing in the bedroom."

The sheriff rounded the bed and picked up the foot-and-a-half length of oak wood. He looked it over closely, then laid it on the bed beside the corpse. He extracted a small notebook and the stub of a pencil from his back pocket, then began to walk around the bed scribbling notes.

Well aware of the fact that the lawman could finish his investigation with no help from him, Summer turned toward the door. "I reckon you're gonna be busy in here for a while yet, Dolph," he said. "I'll just get on out of your way." He stepped through the doorway and joined Kirb Renfro, who stood leaning against the wall of the cabin.

The two friends stood side by side quietly for several minutes; then Summer finally pointed to the ground and broke the silence. "More'n one horse trampled around in this yard yesterday," he said, "and I want to make sure Sheriff Miller sees all these tracks."

"I reckon he'll notice 'em without being told," Renfro said softly. "That's why I kept everybody outta the yard."

Kirb's reckoning proved to be correct, for he had no more than spoken, when the lawman appeared in the doorway with the bloody stick of firewood under his arm. "I'll take this with me when I leave," he said. "Might need it for evidence one of these days." He pointed to the ground. "Did you fellows ride your horses right into the yard when you came home yesterday?" he asked.

Renfro shook his head. "Ain't been none of my animals in this yard in more'n a month," he said.

The sheriff stepped through the doorway and began to walk around looking at the tracks, holding the firewood under one arm and scribbling in his notebook as he did so. Finally, he tore out a blank page and rolled it up, then got on his knees and used it to measure the dimensions of the hoofprints. After several minutes, he raised himself back up to his feet and shoved the paper into his vest pocket. "Three different horses have been in this yard within the past twenty-four hours," he said. "One of 'em was a whole lot bigger than your normal, everyday saddler too." He stood looking from one of the young men to the other for a few moments, then added. "Does that tell either one of you anything?"

Each man shook his head.

The Browning sisters were back now. "You done in there, Sheriff?" Bess asked. "Can we clean that poor little girl up now?"

Miller moved out of their way. "Yes, ma'am," he answered. "I've seen as much as I need to see."

Bess was through the doorway quickly, but her sister, Carrie, lingered for a moment, speaking to Miller for the first time. "Will it be all right to go ahead and bury Ellie after we lay her out, Sheriff?" she asked. "Can we put her in the ground this afternoon?"

"Yes, ma'am," he answered. "Like I said, my work here is done."

She nodded, and followed her sister into the cabin.

Sheriff Miller stepped to the hitching rail and tied the murder weapon behind his saddle, then began to walk among the Lazy Bee men shaking hands. Some of them he had known for a while; others he was meeting for the first time. He asked all of them the same question: had they seen anyone riding an exceptionally large horse lately?

"I reckon about everybody I know rides a big horse at one time or another, Dolph," Bo Ransom answered. "Both of the livery stables rent horses of all sizes, and I imagine every ranch in the area owns at least half a dozen big ones."

"I'm not just talking about a big horse, Bo," Miller said. "I'm talking about an animal that weighs thirteen or fourteen hundred pounds."

Ransom shrugged, then shook his head. "I don't know anybody who rides one that big," he said, "and I don't think I know anybody who would want to."

The sheriff moved on to the Browning brothers. As usual, Dossy deferred to his brother, Gaylord, who was much the better talker. "We hardly ever see any riders except our own, Sheriff," Gaylord said in answer to Miller's question, "but there sure as hell ain't nobody on our payroll who rides a horse that big. Sounds to me like maybe somebody didn't have no saddler and had to go riding around on a draft horse."

The lawman nodded. "I'm afraid you might be right, Mr. Browning. If that's the case, it's gonna make my job a lot harder." He pointed toward the cabin. "The ladies're in there cleaning the little girl up now," he said. "I've gone over the crime scene and made my notes, so you folks can go ahead and inter the body anytime you want to."

Gaylord pointed over his shoulder with his thumb. "Her husband wants her laid to rest in her garden, so that's the way it'll be. The grave's already been dug, so we'll put her down just as soon as he gives us the word."

The sheriff nodded, then stood quietly for a while. Finally, he offered the brothers a parting handshake. "Like I said before, I've done all I can do here. I'll get on back to town and try to figure out how to begin my investigation." He shook hands with both men, then walked back to the cabin. This time, he kept his right hand in his pocket when he reached Renfro. "Let me say once again how sorry I am about your wife," he said. "And you can rest assured that I'll leave no stone unturned till I find her killers." He stood thoughtful for a moment, then added, "I say killers, because I'm convinced that at least three men were on these premises when she died."

Renfro stood looking the lawman in the eye for a moment, then nodded. "Me, too," he said.

The sheriff offered a handshake to Summer. "I appreciate you coming into town after me, Clay, and I won't be getting much rest till I know a whole lot more about this thing than I do now." He motioned to Renfro, who stood staring down the hill with unseeing eyes. "I'm sure you'll be looking out for your friend there."

Summer squeezed Miller's hand, then released it. "You can count on that," he said.

Moments later, the lawman mounted the county horse and cantered off the premises.

One or the other of the Browning ladies dashed water into the yard several times during the next hour, refilling the wash pan from one of the water buckets each time. Finally, they emerged from the cabin together. Bess set the empty pan back on the shelf; then the sisters walked to the barn and joined their husbands. After a short conversation, a man walked to the wagon containing the coffin and climbed to the seat. He drove the team down the slope and was almost to the yard when Bess Browning stepped in front of the vehicle and signaled him to pull up. She stepped forward and stood beside him. "Not yet, Will," she said. "Kirb just walked into the cabin, and we'll give him as much time alone with her as he wants."

"Yes, ma'am," the man said, reaching into his vest pocket for his smoking tobacco. "You just let me know when you get ready."

After half an hour, Renfro stepped through the doorway and headed toward the corral in long strides, pointing to the garden as he walked. Moments later, he disappeared inside the barn.

Just as if the situation had been rehearsed, the Lazy Bee men went into action. The driver brought the wagon to the doorway, and two men had already removed the coffin by the time the vehicle came to a complete halt. They disappeared into the cabin quickly, and when they emerged three minutes later the pine box was a hundred pounds heavier. They slid the coffin three-quarters of the way into the wagon; then one of the men nodded to the driver.

Every man on the premises except Kirb Renfro joined the Browning women and followed the makeshift hearse to the open grave. Without a word from anyone, four men lowered the coffin into the excavation with ropes, then backed away. Once again, it was Gaylord Browning who did the talking. He doffed his hat and held it against his chest, then closed his eyes and lifted his face skyward. "Lord, we're giving you back the body of this sweet little girl that you let us enjoy knowing for a little while.

"The sheriff thinks there were at least three men in on the killing, but we know that you know the whole story. Now, if you intend to be the sole judge of the matter and punish the killers yourself, we'll all understand. But if you want it to be an eye for an eye, like it says in the Book, then we're begging you to help us find out who done it." He stood quietly for a moment, then added, "Amen." He picked up a handful of dirt and let it dribble into the hole on top of the coffin. "Dust to dust!" he said loudly. He nodded to the two men standing by with shovels, then took his wife and his sister-in-law by their hands and led them off the hillside. Moving very slowly, the remainder of the congregation followed. The shovelers filled in the hole quickly, then they too left the garden.

Bess Browning found the driver of the wagon again. "Get somebody to help you take that mattress Ellie died on outta the cabin, Will. Haul it up to the Lazy Bee, and we'll burn it later. There's a brand-new cotton mattress and two pillows in the back of the shed, so I want 'em brought down here and put on Kirb's bed. You go along, now, and try to get all that done before dark."

"Yes, ma'am," the driver said. He crooked his finger at a helper who was standing nearby, then once again drove the wagon to the cabin door.

Gaylord Browning walked straight to the barn, where he found Kirb sitting in the doorway of a stable staring at the wall. Browning stood quietly for a few minutes, then walked to the shed and returned with a three-legged stool. He seated himself so close that he could have touched Renfro, then stretched out his legs and leaned his shoulders against the wall. He would sit with his young friend all night if it turned out to be necessary.

Neither man spoke for the next half hour; then Renfro broke the silence. "Is it done?" he asked.

Browning nodded. "It's done," he answered.

Renfro sat staring at the ground for a long time. "I'm gonna hunt 'em down, Mr. Browning," he said finally.

"And I'm liable to skin every one of 'em alive when I find 'em."

"I don't think you'll even have to look for 'em," Gaylord said. "I talked with Sheriff Miller for quite a while, and he struck me as a man who'll probably find 'em himself. If he does, any jury in this county'll hang 'em all."

"Maybe so," Kirb said softly. "The law moves awful slow though."

"Of course it moves slow," Browning said, "but it's still the best way to go." He was quiet for a while, then changed the subject. "It ain't every man who's got a friend as good as you've got in Clay Summer, Kirb. He not only took right over when he saw that you weren't able to do nothing, but he volunteered to take care of your job till you feel like doing it yourself. He knows the Lazy Bee boundaries just as well as you do, and he said he was gonna spread his bedroll in your kitchen and live with you till you're in better shape."

"Clay's a good man," Renfro said.

The Brownings and the Lazy Bee crew vacated the Circle R premises an hour before sunset, then Summer and Renfro seated themselves at the table and ate a good portion of the food the women had left behind. When darkness closed in a short time later, they called it a night without ever lighting a lamp. Although Bess Browning had seen to it that he had a new mattress and pillows, Renfro spread his own bedroll on the kitchen floor beside his friend's. Very little conversation passed between the two men during the night.

16

★

Although Renfro had insisted on taking care of his own job, Summer had nonetheless been living on the Circle R for six weeks. A few times he had ridden line with Kirb, but most days he was content to cook the food and care for the animals. Two weeks ago, when Clay drove Kirb's wagon into town for supplies, he had had a long talk with Sheriff Miller. "I know who killed Ellie Renfro," the lawman informed Summer right from the outset. "It's gonna take me a little longer to build a case that'll convince the county prosecutor, but in my own mind, I've done got 'em pegged."

Summer smiled broadly. "I'm mighty glad to hear that, Dolph, and I know it's gonna please Kirb. Who are the sons of bitches?"

Miller shook his head. "You're a smart man, Clay; smart enough to know that I'm not gonna answer that question." He sat thoughtful for a few moments, then began again: "According to some of the men who saw him in action here in town last summer, young Renfro can be hell on wheels when he's pushed, and he's damn sure been pushed. Since you're out there with him all the time, I'm gonna ask you to do all you can to keep him in check till I know a little more. Tell him I expect to make some arrests pretty soon, and that when I do, I'll personally pay him a visit at his cabin."

Summer nodded and got to his feet. "I'll tell him all of that, Dolph, but I reckon I don't have to tell you that he intends to put Ellie's killers in the ground. He's plenty capable of doing it too. He's quicker'n a cat with that six-gun, and he'll damn sure hit whatever he shoots at."

The sheriff extinguished his cigarette in an ashtray, then sat with his elbows on his desk and his chin resting on his thumbs. "Is he as good as you are, Clay?"

Summer stood in the doorway for a moment pondering the question, then nodded. "Yep," he said. Moments later, he climbed aboard the wagon and pointed the team toward the Circle R.

When Sheriff Miller's message was relayed to Renfro, the young man was less than jubilant. "If he already knows who they are, why don't he just put the sons of bitches in jail?" was his first question to Summer.

"I don't reckon it's all that simple," Summer answered. "Like Dolph said, he don't want to arrest 'em till he's got enough evidence to convince a grand jury to indict 'em. He says the county prosecutor's a little bit gun-shy too, since both of the last two cases he prosecuted ended in acquittals."

"Well, I ain't gonna concern myself with all that stuff," Renfro said, getting out of his chair. He retrieved his gun belt from the wall and buckled it around his waist, then tied the holster to his right leg with rawhide. "If Sheriff Miller does get a conviction and a jury sentences 'em to hang, I'll be right there watching when the no-good bastards take the slack out of the rope." He moved into the doorway and stood looking toward the barn. "Now if it don't work out that way, I intend to find out how the sheriff knows whatever it is that he knows; then I'm gonna take care of the job myself." He pointed toward the barn, adding, "I'll be down there in the stable."

Summer nodded and watched his friend walk through the doorway, knowing that Kirb would not be back to the house until after he had practiced his fast draw somewhere between fifty and a hundred times.

Sheriff Miller paid his promised visit to the Circle R Ranch during the third week of March. Renfro had finished the first half of his line riding for the day and had returned to the cabin to eat dinner and change horses. With Clay Summer standing beside him, Kirb had just released the Lazy Bee bay into the corral and switched his saddle to his own black when the lawman drove a buggy up the hill. Sitting on the seat beside him, wearing a flannel shirt and a fleece-lined coat that most men would have considered out of season, was Laney Crosley, the Ginseng Man.

Renfro tied his horse to the gatepost, then he and Summer hurried across the hill to the hitching rail. Though Sheriff Miller had already jumped to the ground, the Ginseng Man kept his seat. Miller tied his mare, then addressed Kirb. "I'm sure Clay gave you my message, Mr. Renfro," he said, "and now I'm here to bring you up to date on the things I've learned.

"I deliberately put off coming out here till I had something more than my own suspicions to talk about. I've been hard at it for the past month, and the more work I done, the more convinced I was that I'd had the right men in mind from the very beginning." I also tracked down that fourteen-hundred-pound draft horse. It belongs to Lonny Tripp's brother-in-law. Tripp used the animal for just that one day, then put it back in the corral and left the country on a sorrel saddler." He motioned to the Ginseng Man. "Last week Mr. Crosley walked into my office and gave me enough evidence to clinch the case against all three men.

"I've got warrants for 'em now, but as you might guess, it looks like they've skipped the county. Ain't nobody seen hide nor hair of a single one of 'em since the sixteenth day of January, the same day your wife died. The county commissioners have authorized a two-hundred-dollar reward for the capture of each man, and the newspaper editor says he'll have some wanted posters printed up within a day or two."

Summer fired off a question quickly. "Are you talking about a dead-or-alive reward, Dolph?"

Miller shook his head. "Not exactly. I couldn't get the commissioners to put the word 'dead' on the dodger, but I'll guarantee you that if somebody shoots 'em in my county, he damn sure ain't gonna have to worry about going to jail." He stood quietly for a moment, then nodded to Crosley. "Tell 'em what you saw on the sixteenth day of January, Laney."

The Ginseng Man took off his ancient straw hat and began to scratch his head. He pointed up the slope. "I saw Pat Pollard, Lonny Tripp, and Wally Stovall come runnin' outta that cabin yonder. Their horses wuz tied to that shelf where th' water bucket and th' wash pan is. They passed a whiskey bottle around, then mounted and headed down the road at a gallop.

"Now, th' onliest reason I wuz here myself wuz to see if th' little lady had some leftovers that she'd give me. She'd done it before, so I figgered she might do it again." He pointed southwest. "I wuz comin' from that direction, and jist as I stepped around th' corner uv th' barn, I saw them three men come runnin' outta th' cabin.

"I jist stepped back behind th' buildin' real quick and

stood there peepin' at 'em till they rode off. As soon as they wuz gone, I knocked on th' cabin doorjamb a few times and called out to th' little lady, but I never got no answer. I jist figgered there weren't nobody at home, so I got me a drank uv water at the sprang, then walked on down the road."

Renfro had listened closely. "Is there any chance that you could be mistaken, Mr. Crosley?" he asked.

The man shook his head emphatically. "No, sir. I've been knowin' all three uv 'em since they wuz jist pups."

Renfro nodded. "It's a good thing you hid behind the barn 'cause I believe they'd have killed you if they'd seen you."

"Me, too," Crosley said. "I didn't have no way uv knowin' it then, but I ain't got no doubt about it now."

Renfro spoke to the lawman. "Do you know Tripp and Stovall personally, Sheriff?"

The lawman nodded. "Well enough to know that there ain't neither one of 'em worth killing."

"What do they look like? Can you describe 'em to me?"

"Well, they're both six-footers, about the same height and weight as Pollard. Tripp's got a big shock of black hair, with blue eyes and a real dark complexion. Stovall's sorta light-headed, with a pale complexion that looks like it ain't never seen the sun. I remember that his eyes ain't no dark color, so he might be blue-eyed too."

"Why, those're the same two sons of bitches who were with Pollard the last time I saw him," Renfro said, spitting as if he had a bad taste in his mouth. "They stared at my wife so long that she got scared of 'em, and they didn't exactly quit doing it even after I got back to the wagon. When they finally went back into the saloon I thought about going in there after 'em, but a fellow can't do nothing like that when he's got his wife with him."

Sheriff Miller had been busy building a cigarette. He

touched it with a match and blew a cloud of smoke sky-ward, then untied the mare. "I'll be getting on back to town," he said. "I just thought this morning was a good time to come out here and make good on my word." He climbed to his seat and backed the animal away from the hitching rail, then spoke a final word to Renfro. "I know there ain't nothing nobody can do to make up for your loss, young man, but I want you to know that you have my sympathy.

"I'm gonna do everything in my power to see that all three of 'em are brought to justice. I can't go chasing 'em all over Texas, 'cause my jurisdiction is limited to Comanche County, but I've got several other options, and I intend to use 'em all. You can rest assured that they're not gonna get away with raping and murdering your wife."

Renfro nodded. "I've already assured myself of that," he said. "I intend to put all three of the sons of bitches in the ground."

The lawman smiled and dropped his cigarette butt into a tin can he kept in the buggy for that purpose. "I figured as much," he said. "You probably wouldn't have no other choice with Pollard anyhow. You've done whipped his ass once, so he'll most likely go for his gun the next time you call his name." He sat quietly for a moment, then added, "If you'll drop by my office early next week, I might have some leads for you." He guided the mare onto the road, then left the hill at a trot.

Renfro and Summer stood by the hitching rail talking for several minutes, then walked to the cabin to eat their dinner. Summer had cooked a large pan of corn bread to go with their beans and had opened a jar of okra and tomatoes that Ellie had put up back in the fall. "I reckon I'll be taking up the hunt about next Monday," Renfro said around a mouthful of food. "When I get done riding line this after-noon I'll ride up to Lazy Bee headquarters and talk about it

with Mr. Browning. He's gonna have to make arrangements for a different line rider, but it's all right with me if
the new man stays in my cabin. Ain't nobody gonna want
to live in that line shack anyway. It's so damn little a man
wouldn't be able to find a place to hang his hat."

"I know," Summer said. He refilled their coffee cups,
then reseated himself. "I've been thinking about riding
with you when you go hunting, Kirb. I mean, you just
never know what kind of situation you might run up
against when you're dealing with vultures like Pollard,
Tripp, and Stovall."

Renfro washed down a mouthful of food and sat staring into his cup. "That's mighty kind of you, Clay, but
I've got to say no. You're the best company in the world,
and I've got to admit that having your fast gun along
would probably improve my chances of coming back
alive, but it wouldn't be the same. Putting Ellie's killers in
the ground is something I've got to do myself, and I've
got to do it alone."

Summer sat digesting Renfro's words for a few moments, then said, "You're absolutely right, Kirb. I don't
know why I didn't figure that out on my own. I'll tell you
what I can do though. I can hold your job down for you
while you're gone, and I'll live right here in this cabin. Ransom can just keep putting your brand on a brood cow every
month and pay me the twenty-five dollars that he's been
giving you. That way your herd'll keep right on growing."

Renfro sat quietly for a while. "Did I hear you right,
Clay?" he asked finally. "Are you saying you'd accept
cows with my brand on 'em as part of your pay?"

Summer nodded. "Of course," he answered. "What
the hell are friends for?"

Renfro did not answer the question.

They rode over the southern boundaries of both the
Circle R and the Lazy Bee during the afternoon, and when

they reached the big spring at two o'clock, Renfro's work was done for the day. Then, instead of heading back to the cabin as usual, they turned their horses north and arrived at Lazy Bee headquarters two hours later. Seeing no one about as they rode up the hill, they tied their horses at the bunkhouse hitching rail then walked to the cookshack. Renfro rapped on the doorjamb, then stepped inside. "Two wayward cowhands here needing a cup of coffee, Mr. Kelso," he said. "We've been hoping you'd let us eat supper with you too."

The cook smiled and chuckled softly. He pointed to a big iron pot that had been moved to the back of the stove. "Get some bowls outta that box over there and help yourselves," he said. "The stew's been done for two hours, and I'll be taking some hot corn bread outta the oven in about three minutes."

The visitors filled their bowls and their coffee cups, then seated themselves at the table to await the corn bread. When the cook set the pan on the corner of the table, Renfro carved off a chunk of the bread with his knife, then began to toss it from one hand to the other. Finally deciding that it was simply too hot to handle, he dropped it into the bowl and tore it apart with his spoon. It would cool down quickly in the bowl, for the stew was only a little warmer than the temperature of the room.

Both men ate hungrily and very soon refilled their bowls. "I reckon this stuff's about all a fellow would need to keep him going, Mr. Kelso," Summer said. "Tastes like there's a little bit of everything in it. How long have you been making stew like this?"

"About forty years," the cook answered. He chuckled. "I don't guess you could truthfully say that it's got everything in it, but it's certainly got a little bit of everything I could find around here in it. I'm glad you like it; eat all you want."

The men finished their meal and thanked the cook, then walked outside just in time to see Gaylord Browning step off the porch and head down the path in their direction. The two men waved, then stood waiting as Browning walked to meet them with long strides. They met at the hitching rail, and Browning shook hands with both men. "It's good to see you two again," he said, "and you're both looking mighty good." He locked eyes with Renfro. "Everything all right down at your place?"

"Yes, sir," Kirb answered, chuckling. "Everything's all right on the southeast portion of your place too."

"Good," Browning said. He pointed to the cookshack. "I guess you've done had all the coffee you could drink."

"Had all we could eat too," Summer said. "Mr. Renfro talked the cook into feeding us."

An awkward silence followed, and Browning finally spoke. "You fellows must have something you want to talk about, so let's walk up to the porch and sit down in some comfortable chairs." He headed for the house, and the others followed.

"Sheriff Miller's identified Ellie's killers, Mr. Browning," Renfro said, taking a seat in the cushioned chair he was offered. "He's got warrants for all three of 'em, and the county's already posted a reward."

Browning banged his fist against the table. "By God, that's the best news I've heard in a long time," he said. "I had confidence in Miller right from the start; he just struck me as a man who'd get the job done."

"Dolph's a good fellow and I'm sure he's been working on it day and night," Clay Summer said, "but it was the Ginseng Man who brought it all to a head."

When Browning raised his eyebrows, Renfro picked up the conversation. "Laney Crosley hid behind my barn and watched Pat Pollard, Lonny Tripp, and Wally Stovall come outta my cabin and stand in my yard drinking whiskey. He says there can't be no mistake 'cause he's known 'em all for years."

Kirb stared between his boots for a few moments, then began to sniffle. "Sometimes in bed at night I can just hear Ellie begging 'em, Mr. Browning. She . . . she probably done everything they told her to and gave 'em everything she had, but the no-good sons of bitches beat her to death anyhow." He sniffled once more, then raised his head. He wiped his cheeks on his shirtsleeve, then looked at the rancher misty-eyed. "They're goddam sure gonna pay for it too."

"I know, Kirb," Browning said, putting his arm around Renfro's shoulders and hugging him like a son. "I know."

The three men finally got around to talking business, and half an hour later, after borrowing a Lazy Bee pack-saddle, Renfro and Summer mounted their horses and rode over the hill. Gaylord had been quick to accept the suggestions that Clay Summer himself take over Renfro's job, and that Kirb should continue to gain another cow at the end of every month. The rancher had even offered to bear the expense of Kirb's upcoming manhunt. Renfro had declined the offer, saying that he would make a withdrawal from his own bank account.

Darkness had closed in by the time they reached the Circle R. They stripped their saddles and cared for their animals by lantern light, then headed for the cabin. Renfro lit the lamp, then pointed to the pot on the stove. "You want something else to eat?" he asked jokingly.

"I don't feel like I'll ever want to eat again," Summer answered, then walked to his newly built bunk and pulled off his boots.

"I feel the same way," Renfro said. He sat down in a chair and took off his own footwear, then blew out the lamp and felt his way to his bed. No more conversation passed between the two men, and both slept soundly.

17

Monday morning at nine o'clock, Kirb mounted Midnight and took up the slack in his pack animal's lead rope. Standing beside Renfro's stirrup, Clay Summer offered some parting advice: "Don't talk to no more people than you have to, Kirb, and don't trust no damn body." He pointed to the five-day growth of stubble on Renfro's face. "Just leave your razor in your saddlebag and let that beard keep on growing till the hunt's over. Be careful what you do and what you say, and remember that all three of the men you're hunting know exactly who you are and what you look like. You've got to see them before they see you." He took a step backward to indicate that he had nothing else to say.

Renfro nodded and sat his saddle quietly for a few moments. "I appreciate everything you're doing, Clay," he said finally. "Having a man like you taking care of my job while I'm gone is more than I could have hoped for, and I won't be forgetting it." He clucked to Midnight, then continued to speak over his shoulder as he moved away. "I intend to stay with the hunt, Clay, and you won't see me again till it's over." He rode out of the yard and took to the road at a trot.

By the time he reached the river road and turned toward town, the black had of its own accord slowed to walk. The horse-saving gait pleased Renfro well enough. He was in no hurry; the woman-killers would keep.

Today, Kirb Renfro was a man on a mission, and he was armed to the teeth. Full up and ready for action, his trusty, twelve-shot Henry rifle rode in its saddle scabbard next to his left leg. A wide gun belt was buckled around his middle, with his Colt resting in a holster that was tied to his right leg with rawhide. A double-barrel derringer that was owned by Clay Summer was stashed in his saddlebag. Renfro was more than a little handy with any of the weapons and had an ample supply of ammunition for all in his pack.

Both Renfro and Summer believed that the pack contained everything Kirb was going to need on his manhunt. That had been their conclusion when they put the pack together the afternoon before, and it had been reaffirmed after a close inspection this morning. In addition to the necessary cooking and eating utensils, the pack mule carried three changes of clothing and an extra pair of boots for its master, a tarpaulin and two extra blankets, three quart jars that Kirb expected a restaurant cook to fill with precooked food, and a wide assortment of things that a man would seldom think of until he needed them.

The mule carried no food at the moment. Renfro had no idea how long he would be in Comanche, but he would not leave town until he knew where he was going. Once he had a destination, he would stock his pack with sup-

plies at the grocery store, then have his jars filled at
Sleepy's Restaurant. At that time he would also decide
whether or not to buy grain.

Being reluctant to load his pack animal down unless
it was absolutely necessary, he would hold off on buying
a sack of oats till he knew which direction he would be
traveling in. Some parts of Texas had little or no graze at
this time of the year, while others, such as the Comanche
area, had green grass in abundance. Whatever the case
turned out to be, his pack contained a nose bag for each
of the animals.

Shortly after noon, he dismounted at the livery stable
in Comanche. "I want to leave my mule with you for a
while," he said to Sid Yokum, the aging hostler who had
met him in the wide doorway. "I'd appreciate it if you'd
put my pack in the office, so nobody'll be tempted to go
prowling through it."

"I always do," Yokum said, taking the animal's lead
rope from Kirb's hand. "I guess I'd better tell you right
up front, though, that I had to raise my prices a little. The
cost of feed's gone up so damn high that I couldn't make
it on a quarter a head, so I'm having to charge thirty cents
now."

Renfro nodded. "Thirty cents is fine," he said. "I don't
know how long I'll be leaving the mule, but I'm sure I
won't need him again today." He pointed to the black.
"In fact, I'll probably bring my saddler back to you before
the night's over."

The hostler nodded. "You do that," he said. "I hope
you bring him before ten o'clock though. I give out a lot
quicker'n I used to, so I try to go to bed by that time."

Kirb nodded, then remounted the black and rode up
the street. Moments later, he tied up at the sheriff's hitching rail, then walked to the office and rapped his knuckles
against the doorjamb.

Miller had been lounging behind his desk with his feet propped up on a stool, but he got to his feet quickly when he recognized the man standing in the doorway. "Come right in, Mr. Renfro," he said, crossing the room with his right hand extended.

Kirb shook the hand. "You said you might have some leads for me," he said, "so here I am. I'm ready to go looking for the three men who murdered my wife."

The lawman nodded and led the way back to his desk. "I was expecting you today," he said as Renfro seated himself. "I've got a fellow I want you to talk to, but I doubt that I could find him today. He'll be easier to run down after dark 'cause he comes into town about every night of the week. He knows the three men you're hunting like a book, and he wants to see at least one of 'em dancing at the end of a rope almost as bad as you do. Pat Pollard beat him up for no reason at all about a year ago, then worked his face over with his boot heels after he had him knocked out. Poor fellow's face is scarred up for life."

"I'd like to talk with him," Renfro said. He drummed his fingers on the desk. "There's something else I guess I'd better mention. You said the newspaper was gonna print up some wanted posters, and Clay Summer says I oughtta have some of 'em to carry around with me. He says I'll need some proof that they're running from the law if I have any gunplay with 'em in another sheriff's jurisdiction."

"Clay Summer told you right," Miller said, pulling out his desk drawer. "I got the dodgers two days ago, and I'll give you a few of 'em to carry around in your saddlebag." He separated several copies from the stack, then pushed them across the desk.

Renfro read one of them quickly. It stated that a young housewife had been raped and murdered in her own Comanche County home on January 16, 1871, and that an eyewitness had placed Pat Pollard, Lonny Tripp, and Wally Stovall in her cabin at about the time the crime was committed. It described all three men in detail and stated that the county of Comanche would pay the sum of two hundred dollars for the capture of each individual. A garbled signature that Kirb could not read was scrawled across the lower right-hand corner of the page.

He folded the posters twice, then got to his feet. "I'll walk out to the hitching rail and put these things in my saddlebag," he said.

Renfro spent another half hour in the lawman's office, then rode up the street and rented an upstairs room at the Comanche Hotel. Without even climbing the stairway, he returned to the sheriff's office and gave the lawman his room number, then rode to the livery stable and turned his black over to Sid Yokum. When he returned to the hotel with his saddlebags over his shoulder and his Henry cradled in the crook of his arm, the desk clerk was nowhere to be seen.

Moments later, Kirb stepped into room 216 and relocked the door, then seated himself on the edge of the bed. He sat for several minutes reliving his conversation with Sheriff Miller. The lawman had singlehandedly put together enough evidence to convict the killers in any court in Texas. He even knew the identity and the whereabouts of a young woman who had listened to Wally Stovall's confession of the rape and murder. The man Miller expected to deliver to Kirb's hotel room before the night was over was a brother to that woman.

Renfro spent a long afternoon in his room, then ate supper in the hotel restaurant at sunset. He bought a newspaper from a vendor on the street corner, then climbed the stairway again. He read a few articles in the paper by the light of a coal-oil lamp, then pulled off his boots and lay on the bed dozing. He was dreaming that he and Ellie were back home in Tennessee when a loud knock brought him wide awake. With his Colt in his right fist, he crossed the room and unlocked the door quickly. Sheriff Miller poked his head through the doorway and looked at the Colt in Kirb's hand. "I can see that you're on your toes," he said.

A slender, blond-haired young man, who stood a couple inches less than six feet tall, followed the lawman into the room. His complexion was extremely fair, and his otherwise handsome face was so badly scarred that it was almost repulsive to the eye. His lower lip looked as if it belonged on a different mouth, and deep scars ran along both cheeks and around his eyes, some of them a reddish pink, others purple.

"This is Ollie Blanding, Kirb," the sheriff said, as the two men shook hands. "He's the young man I was telling you about earlier today."

Renfro pumped Blanding's hand a few times, then pointed to the only two chairs in the room. "Make yourselves at home," he said, then seated himself on the side of the bed. He sat quietly for a moment, then spoke to Blanding. "The sheriff tells me that you know quite a bit about Pat Pollard, Lonny Tripp, and Wally Stovall," he said. "Since that's a whole lot more than I know, I'd appreciate anything you can tell me."

Blanding nodded. "I'd certainly like to see those scumbags brought down, so if you think I might know something that'll help, I'll answer any questions you've got."

"Thank you, Ollie," Renfro said. "Just tell me whatever you can think of about 'em. The sheriff says your sister heard Stovall talking about the murder. I'd like to hear what you know about that."

Blanding nodded, then began to talk. He had known all three of the wanted men for most of his life, he said, and his sister, Blanche, had even allowed Wally Stovall to court her a few times. The fact that she had eventually decided that she wanted nothing to do with a man who was a hard drinker did little to discourage Stovall, however, for he continued to seek her out at every opportunity.

On a few occasions, he had even shown up at her home drunk, begging for any scrap of affection. One of those occasions had been the day after Ellie Renfro was murdered. With a whiskey bottle in his hand and tears rolling down his cheeks, Stovall had begged the girl to go away with him. When it became obvious that his drunken plea was falling on deaf ears, he had begun to cry like a baby, then confessed that he was in big trouble.

As Blanche Blanding sat listening, Stovall admitted to raping Ellie Renfro, but claimed that the killing blows with the stick of stove wood had been delivered by Pollard and Tripp.

"You say Stovall wanted your sister to go away with him," Renfro said, when Blanding stopped to get his breath. "Did he tell her where he wanted to take her?"

"Sure did," Blanding answered. "Said he was gonna go to Round Rock. Said he knew a rancher there who'd not only give him a job, but who would furnish him a cabin to live in if she'd go with him and claim to be his wife. Blanche finally quit listening to him. She locked the front door and left him standing on the porch talking to himself. She said she watched him through the window, said he hung around for a few more minutes, then threw his empty whiskey bottle in the yard and rode off toward town."

"Do you know what color horse he was riding?" Renfro asked.

Blanding nodded. "Same one he always rides. Good-looking bay with three stockings and a blaze. The horse has got a big ox yoke burnt into his left hip, and that brand sure don't belong to nobody around here."

Renfro was writing down the information in a small notebook. He paused for a moment, then asked, "Did Stovall say what the Round Rock rancher's name is?"

Blanding shook his head. "I asked my sister the same question, and she said he never mentioned the man's name. He did tell her that the ranch is real close to town though."

Renfro continued to write. "Ranch . . . close to town," he mumbled, as if talking to the notebook. He turned the page, then spoke to Blanding again. "Did Stovall say anything about where Pollard and Tripp might have gone?"

Blanding nodded. "Sure did. He said they'd done lit out for Pleasanton the night before. He said Pollard got real scared after he sobered up some 'cause he was afraid the Texas Rangers might get involved. According to Stovall, Pollard said that all three of 'em would have a better chance if they went in three different directions. He told Stovall to go his own way, and even said that him and Tripp were gonna split up once they got to Pleasanton.

"Now I happen to know that one of Pat Pollard's cousins lives at Pleasanton 'cause I met him the year I was in the sixth grade. He spent part of his summer vacation with the Pollard family, and I got to knowing him pretty well. Of course, I don't have no way of knowing whether he still lives down there or not, but he sure did then. His name is Cecil Bray."

"Cecil Bray," Renfro repeated, jotting the name down in his notebook. "Bray would be about your age then?"

Blanding nodded. "I don't have no idea when his birthday is, but he'll be twenty-three sometime this year."

Renfro nodded and laid his notebook on his pillow. He walked across the room and stood looking through the window for a few moments, then turned and spoke to Blanding again. "I can't help wondering why your sister didn't bring all this information to Sheriff Miller right away, Ollie. Did she say anything about that?"

Blanding nodded. "She said she didn't want no part of an investigation, and that there wasn't a thing she could say or do that would bring the dead woman back. She went up to Stephenville to live with our Aunt Martha two days after talking with Stovall, but she says she'll come back and give her testimony in court if it's ever needed. Otherwise, she intends to stay in Erath County."

"I see," Renfro said. He stood quietly for a moment, then moved back to the footboard of the bed. "I reckon you've given me all the information I need, Ollie, so I won't ask any more questions. It was awful nice of you to come forward, and I want you to know that I appreciate it."

Blanding sat looking at the floor. "Well, I didn't exactly come forward," he said sheepishly. "Sheriff Miller came looking for me."

The lawman, who had not spoken in several minutes, was on his feet now. "I reckon what Mr. Renfro's saying is that me and him both appreciate what you've done, Ollie. Thank you for coming, and you can go on about your business now."

Blanding got to his feet quickly and was out the door without another word.

"Well, where do you intend to go looking first?" the sheriff asked, reseating himself in one of the chairs.

Renfro was slow to answer. "Round Rock's closer than Pleasanton," he said finally. "Blanding says that's where Stovall went."

Miller nodded. He sat thoughtful for a moment, then spoke again. "Clay Summer says you're as good with a six-gun as he is, Mr. Renfro, and by God that's saying something."

Kirb raised an eyebrow. "Clay said that?"

"Sure did, and that tells me right off that you're plenty good enough to bring down such riffraff as Pat Pollard, Lonny Tripp, and Wally Stovall. I have no doubt that you'll do it; and when you do, just leave the sons of bitches lying wherever they fall.

"I hunted up two of the county commissioners this afternoon and told 'em about Wally Stovall's confession. After hearing that, they gave me permission to put 'Dead or Alive' on the wanted posters. The people at the newspaper promised to print up a few dozen copies for me first thing in the morning, and I'll make sure you get a handful of 'em before you leave town." He headed for the doorway, continuing to speak over his shoulder. "I'll deliver 'em to you right here about nine o'clock in the morning." He let himself out, and Renfro locked the door behind him.

18

★

Renfro rode out of Comanche an hour before noon the next morning and headed south by southeast. After eating an early breakfast at Sleepy's Restaurant, he had spoken to the cook about filling his jars with precooked food. "I can handle that," the fat man had said. "Had nearly half a pot of stew left over from supper last night."

"The jars are in my pack at the livery stable," Kirb said. "I'll bring 'em to you on my way out of town this morning. Can you bake an extra pan of biscuits for me too?"

"I can bake as many pans as you want," the cook said.

Kirb smiled. "One'll be enough," he said. "I'm gonna be traveling, so if you'll wrap 'em up or put 'em in a paper bag, I'll appreciate it.

The cook nodded, then returned to the kitchen.

Sheriff Miller delivered the new posters to Kirb's hotel room right on time. Renfro put them in his saddlebag and laid it across his shoulder, then said good-bye to the lawman. He headed for the livery stable, and half an hour later, led the mule to the grocery store and loaded its pack with supplies. Then he headed for the restaurant and turned his jars over to the cook. He ate a piece of pie and drank a cup of coffee while he was waiting, then left the restaurant with his stew, a dozen biscuits, and two wedges of apple pie. His last stop before leaving town was the bank, where he made a cash withdrawal and discussed his business with no one.

Today he was headed for Round Rock, a town his map showed to be located halfway between Waco and San Antonio. His pack animal carried everything he was likely to need, and the weather was comfortable. Like most other people, this was his favorite season, and the spring flowers growing by the roadside reminded him of his beloved Ellie. She had been a devout student of nature and could put the correct name to almost any plant that bloomed.

Just thinking of her always sent a chill through his spine, and he missed her more than words could describe. She had truly been his better half and had made it plain right from the start that her main concern in life was to make him happy. And she had succeeded. Even now Kirb rode around talking to her in the daytime and sometimes walked into the garden and sat beside her grave for hours before going to bed at night. She knew that he was going on a manhunt this week. He had told her dozens of times, and each time he mentioned it he got the feeling that she agreed with his decision.

Kirb had contacted no one back in Tipton County about his wife's murder. One of his reasons was to shield them from grief, and another was because there had been no closure in the case. He had already decided that if he was successful on his manhunt, he would notify Ellie's grandmother and fill her in on the details. Lady Kerrington would see to it that the word was spread throughout the county.

He rode at a steady pace for the remainder of the day, and about an hour before sunset, forded the Lampasas River and made camp on the west bank. There was plenty of green grass in any direction, and he picketed his animals less than forty yards from his campsite.

He found kindling easily, and once he had a fire going, walked to the river and filled his coffeepot. He dropped a handful of grounds into the pot and set it on the fire, then emptied one of the jars into his skillet. In a matter of minutes, he was washing the tasty beef stew and cold biscuits down with strong coffee. He ate a wedge of the apple pie afterward, then raked dirt over his fire.

He dragged his bedroll into a cluster of leafy bushes as darkness closed in and, with his Henry and his Colt close to hand, pulled off his boots and stretched out. His bedroll, which was actually a thick quilt sewed to a piece of waterproof canvas, felt comfortable enough on the sandy terrain of the riverbank. And though he had a blanket nearby, he doubted that he would be needing it for the night was unseasonably warm. After tossing and turning for a while, he folded the blanket and placed it under his head for a pillow, then slept soundly.

He was up long before the sun next morning and built a fire at the first hint of daybreak. He reheated his leftover coffee, and daylight found him sitting beside his pack eating Bologna sausage, strong cheese, and cold biscuits. When he was done, he extinguished his fire and reorganized his pack, then headed for the meadow to retrieve his animals.

He was on the move again at sunup. Riding more or less parallel to the river, he was seldom out of sight of the water. Since the road held to a steady course whenever possible, and the river curved back and forth repeatedly in its constant search for the path of least resistance, he had to ford it several times during the morning. None of the crossings had been difficult, however, for the water in most places had been less than a foot deep.

He forded the wide stream again at noon, then dismounted beside a big oak. He was back on the east bank now, and for some reason the grass seemed to grow thicker on the east side of the river. He left the saddle and the packsaddle on his animals, then staked them out where the green grass appeared to be the thickest. He built no fire. He had been sweating all day long, and the last thing he wanted at the moment was a hot cup of coffee. He ate more Bologna sausage and cheese, then drank two cups of cold water from the fast-moving Lampasas.

He leaned against the trunk of the oak and was about to doze off when he heard the rattle of trace chains and the sound of wheels crunching the hard, dry earth. An eastward glance revealed an oversized freight wagon drawn by four large draft horses. Two men sat on the seat. Traveling a little-used road that Renfro had hardly noticed before, the vehicle was headed west, and the driver no doubt intended to take the main road when he reached the intersection, which was very close to where Kirb was sitting. He got to his feet and stood leaning against the tree.

Instead of taking the main road, the man drove across it, pulling up only a few yards from where Renfro stood. The driver wrapped the reins around the brake and climbed over the sideboard, and his partner was on the ground almost as quickly. Both men appeared to be about fifty years old. "Howdy," the driver said. "My name's Will Easter, and this is my brother, Clem."

Renfro nodded, and said nothing.

Will Easter pointed back the way he had come. "Looks like the county'd finally do something to that damn road," he said. "I know there ain't many folks that use it, but people going from Hamilton to Goldthwaite ain't got no choice." He pointed down the main road. "Now that's a good road there, but we won't get to stay on it but about three miles, then that same pig trail splits off and goes on to Goldthwaite."

Renfro shook his head sympathetically but remained silent.

The man named Clem took an armful of deadwood from the wagon and began to kindle a fire, while his brother, Will, continued to talk. He stood looking at Renfro for a moment, then asked, "You headed north or south?"

"South," Kirb answered.

"Guess you must live up around Comanche then."

Renfro nodded again.

"We've got a cousin lives up there," Will Easter said. "His name's Moe Jilly White, and he's about our own age. Know him?"

"No, sir," Kirb said. "I've never heard that name before."

The man was busy putting nose bags on his horses but continued to talk as he worked. "Moe Jilly rode up there for the weekend back in the summer of sixty-five and liked it so much he just stayed.

"Me 'n' Clem still live in Hamilton though, and I reckon we'll be there for the rest of our days. Right now, we're taking this load of bricks to Goldthwaite. Gotta do it two more times too; a fellow over there bought three wagonloads." He hung a bag on the last of the horses, then leaned against a front wheel. "Sure was bad about somebody killing that young woman up there in your county last winter. From what I hear, they ain't never caught nobody, neither, and I'd be willing to bet that they never will." He produced a plug of tobacco and bit off a chew, then turned it over in his mouth several times and spat a mouthful of juice between his feet. "I guess you know the killing I'm talking about, huh?"

Renfro stood thoughtful for a long while. "Yes, sir," he finally answered. "I know exactly what you're talking about." He hung the black's bridle over his shoulder and picked up his cup and the remainder of his food, then stepped around Easter's wagon and headed for the meadow. He caught up his animals and stowed their picket ropes in his pack, then tightened the saddle cinch and mounted the black. Seeing the Easter brothers standing beside their wagon staring, he waved good-bye to them and took the road south. He was out of sight quickly.

He rode at a fast walk for the remainder of the day, and the sun had already dropped out of sight when he finally pulled off the road. He had not been concerned about finding the perfect place to camp for the night, for there was plenty of green grass everywhere. And the fact that he intended to build no fire meant that he only needed enough time to picket his animals before night closed in. He would eat a cold supper in the dark, then spread his bedroll wherever he found a level spot. An hour after leaving the road, he was sleeping soundly between a fat cedar and a fallen log.

He was in the saddle again at sunup next morning, and by late afternoon had traveled a distance that he estimated to be at least forty miles. The sun was still an hour high when he topped a steep hill and sat looking down at the community of Copperas Cove.

Lying in a bowl that was completely surrounded by hills, with an abundance of spring water that was said to taste like copper, the tiny settlement was a stopping point for drovers bringing their herds to the Chisholm Trail. And though the area was inhabited by law-abiding farmers and ranchers for the most part, the town had seen more than its share of violence, for wherever drunken cowhands congregated, drunken disputes were sure to follow. Fistfights were a common occurrence and often escalated into gunplay.

Renfro sat looking for only a short time, then kneed the black down the hill. He had already decided to buy his animals a good feed of oats and put them up at the livery stable for the night, and he intended to treat himself at least as well. Riding down the town's only street a few minutes later, he counted three saloons and only one hotel. A restaurant was adjacent to the hotel, and he immediately decided to eat his supper there.

He looked the establishment over for a moment, then trotted on to the livery stable at the end of the street. As Kirb rode through the open doorway, a skinny, middle-aged man stepped from the office. "Thank you for stopping in, young fellow," he said. "Want me to feed 'em and put 'em up for the night?"

"Yes, sir," Renfro answered, dismounting. "Give 'em a feed of oats tonight and again in the morning, if you will."

The man took the black's reins and the mule's lead rope. "I can handle that," he said. "You need anything outta your pack before I lock it up in the office?"

"No, sir," Kirb said. He unsheathed his rifle and cradled it in the crook of his arm. Motioning up the street with his thumb, he asked, "Is the Ferguson the only hotel in town?"

The hostler nodded. "Yep," he said. "I reckon it's the only one we need. The only times it ever fills up is when the trail hands are in town, and they ain't due for another month yet. You just walk on up there now and tell 'em what you want. I'll guarantee you that they'll put you up right and they'll feed you right. They won't charge you an arm and a leg for it neither."

Kirb thanked the man, then headed up the street.

A white-haired, fat man got to his feet when Renfro stepped to the counter at the hotel. "Thank you for stopping at the Ferguson, sir," he said in a high-pitched voice that sounded very much like Bess Browning. "Will you be needing a room for the night?"

Renfro nodded. "I guess the top floor's a little cooler, huh?"

"It sure is," the man said, pushing the register forward. "I'll give you the upstairs room on the northwest corner. It has a window on two sides, and you should be able to create a breeze by raising both of 'em." He dropped a pencil on the counter. "I need eighty cents in advance for the room, and the law says you've got to sign the register."

Renfro wrote the name "Bill Alexander" in the book, then counted out the money.

The clerk handed him a key. "Room two-ten," he said. He motioned toward the bat-wing doors on the south side of the lobby. "The restaurant opens at six o'clock in the morning and stays open till midnight. Everybody I know says we serve the best food in town."

Renfro put the key in his pocket. "That sounds good," he said. "I'll be testing it myself within the next few minutes." He took the stairs two at a time, and a few moments later let himself into the room and relocked the door. He raised both of the windows, then sat down on the edge of the bed. He had been uncomfortably warm for most of the day, and the draft created by the opposing windows cooled him off and dried the back of his sweat-stained shirt quickly.

He sat for half an hour with his feet on the bed and

his shoulders leaning against the headboard, then as darkness closed in, put a burning match to the wick of the coal-oil lamp. He replaced the globe and adjusted the light to a softer glow, then stepped into the hall and locked the door. A moment later, he walked past the desk clerk and made his way into the restaurant.

The establishment was both large and clean, with half a dozen stools at the counter and four long rows of tables. Though he could see no more than a dozen diners from where he stood, he decided very quickly that the restaurant could probably feed a hundred people at a time. He stood just inside the doorway for a few moments, then stepped forward and seated himself at the nearest table. A tall, young waiter was there quickly. He laid a bill of fare on the table. "Thank you for dining with us, sir," he said, with a slow drawl. "Our special tonight is sirloin tips and potato salad."

Renfro smiled, then picked up the menu and handed it back. "You whetted my appetite right off," he said. "I'll have the special."

"Yes, sir," the young man said, then headed for the kitchen.

When his meal arrived twenty minutes later, Renfro became convinced very quickly that what the desk clerk had said about the restaurant's food had been no idle boast. The meat was tender enough to tear apart with a fork, and the gravy was second to none he had ever tasted. The two large biscuits he had been served were still warm from the oven, and the potato salad had a tangy aftertaste that reminded him of the salad he had occasionally eaten at Lady Kerrington's table.

He declined the dessert the waiter suggested but did accept a second cup of coffee. He gazed about the room continually as he sipped the strong liquid but looked no one directly in the eye. The number of diners had re-

mained constant since his arrival, for although several
people had eaten and left the premises, others had come
along to take their places. Without actually making a head
count, he decided that there were probably fifteen people
in the building, most of them middle-aged couples.

He finished off his coffee and laid a dime on the table
for the waiter, then walked to the counter and paid for
his supper, surprised that the price was only thirty cents.
Passing up the bat-wing doors leading to the hotel lobby,
he stepped through the front doorway of the restaurant
and onto the plank sidewalk. He stood looking up and
down the street for a while, then decided on the spur of
the moment that he wanted a cold beer.

Two of the three watering holes he had counted earlier
were within a stone's throw of where he now stood. Since
each of them had only three horses tied at its hitching rail,
he chose the one directly across the street for no reason
except that it was a few steps closer. Moments later, he
shouldered his way through the bat-wing doors and
stepped inside.

The saloon was large, even by Texas standards. A
forty-foot bar with stools on all sides was located in the
middle of the building, and what appeared to be a half
acre of tables and chairs were scattered about the huge
room. Double booths, facing each other across tables
adorned with colorful cloths, lined all four walls, and a
small stage was located against the rear wall. The dance
floor played out beside a narrow staircase that no doubt
saw lots of use when the trail hands were in town.

There was a billiard table in the northwest corner of
the building, and two men stood beside it knocking the
balls around. And although the bar had working stations
for four bartenders, only one man was on duty at the
moment. He eased himself off of his stool as Kirb approached the bar. "Howdy," he said. "Business'll pick up

in about two hours, but right now, I'd say you've just about got the place to yourself. What'll you have?"

"I've been wanting a cold beer for a week," Kirb said, sliding onto a corner stool. "I'll even buy you one if you'll drink it."

The man chuckled. "I try to limit myself to about six hundred a day," he said, "but I ain't had near that many yet." He drew two beers and slid one down the bar to Renfro. "My name's Perry Younglove," he said, lifting his mug into the air. "I always introduce myself to a man before I start drinking up his money."

"I'm Bill Alexander," Renfro said, offering a handshake across the bar.

Younglove set his mug down and wiped his right hand on his apron, then pumped Kirb's arm a few times. "I don't reckon there's anybody in this town that I don't know," he said, "so you must be on your way to someplace else."

Renfro nodded. "Headed south," he said.

"Austin?" the barkeep asked.

Kirb shook his head. "Austin's too big for me," he said. "I'm more likely to pull up when I get to Round Rock."

Though the bartender was shorter that Renfro, he was probably heavier, for he was a very muscular man. With a ruddy complexion and thinning brown hair that was graying at his temples, he appeared to be in his late thirties. He took another sip of his beer, then wiped his mouth on his sleeve. "I've never been to Round Rock myself," he said, "but there damn sure must be something awful important down there. Seems like every man who's stopped in here this year has been headed for Round Rock."

Renfro wet his lips with beer. "Did any of 'em say what they were gonna do when they got there?"

The bartender topped off Kirb's mug and refused payment. "I didn't actually ask none of 'em what their business was. Best I remember, three or four of 'em said they had relatives there, and a couple more said they were hunting work." He chuckled softly. "One of 'em sat on that same stool you're on for two days and nights back in January. Said he was gonna go to work on the Seesaw Ranch when he got to Round Rock, but he was probably just shooting the shit. He was drunk when he got here, and he was drunk when he left.

"He sat right here at this bar drinking for a total of about thirty hours. Got here right after we opened up each morning and stayed till we closed at night. What amazed all of us bartenders was the fact that he never did pass out." He chuckled again and pointed. "He fell over that table there on his way out of the building the last night he was here, but it didn't seem to bother him none. He just picked his gun up off the floor and shoved it back in his holster, then got up and walked through the front door like a sober man."

Renfro chuckled. Then, for no other reason than to make conversation, he said, "Sounds like somebody I know."

"Well, he ain't one you'd be likely to forget," Younglove said. "Told all of us his name was Stovall."

Renfro set his mug down slowly. He repeated the name to himself, then spoke to the bartender again. "Wally Stovall?" he asked.

"That's him," Younglove said quickly. "I reckon, by God, you know the fellow all right."

Renfro sat quietly for a moment, then pushed his mug across the bar for a refill. "Stovall said he was going to work on the Seesaw Ranch, huh?"

The bartender nodded. He drew the beer and set it at Kirb's elbow. "That's what he claimed. I can't imagine anybody hiring him unless he straightens his ass out though. Especially a big outfit like the Seesaw."

Kirb had one last question for the bartender. "Is the Seesaw located close to Round Rock?" he asked.

"It's damn near in Round Rock, from what I hear," Younglove answered. "The ranch begins where the town ends, and I've heard it said that Pete Turner's cattle stroll down Main Street anytime they feel like it."

"Pete Turner?" Kirb asked.

Younglove nodded. "He owns the Seesaw."

Renfro had heard enough. He finished off his beer, then slid off the stool. "I'm not quite as good a drinker as Wally Stovall is," he said with a chuckle. "Besides, I've been in the saddle all day and I need some rest." He pushed a dime across the bar, adding, "Have another beer on me." He waved his arm in a good-bye gesture, then headed for the front door.

19

★

Renfro rode out of Copperas Cove an hour after sunup next morning. He had eaten breakfast at the hotel restaurant, then bought a dozen hard-boiled eggs and some biscuits from the cook. He had picked up three pounds of smoked ham and a box of sulfur matches at the general store, then headed south. For the next several mornings, the preparation of his breakfast would be both quick and easy.

He crossed the Lampasas River on a heavily timbered bridge two hours later, then saw an immediate improvement in the condition of the road. Gone were the deep ruts and ditches that often played havoc with wagon wheels, and it even appeared that a large amount of dirt had been hauled in from somewhere else. The fact that heavy machinery had been used was obvious, for the road was now wide enough for two large vehicles to pass each other with ease, and the drainage ditches on each side were deep.

Renfro rode for a while pondering the many possible reasons for the strong bridge and the sudden change in the condition of the road. Finally, he pulled over and brought his animals to a halt. He fished his map out of his saddlebag and spread it across his lap, then sat smiling as the picture became clear. The reason for the improvements was no longer a mystery: he had just left Lampasas County behind, and Burnet County was obviously more concerned with the condition of its roads.

He allowed his animals to graze for an hour at midday, while he sat beside a spring washing soda crackers and smoked ham down with cold water. Two freight wagons traveling in opposite directions stopped while he was there, but neither driver lingered to rest or prepare a meal. With no more than a nod in Renfro's general direction, each man watered his horses from the spring's runoff, then guided them back onto the road.

Kirb emptied both of his canteens and refilled them with the sweet spring water, then caught up his animals and continued on his way. He rode at a steady pace for the remainder of the day and an hour before sunset pulled up at another spring two miles out of Georgetown. He had been paying close attention to his map and knew that he was now no more than ten miles from Round Rock. He selected a campsite fifty yards east of the spring, then picketed his animals a hundred feet away.

That done, he began the search for fuel. He had to walk a little farther than usual but had an armload of deadwood and kindling when he returned. He filled his coffeepot with water and dumped in a handful of grounds, then began to concentrate on kindling a cook fire. He had barely coaxed a flame into existence when a covered wagon rolled around the curve from the north and pulled up at the spring. As the driver climbed down and helped his woman to the ground, three half-grown children poured over the tailgate and began to chase each other round and round.

Although Kirb gauged the people to be completely harmless, he nonetheless scooted around to the opposite side of his fire so he could watch them without appearing to do so. From this position he could keep track of their activities out of the corner of his eye. He would not look directly at any of them, for an exchange of glances was almost always followed by conversation. Conversation brought on familiarity, and he did not intend to discuss his business or his identity with anyone. He smoothed out his fire, then went about preparing a meal.

Using his pocketknife, he cut several ounces of smoked ham into bite-size chunks, dropping them into a pan that was already half full of precooked beans. Moments later, with the pan on the coals beside the coffeepot, he stretched out his long legs and leaned on his elbows anticipating the upcoming meal. Since neither the beans nor the ham needed cooking, he left them on the fire for less than five minutes. Then he poured himself a cup of coffee and began to eat his supper right from the pan.

The sun had disappeared behind a distant hillside by the time he finished his meal. He filled his cup one last time, then set the coffeepot aside. It was still half full of coffee that he would reheat at breakfasttime. The family at the spring had their own fire going now, and even as Kirb watched, one of the boys left the camp and headed up the hill in his direction.

"Pa wants to know if you got any salt to spare," the youngster said, when he reached Renfro's fire. "We don't need much 'cause we're gonna be where we can buy some tomorrow."

Kirb nodded. "Did you bring something to put it in?"

The boy pulled a small paper bag from his pocket. "Pa said to just put a little in here. Enough for supper and breakfast is all we need 'cause we're gonna be in Round Rock before dinnertime tomorrow."

Renfro divided his salt with the boy, then sat watching him walk back down the hill. The kid was gonna be a hell of a man when he stopped growing, Kirb was thinking. Broad shouldered and thick chested, he appeared to be no more than ten years old, yet he stood at least five feet, eight inches tall. Kirb continued to watch as the youngster reported to the campfire and handed the salt to his mother, then disappeared behind the wagon. Renfro smiled at his thoughts. No doubt about it, the young man was gonna cover an awful lot of ground about ten years from now.

Kirb extinguished his fire and sat beside the ashes till there was no hint of daylight left. Although he knew that the folks down the hill could not see him, he could see them very clearly, for even though they had already eaten their supper, the children continued to feed the fire. Knowing that deadwood was not always easy to come by and that the family had been hauling their fuel in the back of their wagon, Kirb expected one of the parents to put a stop to the wasteful practice very soon. Almost as if he had read Renfro's thoughts, the father got to his feet a moment later and pushed several sticks of wood off the fire with the toe of his boot, then kicked dirt over the remaining coals. The entire area around the spring was suddenly as dark as pitch.

With his Henry in one hand and his bedroll in the other, Kirb felt his way up the hill for a hundred feet of so, then stretched out for the night. He was unable to go to sleep right away however. It was not that he distrusted the folks at the spring, but that he had a headful of questions and no answers. For instance; How was he going to move about once he got to Round Rock without being spotted by Wally Stovall? And was there any possible way for him to know whether or not he had been seen by the wanted man?

Kirb had no answer for either question but had already decided that walking the streets of Round Rock in broad daylight was not even to be considered. He had asked himself a hundred times how well Wally Stovall had looked him over the day the three men stood in front of the saloon staring at Ellie. Had the man paid such close attention to Renfro that he would recognize him anywhere? Even with such a thick growth of beard? Kirb had no way of knowing, for he could not remember whether Stovall had given him a serious looking over or merely a casual glance. Maybe there was a chance that the man would not recognize him until it was too late, Kirb was thinking, but he was not going to bet his life on it. He intended to walk the streets of Round Rock, all right, but never during the daylight hours.

The talking and giggling of the kids at the spring finally ceased after some loud admonishment from their father, and Renfro was asleep a short time later. He awoke only once during the night. He stepped away from his bedroll and peed on the top of a small cedar, then stretched out again. The sun was up the next time he opened his eyes.

The people at the spring were already sitting around their cookfire eating breakfast, and Kirb was wondering how he had managed to sleep through as much noise as they must have made during its preparation. He finally decided that they had deliberately moved around as quietly as possible so as not to disturb his sleep. It was a different story now that they knew he was awake however. The kids were all talking at the same time, each one trying to drown out the others. Once again, a loud bark from the father brought a quick hush over the camp.

Renfro kindled a small fire and reheated his coffee,

then sat watching as the people broke camp and hitched up their animals. The boy who had borrowed the salt loaded the few sticks of wood they had left, then climbed into the wagon with his siblings. The father walked around the camp making sure they were not leaving anything, then helped his wife to her seat. He climbed the front wheel and sat down beside her, then picked up the reins and released the brake. After waving good-bye to Renfro, he slapped the horses' rumps with the reins. The big canvas-covered vehicle moved onto the road and was out of sight quickly.

Renfro heated up the remainder of his ham and beans, then had a leisurely breakfast. And the fact that most folks would hardly consider such food breakfast fare bothered him not in the least. A few times in the past he had actually spent a little time trying to figure out who it was that decided which foods should be eaten at which meals. He had always believed that if something was suitable for one meal, it was suitable for all meals: breakfast, dinner, supper, or anytime in between. Albert Renfro had been of the same opinion, and Kirb could easily recall seeing his father eat bacon and eggs for supper, then breakfast on possum and sweet potatoes next morning.

When he was done eating, Renfro put on a fresh pot of coffee, then moved his animals to new grass. He would allow them to graze till midafternoon, then saddle up and head for Round Rock. He wanted to reach town under cover of darkness, but not so late that the livery stable might be closed. Knowing that most stables stayed open till nine or ten o'clock, he felt that he would have no problem timing his arrival to suit the circumstances.

He added a stick of wood to his fire, then walked to the spring and filled his pot with water. He dumped in a few handfuls of dry kidney beans, then put the pot on to boil. He intended to fill his jars with the precooked beans while he had the chance. They would come in handy when he was sitting in a hotel room hungry, reluctant to visit a restaurant during the daytime for fear of being recognized.

He moved his animals to new grass again at mid-morning, then returned to his camp and put out the fire. He allowed the beans to cool for a while, then filled two jars and sealed their lids. He washed the remainder of the beans down with lukewarm coffee, then cleaned up his cooking and eating utensils at the spring.

He lounged around his camp till four o'clock in the afternoon, then tied up his bedroll and dropped it beside his loaded pack. He headed for the meadow to retrieve his animals just as a middle-aged couple pulled away from the spring in a multicolored buggy. The driver waved, and Kirb acknowledged the greeting with a nod. Dozens of people had stopped at the spring throughout the morning and early afternoon, many of them traveling on horseback but most driving some type of vehicle. Kirb had kept his distance each time, speaking only if spoken to.

When he rode away from the spring half an hour later, he held the black to a walking gait. He had glanced at his watch just before mounting and decided that he was right on time. The road he was following passed through Georgetown before it reached Round Rock, but Kirb had no intention of staying with it that far. Within the next hour he would skirt Georgetown on the west, then travel the remaining seven or eight miles to Round Rock cross-country. According to his calculations, he should get there about an hour after sunset.

He was actually within sight of Georgetown when he pulled up and could tell even at a distance that he was looking at a prosperous community. None of the homes appeared to be a single-story affair, and most were made of stone or bricks. Facing each other across a level street that was wide enough to turn a six-horse team around in, the commercial buildings stood in neat rows, and the fact that much thought had been put into selecting their locations was obvious. Making a mental note to ride right through the middle of town the next time he was close, Kirb guided the black off the road and headed west.

After traveling for a mile or so, he turned due south and began riding parallel to the road, a course he expected to take him to Round Rock without his seeing another human being. He allowed the saddler to choose its own gait. He was in no hurry and was thoroughly enjoying the terrain he was passing through.

Having been raised on a farm, he could tell at a glance that he was riding through some very good farming country. Occasionally standing up in his stirrups so he could see over the pole field fences, he noted that most of the black, fertile soil had been turned over with plows. He could not tell for sure, but it appeared that much of the acreage had been planted already. He was thinking that he would certainly like to be around at harvesttime, for he had no doubt that this land would produce crops in abundance. And it would do so with no assistance from man-made fertilizer.

After riding for what he estimated to be seven miles, he crossed a shallow creek and pulled up at the top of the next rise. He realized immediately that he was ahead of his schedule, for he could see the town of Round Rock no more than half a mile away. He sat his saddle looking down the slope for a few moments, then rode back into the trees. He dismounted and tied the black to a sapling, then seated himself cross-legged on the ground. His wait would not be a long one. The sun was already slipping behind the hills to the west, and total darkness would be along within the hour.

He rode to the edge of town during the last few minutes of twilight. Then, seeing that the livery stable was located at the end of the street on the opposite side of town, he began to circle the small community. Making every effort to move as quietly as possible, he ignored the barking of a dozen dogs and finally reached the stable. He dismounted outside the glow of lanternlight, then led his animals into the wide doorway. A middle-aged, bald-headed man stepped from the office with a limp. "You gonna call it a day?" he asked.

Renfro nodded, then handed over the reins. He laid his saddlebags across his shoulder and eased his Henry out of its scabbard before speaking. "I'll be back in touch with you later on," he said. "As far as I know now, I might be in town for several days."

The man nodded, then pointed. "Your pack'll be there in my office if you need to get into it." He began to un-buckle the mule's packsaddle. "It'll be thirty cents a night for each one of the animals, in case you get to wondering how big a bill you're running up."

Kirb nodded, then left the building, with the fact that he carried two quart jars in his saddlebags evident by the bulges they created. Keeping to the shadows, he walked north in search of a hotel. The search was a short one. He had walked no more than a block when he found him-self standing directly in front of a hotel that might very well be Round Rock's best. He let himself into the lobby, then walked across the heavily carpeted floor to the counter. "I'd like an upstairs room with a window," he said to a dark-haired clerk who appeared to be in his twenties.

The young man smiled. "How about a room with two windows?" he asked.

Kirb nodded. "That sounds even better," he said.

With his commercial smile remaining constant, the clerk pushed the register across the counter. "Thank you for choosing the Saint Charles," he said. "You're the type of man we appreciate. If you'll sign the register and give me a dollar twenty, I'll give you the key to room two-fourteen."

Kirb wrote the name Bill Alexander across the page, then counted out the money. With his key in one hand and his Henry in the other, he took the stairs two at a time. He unlocked his room to find that the lamp was already burning, though it was turned down to a soft glow. He stepped inside and relocked the door, then adjusted the wick to provide more light.

He was not surprised to find that the room was well-appointed, for he had no doubt that the Saint Charles was the best the town had to offer. He raised the windows and stood enjoying the cool breeze for a moment, then seated himself on the edge of the bed.

A few minutes later, he swung his booted feet onto the bed and put both pillows under his head, then lay down on his back. He was trying to figure out which side of town the Seesaw Ranch was on. He had already ruled out the north side, for although he had seen a few longhorns as he rode in from that direction, none of them had been wearing the Seesaw brand. He had thought about asking the hostler for that information but had decided against it. He believed that the less other people knew about his business, the better off he was likely to be.

Anyway, would knowing the location of the spread put him any closer to his quarry? Did Wally Stovall even work there? Renfro had no way of knowing. It could be that the bartender in Copperas Cove had been right. If Stovall had been under the influence of liquor when he applied for work, the ranch foreman, or maybe even Pete Turner himself, had probably shown him the road. Kirb had been told by Clay Summer and several other cowhands as well, that ranchers or foremen who would tolerate drinking on the job were practically nonexistent.

If Stovall was not on the Seesaw Ranch, where was he? Renfro shook his head, refusing to ponder the multitude of possibilities. He would just assume that his quarry was at this very moment in this county and maybe even in this town. He allowed yet another thought to creep into his mind: Hell, the man could be right here in this hotel, for all I know, he said to himself.

He got to his feet and drew the shades on the windows, then stepped to the middle of the room and began to practice his fast draw. The big Colt felt like an extension of his right arm, and the speed with which he brought the weapon to bear on an imaginary target was nothing short of phenomenal. He stood slapping his leg and emptying the holster for about twenty minutes, then returned to his seat on the bed.

He was probably as fast right now as he was ever going to get, he was thinking. He had often read that a man reached his peak at the age of twenty-one, and next Tuesday would be his twenty-first birthday. Was he really as good as Clay Summer? Clay had told Sheriff Miller that he was, but had he been serious? Maybe, maybe not. He had certainly never said any such thing in the presence of Renfro.

A man did not have to be as good as Summer to win a gunfight, however, for Kirb considered Summer to be one of a kind. He believed that a man who was a little slower than Clay might still be faster than anybody else around. And deep down, Renfro felt that he himself fell into that category. He had watched Summer's awesome prowess with a six-gun too many times to start kidding himself. He was not as fast as Clay Summer, but he was close. Damn close.

He took the jars out of his saddlebags and set them on the table, along with a spoon and two hard biscuits wrapped in a piece of newspaper. Then he sat back down on his bed to think. He was hungry, but did not like the thought of walking into a well-lit restaurant. He also knew that he could eat the beans and biscuits, but the longer he sat looking at them, the less appetizing they appeared. After a while, he began to imagine himself chomping on a T-bone steak.

What the hell, he finally said to himself. Wally Stovall ain't gonna come to me, so if I'm gonna find him, I've got to go looking. He got to his feet and turned the lamp down low, then headed for the door. He would have his T-bone steak at the first restaurant he saw, then go hunting.

20

He turned north when he reached the boardwalk, then walked half a block to a small restaurant. A Mexican waiter met him just inside the door and attempted to seat him at a nearby table. Renfro shook his head. "I've always made it a habit to sit where I can see everybody else," he said, motioning toward the rear of the building. "How about a table along the wall back there?"

"Why, of course, sir," the young man said in perfect English. He retrieved the bill of fare from the table, then smiled broadly. "Just choose your own, and I'll follow you."

Kirb was soon seated in the northeast corner of the building, the rear wall at his left elbow. From his chair he could see everyone in the room except the cook. "Just bring me a T-bone steak and some potatoes," he said to the waiter, declining the printed menu that was offered. He returned the young man's smile. "If you'll bring me a cup of coffee to sip while I'm waiting, you'll have a friend for life."

The waiter smiled again, then left for the kitchen. He was back with the coffee in a matter of seconds. "Here you are, sir," he said. "Your food should be ready in about twenty minutes." He set the steaming cup on the table, then disappeared again.

Renfro scooted his chair close enough that he could lean his shoulder against the wall, then sat sipping his coffee and watching the other diners. There were four men in the establishment besides himself, none of them bearing the slightest resemblance to Wally Stovall. Nor had they paid any attention to Renfro, seeming to be completely unaware of his existence. By the time Kirb's food arrived, two of the men had finished their supper and disappeared through the doorway.

"I think you're gonna like this," the waiter said, as he set the long platter on the table. "I brought you a little bowl of salt, too, in case you need it." He took Renfro's cup to the kitchen for a refill and was back quickly, adding, "We've got something special for dessert tonight. The cook baked several lemon pies this afternoon, and they sure turned out nice."

Kirb nodded. "Good," he said. "I'll be more than happy to help him get rid of 'em."

The waiter disappeared again, and Renfro sat eating his meal leisurely. The beefsteak was both large and tender, and it appeared that the platter contained at least a double helping of fried potatoes. Kirb was thinking that, since he himself was now the only customer in the building, the cook might be stuck with half a panful of potatoes. He smiled at the thought, then sprinkled salt on the heap and continued to enjoy his supper.

The waiter delivered a wedge of lemon pie to the table

a few minutes later, then seated himself on a stool a short distance away. As Renfro sat eating the pie and looking at the young man, an idea slowly began to take shape in his mind. He drained his cup and held it up for a refill.

The waiter reacted quickly. "My name's Bill Alexander," Kirb said, when yet another cup of coffee had been delivered. "What's yours?"

"My name is Manuel Alverez, sir."

Kirb made a show of looking around the room, then shrugged. "Looks like your business might be about over for the day," he said. "Are you allowed to sit with the customers?"

"Mr. Cantrell don't care where I sit when there's nothing to do," the waiter answered. "Are you inviting me to sit down?"

"Absolutely," Kirb said, pushing out a chair. "Take the load off your feet."

The young man seated himself. "I always dread these last two hours," he said. "I'll bet we don't have three customers the rest of the night, but we have to stay open anyway. Mr. Cantrell's afraid we might miss somebody who forgot to eat at mealtime. The stragglers, as he calls them."

Renfro sat quietly for a few moments, then asked, "Did you grow up here in Round Rock, Manuel?"

"Yes, sir. Been here all my life."

"Then you'd know where the Seesaw Ranch is, right?"

Alverez smiled. "Of course," he said. "It's anywhere you look south and east of town. I mean, it ain't more'n a quarter of a mile from here to the Seesaw."

Renfro nodded. "Somebody told me it was close," he said. He paused for a moment, then continued. "I'm not really hunting the ranch though. I'm looking for a horse, a big bay with three white stockings and a blaze. Now there ain't nothing unusual about that description, but there is something different about the brand. The animal's got a big ox yoke burnt into its left hip."

"An oxbow?" the young man asked. "I've seen that horse right here in Round Rock, and I remember asking somebody if they'd ever seen that brand before. Big bay like you were saying, and he's got the stockings and the blaze, all right."

Thinking that he might have hit pay dirt, Renfro continued the questioning. "Do you remember exactly where you saw the horse, Manuel?"

Alverez shrugged. "I've seen him standing at several different hitching rails around town, but I've never seen anybody riding him." He pointed to the street. "I've seen him right out there at our hitching rail, but I ain't got no idea who rode off on him."

Renfro leaned across the table, beginning to speak a little softer. "I'm new in this town, Manuel, and I need some help. I believe you're the man who can help me, too, and I certainly don't mind paying you for it." He fished a half eagle out of his pocket and pushed it across the table. "Put that in your pocket and don't say a word to anybody about it. You're gonna have another one just like it coming if you help me solve a little problem."

The young man picked up the coin and turned it over in his hand a few times. "A half eagle now and another one later on?" he asked. "Ten bucks? That's almost half as much money as I earn here in a month." He was quiet for a while, then asked, "What in the world would I have to do to get it?"

Renfro continued to speak softly. "The blaze-faced bay is not really what I'm looking for, Manuel. I'm hunting the man who owns the animal." He waited for the words to sink in, then continued. "Now it's absolutely essential that nobody knows about this but the two of us. Do you understand what I'm saying?"

The waiter nodded. "Yes, sir. I don't tell nobody my business anyway."

Renfro raised his eyebrows. "You're willing to help me find my man then?"

Alverez nodded. "Yes, sir," he said. "Ten dollars is enough money to finish paying off my new saddle."

"All right," Kirb said. "I'm in room two-fourteen at the Saint Charles Hotel, and what I want you to do is locate the man who rides that horse. He's a light-complected, blond-headed fellow with blue eyes and stands about six feet tall. He weighs about two hundred pounds, and he's somewhere in the neighborhood of twenty-five years old. When you find him, I want you to come to the hotel and tell me where he is. That's when you can pick up the other half eagle I promised you." He paused for a moment, then added, "I hope you're gonna get right on it now, 'cause I'm gonna be stuck in that room till I hear from you."

"I'll start on it as soon as we close up for the night," the waiter said. "I'll keep an eye on every hitching rail in town till I see that bay. I'll be checking out the corral down at the livery stable too."

Renfro was on his feet now. "You're a good man, Manuel, and I'm hoping to hear from you real soon. Not a word of this to anybody now."

Alverez dragged a forefinger across his chest in the sign of a cross. "Not a word," he said. "I swear."

Renfro nodded. He stepped to the counter and paid for his food, then headed for his hotel room.

21

Manuel Alverez made good on his promise the following afternoon. Renfro had eaten half a jar of beans for breakfast, then spent the entire morning sitting at the window watching the traffic on the street. He finished off the beans at three o'clock and had just stretched out on his bed when he heard a faint knock and a soft voice calling for Mr. Alexander. Drawing his Colt, he crossed the room and cracked the door, then swung it wide. "Come in, Manuel," he said, reholstering the gun.

The young man stepped inside quickly, and Renfro relocked the door. "The horse you've been hunting is standing at the Buckhorn Saloon's hitching rail right now," Alverez said. "I walked down that side of the street on my way to work, and there stood that bay, just as big as you please."

Renfro laid a half eagle in the waiter's hand. "You've earned this, Manuel," he said. "Did you happen to notice how many other horses were at the rail?"

"The saloon's got three hitching rails," the waiter answered. "Two horses and a mule are tied at one of 'em, and the bay's standing by itself at another one."

Kirb was thoughtful for a moment, then spoke again. "I reckon that means four drinkers are inside the place then."

Alverez shook his head. "Probably more," he said. "Most of the business we get at the restaurant is from foot traffic, and I'd say the same might be true for the saloon."

Renfro stared through the window for a few moments, then motioned to the chair. "Have a seat, Manuel," he said. When the young man had seated himself, Kirb continued, "I hate to keep putting you on the spot, but I need one more favor. If you don't want to do it, I'll understand 'cause I know that you have to live in this town." He flipped a half eagle into the air and caught it. "There's another five bucks in it for you though."

Alverez nodded. "I don't see no reason not to," he said. "Seems like easy money to me. Hell, I don't make but ninety cents a day at the restaurant." He was thoughtful for a moment. "What else do you want me to do?"

Renfro laid the money in his hand, then gave the young man his instructions. A short time later they walked through the lobby and stepped out onto the plank sidewalk.

The Buckhorn Saloon was one of the largest single-story buildings in town, occupying two corner lots a block south of the hotel. Getting right down to business, Renfro and Alverez headed for the oversized watering hotel at a fast clip. When they reached the saloon, Kirb took up a position behind the corner of the building, then nodded to the waiter, who was now standing at the hitching rail.

As had been his instructions, Alverez untied the bay and shooed the animal away from the rail, then stepped across the boardwalk to the saloon. He poked his head over the bat-wing doors and shouted at the top of his lungs, "Somebody's horse is loose out here! Big bay with three stockings and an oxbow on its hip!" With his assignment completed, the young man moved away from the doorway quickly, then ran down the side of the building.

A man suddenly burst through the bat wings and trotted to the big bay, which was now standing in the middle of the street with its reins lying on the ground. Renfro held his position behind the corner of the building as the man caught the animal and led it back to the hitching rail. There was no doubt about it, Renfro was now looking at Wally Stovall, one of the men who had raped and killed his beloved Ellie. Even now Kirb could see her undergarments scattered around the bedroom and the red-and-purple bruises left by the heavy stick of oak firewood that had come crashing down on her beautiful face.

Renfro waited no longer.

Just as Stovall finished retying the bay and turned to go back into the saloon, Kirb stepped around the corner quickly. Though he was facing his quarry from a distance of less than thirty feet, he nonetheless spoke loudly, almost shouting, "Have you raped and murdered any more defenseless women lately, Stovall?"

"What . . . who are you, fellow? I don't know what the hell you're talking about. My name ain't Stovall neither. It's Payne. Daniel Payne."

Renfro nodded. He was standing with his legs spread apart and his body bent slightly forward. "Oh," he said, "I guess a name like that does sound a little better to you nowadays. Daniel Payne probably ain't wanted for rape and murder, like Wally Stovall is."

"What's your—"

"The name's Renfro," Kirb interrupted. "The woman you helped Pat Pollard and Lonny Tripp rape and murder last January was my wife." He stood staring into the man's eyes. "It's all over for you, Stovall, and it's gonna be over for Tripp and Pollard pretty soon now. Are you gonna tell me where to find 'em?"

"I don't know what you're talking about, fellow. You—"

He would never finish the sentence, for Renfro had shot out his throat. Kirb had made the fastest draw of his life and had been right on target. Stovall had managed to get his own weapon out of its holster but had died before he could raise his shooting arm. He now lay face down directly in front of the saloon, his upper body on the sidewalk and his legs and feet in the dirt beneath the hitching rail.

A crowd gathered quickly, Manuel Alverez among them. He stood staring at the dead man for a moment, then shook his head and headed up the street toward the restaurant.

Three men had come from inside the saloon, one of them wearing an apron. He pointed to the corpse, then spoke to Renfro, who still had his Colt in his hand. "Ain't that Dan Payne? he asked. "What did he do to bring all this on?"

Renfro shook his head. "Daniel Payne is just a name the man pulled out of the air after he started running from the law," he said. "His true name was Wally Stovall, and he was a rapist and a woman killer."

"Well, I'll be goddam!" a fat, middle-aged man said loudly. "Who in the world woulda ever thought that?"

Kirb spoke to the same man. "Have you got a marshal in this town? Would you ask somebody to get him down here?"

The man pointed. "Ain't nobody gonna have to hunt him, mister. His name's Wink Goodman, and that's him coming down the other side of the street there."

The middle-aged lawman, followed by two deputies,

crossed the street and stopped at the hitching rail. He was a small man, about five-eight with a slender build, and one of his copper-colored eyes appeared to have a permanent squint. He stepped up to the boardwalk, then addressed Renfro, "Your name?"

Kirb identified himself.

The marshal nodded, then pointed to the dead man. "Who's that?"

Renfro took one of the wanted posters out of his pocket and handed it over, saying, "His name was Wally Stovall, and he's the one listed at the bottom of the page."

The lawman studied the document for a while, then turned the corpse over. He stood comparing the dead man's appearance with the description on the poster for several seconds, then tapped it with his forefinger. "You killed him because he fit this description?" he asked.

"No," Kirb answered quickly. "I knew who he was 'cause I recognized him on sight."

"You two were acquainted beforehand then?"

"We weren't friends, but I'd seen him before."

The marshal nodded. He read the last paragraph of the poster again, then asked, "You shot him for the reward?"

"No!" Renfro answered loudly. "The woman he raped and murdered was my wife."

The lawman began to shake his head slowly. "I'm mighty sorry about that, son," he said, sounding as if he really meant it. "I reckon I understand how you feel." He folded the dodger and shoved it into his vest pocket. "I'd like to keep this if you don't mind. You've got some more of 'em, I suppose."

"Yes, sir," Renfro answered. "I'd also take it as a favor if you'd write a note of some kind for me to carry to Sheriff Miller, in Comanche County. Something saying that you witnessed Wally Stovall's dead body."

The marshal nodded. "Be glad to. I ain't gonna put no name on the body, but I'll write that I saw a corpse that fits the description on this dodger."

"Thank you, sir. That'll be all I need."

The lawman pointed to Stovall's remains. "Are you willing to pay for putting him in the ground?"

"Yes, sir," Renfro said. "I'd rather let the son of a bitch pay for his own funeral if he's got the money though."

The marshal stood thoughtful for a moment, then spoke to the youngest of his deputies. "Go through the dead man's pockets and see what he's got, Joe."

The deputy complied, then announced his findings. "He's got eigthty-three cents on him, Marshal."

"I'll take care of the burial expense then," Renfro said to the lawman. "How much will it cost, and who do I give the money to?"

The marshal pointed to a skinny old man a few feet away. "That fellow right there's the undertaker," he said, then spoke to the man he had pointed out. "What's it gonna cost to put this man in the ground, John?"

The old man stepped forward. "Well, let me see," he began. "The deceased is gonna weigh a right smart, so I'll have to hire two strong men to move him about. Then there's the price of a coffin, and the price of the grave diggers. The diggers'll have to be paid extra for filling the hole back in, you know, and then there's—"

"How much is it gonna cost to put that dead dog in a hole?" Kirb interrupted.

"Is . . . is fifteen dollars too much?"

"Of course it's too much," Kirb said. He handed the scrawny man an eagle. "Here's ten dollars, and that's at least twice what it oughtta cost."

The old man accepted the coin and dropped it into the breast pocket of his overalls. "Yes, sir," he said. "This'll take care of everything."

The marshal dispersed the crowd, then Kirb followed him to his office. The lawman wrote a short note to Sheriff Miller and had both of his deputies sign it as witnesses, then handed it to Renfro.

Kirb read it at a glance, then shoved it into his pocket. "I certainly appreciate all of this, Marshal Goodman, and maybe I'll get a chance to visit your town under different circumstances sometime." He waved good-bye. "I'll be on my way now." He turned his back and stepped through the open door.

The older of the two deputies followed Kirb out and stopped on the small porch. "The marshal wasn't lying when he said he knew how you felt about losing your wife," he said. "Indians killed and mutilated his wife fifteen years ago."

Renfro froze in his tracks. He stood staring down the street for a few seconds before speaking. "I'm awful sorry to hear that, Deputy," he said over his shoulder. "Tell Marshal Goodman that I said so, will you?"

"Sure will, Mr. Renfro. You be careful now."

Kirb stepped into the street and headed for the livery stable. He had a good three hours of daylight left, and he intended to spend it putting some distance between himself and this town.

The liveryman helped him ready his animals for the road, and Renfro gave him a gratuity that left him smiling. A few minutes later, Kirb tied up in front of the hotel. The retrieval of his belongings took no more than three minutes, then he was back at the hitching rail. He shoved the Henry in the boot and remounted the black, then led his packmule out of town.

22

Alternating between a slow trot and a fast walk, Renfro was halfway to Austin when the sun went down. He watered his animals at a shallow creek, then forded the stream and pulled off the road. He rode into the meadow for a hundred yards, then dropped his bedroll, saddle, and packsaddle behind a cluster of bushes. By the time his saddler and his mule were on picket ropes, darkness had already closed in. He raked the sticks and stones from a small area that was relatively level, then stretched out on his bedroll, his weapons close to hand.

Sleep did not come quickly, however, for it seemed that a thousand thoughts were racing through his mind. Today he had killed a man, and the strangest part of it was that he felt no remorse whatsoever. He had wanted Wally Stovall dead and had actually experienced an inward feeling of jubilation at seeing the man drop his weapon and fall to the boardwalk. Now, just thinking about it caused Kirb to clamp his jaws together and grit his teeth. Stovall would never rape or kill another woman, he was thinking, and if the religious views of Lady Kerrington were to be believed, the son of a bitch was burning in hell at this very moment.

He lay awake for a long time, eventually beginning to talk to his beloved Ellie. He told her everything he had done lately, then decided that she already knew; she had been watching his every move. "I hope I'm doing the right thing, Ellie," he whispered softly. "It's the only thing I know to do, and you yourself told me more'n once that the Bible says we're supposed to take an eye for an eye." He paused for a few seconds, then continued to whisper, "Please figure out some way to let me know whether I'm doing right or not."

It would have been impossible for someone to convince Kirb Renfro that his wife had not just communicated with him from the grave for he suddenly felt that his actions were as right as rain. The dispatching of Wally Stovall had been an act of kindness toward the rest of the world, Ellie seemed to be saying, and the man's accomplices deserved the same fate. Kirb could almost hear her telling him to complete his mission. "Thank you, honey," he whispered into the darkness, "and good night." He relaxed immediately, then turned on his side and slept soundly.

The next time he opened his eyes the sky in the east had taken on a pinkish hue, informing the world that daybreak was only minutes away. He looked over the tops of the bushes to check on his animals, and the fact that he could see two dark objects about forty yards away told him that all was well. He seated himself on his bedroll and pulled on his boots, then laid the bridles over his shoulder and headed across the meadow.

He watered his animals and led them to his campsite, then stood around for a few minutes waiting for more light. He intended to skip breakfast this morning, and since all of the available kindling was wet with dew, he would not even try to build a fire for coffee.

He would be doing some cross-country traveling today. Riding more or less parallel to the road, he would skirt the town of Austin at midmorning, then stop and eat the remaining jar of beans at dinnertime. Later in the afternoon, he would stop at the first grocery store he saw and replenish his food supplies.

He saddled up during the early morning twilight, but waited for full daylight to buckle on the mule's packsaddle and balance the individual packs. When he finally mounted and guided his saddler back to the road, he saw that he was not the only man who had spent the night in the area. Two covered wagons were parked on the opposite side of the road, and a canvas tent had been erected between them.

Renfro pulled up for a moment and sat shaking his head, wondering how he had managed to sleep through their arrival. Whoever had set up that tent in the dark was undoubtedly an expert, he was thinking. Kirb had done it himself a few times and knew that it was not always an easy task even in broad daylight. He was still sitting his saddle watching when a man crawled from the tent and began to kindle a fire. Kirb waved a greeting to him, then kneed the black onto the road.

He had been traveling for two hours when he made the decision to leave the road. Now that he was closer to Austin the area was more densely populated, and he wanted to be seen by as few people as possible. A quick study of his map had told him that he could bear off to the east and ride in a half circle, then pick up the same road a few miles south of town. He guided the black across a ridge that was dotted with scrubby cedars and soon put a mile or more between himself and the road.

With only an occasional variance to get around a barrier of one type or another, he held to the same course for almost three hours, then turned west. When he picked up the main road again he was at least four miles south of Austin, and the traffic had dropped off accordingly. Shortly after noon, he pulled up at a roadside spring. Leaving the saddle on the black and the packsaddle on the mule, he staked the animals out where the grass was tall and green.

He found kindling for a cook fire easily enough and soon had coffee boiling. He sliced the last of his smoked ham into a skillet, then trimmed the mold off his last chunk of cheese with his pocketknife. No doubt about it, he was thinking, his food supply was woefully inadequate, and a visit to a general store had become a necessity.

He ate his dinner and extinguished the fire, then emptied the coffeepot into his cup. He had made only two cups of coffee. Making a full pot at noon would be a waste of coffee grounds, for he would have to pour out all he could not drink. The evening meal was different, however. He almost always made a full pot at night for he could reheat and drink whatever was left next morning.

He washed his utensils at the spring, then put them back on the packmule. Both animals were grazing like there was no tomorrow, and he decided to give them another half hour on the lush, green grass. He found a shady spot beneath the canopy of a leafy oak, then seated himself on the ground cross-legged. He had scarcely begun to relax when two wagons traveling in opposite directions left the road and pulled up at the spring.

The first driver watered his team and continued on his way, while the occupants of the second wagon, which had been headed north, made it obvious that they intended to stay around for a while. Two middle-aged men and a woman who appeared to be several years younger climbed down from the canvas-covered vehicle, and one of the men set about building a fire. Renfro sat watching for a short while, then got to his feet and walked to his grazing animals.

Moments later, he rode within a few feet of the wagon on his way back to the road. "Howdy!" the man who had kindled the fire said loudly. "Going to San Antonio?"

Renfro shook his head. "Farther south," he said.

The man smiled. "We live south of there ourselves," he said. "We always tell everybody we live at San Antonio, though, 'cause most folks ain't never heard of Pleasanton."

"Well, I certainly have," Kirb said quickly. "Fact is, that's where I'm headed right now."

"Well, I'll be dad-burned," the man said. He turned to the woman, who was busy situating a pot on the fire. "You hear that, Flo? This young man's headed for Pleasanton."

"I heard him," she answered, then nodded in Kirb's direction. "Howdy do."

Renfro touched the brim of his hat, and returned the greeting.

"Ain't no use in you rushing off in the heat of the day," the man said. "We're gonna have vittles and coffee here in a few minutes."

"Thank you," Kirb said, "but I just had a good meal and all the coffee I could drink." He slid to the ground and led his animals toward the spring's runoff. "I am gonna take this opportunity to offer my stock another drink of water though." Both the horse and the mule sniffed the water and wet their muzzles, but neither drank. "It's like the old saying goes," Kirb said, leading the animals away from the ditch. " 'You can lead a horse to water, but you can't make him drink.' "

"They don't really need water more'n about twice a day at this time of year. They will about two months from now though. During June, July, and August, a working animal's liable to keel over if a man don't see after its water."

Renfro nodded, then turned to remount.

"You say you're going to Pleasanton," the man said. "What're you gonna be doing down there?"

Kirb turned back to face the man. "I don't know for sure. I just heard that it's an awful pretty place, so I thought I'd go down and look it over. A man told me I oughtta look up a fellow named Cecil Bray when I got there. Do you happen to know him?"

"Cecil Bray," the man repeated, then stood thoughtful for a few moments. "What age fellow are you talking about?"

"Early twenties," Kirb answered.

The man shook his head. "The only fellow I know by that name is Hanson Bray. I remember that he's got a coupla grown sons, so I suppose one of 'em could be named Cecil."

"I see," Renfro said. He threw a leg over his saddle. "Do you know where Hanson Bray lives?"

The man nodded. "He owns a good-sized spread northeast of town. As soon as you cross the Atascosa River, you'll be on his property. His brand is a four-pointed star."

"Thank you, sir," Renfro said. "I appreciate the information." He kicked the black in the ribs and took to the road at a trot.

Two hours later, he came to a fork in the road that a roadside sign identified as Shinbone Forks. Another sign informed travelers that a right-hand turn would lead them to San Marcos, and that the road to the left continued on south to the town of Lockhart. Renfro would be riding south, but not until after he had bought some food supplies.

Situated in the fork between the two roads, with a tall sign advertising a wide assortment of goods, was a general store. Two large oaks shaded the building and its huge yard, and three hitching rails lined the front. A saddle horse and a wagon team were standing at two of them, and Renfro rode into the yard and tied his own animals at the third.

Even as Kirb stood at the hitching rail, a stoop-shouldered, middle-aged man stepped through the doorway and onto the porch. He bit the corner off a plug of chewing tobacco and wallowed it around in his mouth a few times, then walked into the yard and untied his sway-backed roan. He spat a stream of tobacco juice at a nearby rock, then mounted and took the road to San Marcos. Kirb supposed that the man had stopped at the store for no other reason than to buy the plug for he had carried nothing else in his hands. Renfro found the idea repulsive. He himself had tried chewing tobacco once, and once had been enough.

Moments later, Kirb was inside the store. He moved away from the doorway and stood leaning against the wall, for he could see that the proprietor was very busy. A couple appearing to be in their mid-thirties stood at the near side of the counter, which was piled high with merchandise. A tall man with silver, shoulder-length hair stood behind the counter boxing up their purchases and tallying up the cost. He craned his neck to look over the heads of his customers, then spoke to Renfro. "I'll be with you as soon as I can, sir," he said. "Won't be long."

Kirb nodded, then began to move around the room. He could see right away that the establishment probably had most anything a man might be looking for, but doubted that even the proprietor would be able to find it. The aisles were not actually aisles, but crooked avenues of merchandise lying about in such haphazard randomness as to make it obvious that no thought whatsoever had been given to stocking goods of a kind in the same section.

The store was unquestionably overstocked, and it appeared that everything in it had literally been dropped off any old place there was room. Renfro had just found some tinned meats and fish on the same shelf with saddle blankets and shotgun shells, when he was rescued. "Sorry it took me so long, mister," the old man said, "but that couple almost bought me out." He was standing beside Kirb now with a pasteboard box in his hand. "My name's Lovell, and I appreciate you coming in. You need a little help?"

Renfro stifled a chuckle, then raked about a dozen tins of meat and fish into the box. "I need a lot of help," he said. "I stopped off to restock my food supplies, and if you'll show me where things are, it'll save us both some time."

"A lot of that kinda stuff is along this wall," Lovell said, "but there's a bunch of it in the back of the store too." He pointed. "Right over there in the middle of the room, and over yonder in that far corner too, there's—"

"Just lead the way," Renfro said. "I'll be right behind you."

Kirb stayed inside the store much longer than he had expected to, but when he finally loaded his supplies on the mule and took to the road, he knew that he would be eating well for many days to come. He kicked the black to a easy trot, intending to make camp as soon as he reached good grass and water. Even now the sun was less than two hours' high, and he was hungry. Very hungry.

He picketed his animals on the west bank of a shallow creek within the hour and had a pot of coffee brewing less than ten minutes later. He laid several slices of Bologna sausage in his skillet and placed it on the fire, then opened two tins of fish. He leaned back on his elbows till his coffeepot began to boil, then pulled it off the fire and poured in a little cool water from his canteen. The coffee grounds would settle to the bottom in about two minutes, then it would be suppertime.

He was soon enjoying a meal of Bologna sausage, cheddar cheese, sardines, and soda crackers, and would be having a handful of oatmeal cookies with his second cup of coffee. Later on, when his fire burned down a little, he would bury two large sweet potatoes in the hot ashes and gray coals. Maybe he would eat one before he went to sleep. If not, he could easily put away both of them early in the morning. Sweet potatoes were not only nourishing but tasted good, and their preparation could hardly be easier.

The same thing could be said for soda crackers. Although Renfro preferred biscuits, corn pone, or even hoe-cakes with his food, cooking bread of any kind on the trail was a bigger headache than it was worth. Crackers were a fair substitute and were always ready to eat. He had at least a week's supply in his pack, and had bought as many sweet potatoes as he dared. The potatoes were heavy, and he had bought the smallest bag the general store had out of consideration for his pack animal.

He had finished his meal and was sitting beside his fire eating cookies and sipping coffee when he saw a man riding down the hill from the south on a tall gray. The rider pulled up and sat thinking for a while after spotting the fire, then left the road and headed across the meadow in Kirb's direction. Renfro checked his Colt to make sure it was riding loose in its holster, then sat waiting for the man to cover the fifty or sixty yards between the road and his campsite.

A sandy-haired man who appeared to be in his thirties, the rider pulled up at the fire a few seconds later but made no effort to dismount. "Howdy," he said, flashing two rows of near-perfect teeth. "I'm on my way up to Austin, and since I ain't gonna get there till about midnight no-how, I was hoping maybe you could spare a cup of coffee."

Renfro nodded and pointed to the coffeepot. "Get down and help yourself," he said. "I believe it's still hot."

The man took a tin cup out of his saddlebag, then dismounted. He filled his cup with coffee and remained standing. "It was way after dinnertime when I left Lockhart," he said. "I didn't bring no coffeepot or nothing else with me 'cause I didn't expect to even slow down till I got to Austin." He took a sip of the coffee, adding, "That's mighty good stuff, mister, and I certainly appreciate it."

"Drink all you want," Kirb said. "Cookies over there, too, if you want some."

The man shook his head. "I decided a long time ago not to drink no more'n one cup of coffee at a time," he said. "That's all my kidneys'll stand. I reckon I'll pass on the cookies too. Never was much on sweets." He said nothing else till after he had finished off his coffee and put his cup back in his saddlebag. "I'll be getting on now," he said, throwing a leg over his saddle. "It's gonna be dark here in a few minutes, but my horse knows the way. Thank you again for the coffee." He kicked the gray in the ribs and headed for the road at a fast trot.

Renfro ate another handful of cookies, then spread his bedroll in a cluster of bushes about twenty yards up the slope. He had decided against eating one of the potatoes before going to bed and would just leave them in the ashes. They would not only taste good in the morning, they would still be warm.

He moved his animals to new grass, then returned to his bedroll. He pulled off his boots and, with a folded blanket under his head for a pillow, stretched out for the night. A few minutes later, he was sleeping soundly.

23

Lockhart was located near the site of a fierce Indian battle
that had taken place on August 12, 1840. A large party
of Comanches had successfully swept down the Guada-
lupe Valley all the way to the Gulf Coast, killing settlers,
stealing horses, and plundering and burning one settlement after another. Texas Rangers and a volunteer force
of settlers met the returning war party and defeated them
soundly in what would become known as the Battle of
Plum Creek. The town that sprang up nearby was named
in honor of a pioneer surveyor named Byrd Lockhart, and
was now the southern terminus of the Chisholm Trail.

Renfro led his animals into Lockhart at midafternoon.
His horse had thrown a shoe an hour ago, and he had
traveled the last three miles on foot. He asked the first
man he met for directions to a blacksmith shop.

"Just keep following this street," the man said, pointing. "It curves around to the east right up yonder aways,
but you'll see the livery stable at the end of it. The livery-

man's a farrier too, so he can take care of your horse's problem."

"Thank you," Kirb said, then continued on. He met a few wagons and several men on horseback as he walked through town, and though every man nodded a greeting, none spoke. The plank sidewalks were also busy. Men seemed to be in a hurry to get from one building to another, and quite a few women and children were moving about. Knowing that he would be visiting both places before the day was out, Kirb stood looking at the Clancy Hotel and its adjacent Salty Dog Saloon for a few moments, then led his animals on to the livery stable.

When Kirb stopped in the wide doorway and stated his business, the hostler picked up the left hind leg of the black and rattled the shoe with his hand. "Ain't no problem here I can't fix," he said. "He needs his hooves trimmed and a new set of shoes. Probably take me the rest of the day to do it though. You got that much time?"

Renfro nodded. "Yes, sir," he said. "I intended to leave both of 'em with you overnight anyway. Just grain 'em and hay 'em, and I'll pick 'em up early in the morning."

"Consider it done," the hostler said. Though hatless and standing in low-heeled brogans, the man was still as tall as Renfro and probably weighed fifty pounds more. With thinning brown hair and a ruddy complexion, he had a red nose and bloodshot eyes, both of which were often attributed to heavy drinking. Though Renfro had no way of knowing whether the man was a drinker or not, he decided to take a chance. "If you want to meet me up at the Salty Dog later on, the drinks'll be on me," he said.

The man was busy unbuckling the mule's packsaddle. "I reckon that's the best offer I've had this week," he said. He chuckled loudly. "Don't waste all your money on a bunch of other stuff now 'cause I can sure as hell put that liquor away."

Kirb smiled broadly. "I'll try to hang on to enough money to pay for it," he said. He offered a handshake, adding, "My name's Bill Alexander. What's yours?"

The hostler grasped the hand with a firm grip and chuckled again. "I reckon every man in Caldwell County knows that my name's Hank Macon except you, so you must be from somewhere else."

Kirb nodded. "I live in Comanche County."

"Comanche County," Macon repeated. "You sure ain't the first one to come through here from up thataway lately, and I reckon I met most of 'em. Two of 'em started a brawl in the Salty Dog Saloon about two or three months ago and spent a week in Marshal Dewberry's jail for their trouble."

Renfro nodded. Though he was anxious to learn the names of the two men who had touched off the brawl, he did not ask, for he expected to hear the whole story in the saloon later on. Nobody in any town knew more about what was going on than did the local liveryman, and Kirb had invited this particular one to drink with him for that very reason. He could not even make a guess as to how much the hostler might know about Pat Pollard and Lonny Tripp, but he intended to find out before the night was over. "What time should I be expecting you at the Salty Dog?" he asked.

Macon spat a stream of tobacco juice. "It'll take me about an hour and a half to shoe the horse," he said. "Then if the mule don't need nothing done, I'll just grab a bite and come on up there."

"The mule's hooves are in good shape," Kirb said. "I looked 'em all over about two hours ago."

"I oughtta be up there in about two hours then," the

big man said, stripping the saddle off the black and laying it across a sawhorse. "I'll get me something to eat first though. Putting away hard liquor on an empty stomach is something I wouldn't recommend to my worst enemy."

Kirb nodded. "I'll see you up there," he said. With his saddlebag across his shoulder and his Henry in his hand, he headed up the street. Moments later he stepped into the lobby of the Clancy Hotel and requested a second-story room.

"That'll be ninety cents," the middle-aged desk clerk said, then slid a key across the counter. "Number two-eighteen, at the end of the hall."

Renfro handed over the money, and when it became obvious that he was not going to be asked to sign a register, put the key in his pocket and climbed the stairway. Moments later, he let himself into the room to find that someone had already raised both windows to keep the air circulating. He silently thanked the guilty party, then re-locked the door and walked across the room. He laid his rifle and his saddlebags on the bed, then moved to the window and looked down.

He knew immediately that he would not spend much time at the window for the only things he could see were the second story of a building across the street and the roof over the first floor of the hotel. His view of the street was completely obscurred by the roof, for the second story of the hotel was much smaller than the ground floor.

He pitched his hat on the bed and combed his hair with his fingers, then stepped in front of the mirror and stood looking at his image for a while. His thick, jet-black beard grew almost to his eyes and concealed his facial features entirely. He hardly recognized himself and was hoping that Pollard and Tripp would have the same prob-lem. He took off his shirt and washed his face and upper body in the wash pan, then dried himself and rehung the towel on the nail behind the table.

He stood in front of the mirror fluffing the last of the moisture from his beard, pleased with the degree of camouflage it offered. He scraped his fingernails across one jaw then the other. The incessant itching had begun two days after he stopped shaving and would continue until he began to use a razor again. He took one last look at his reflection in the mirror. Pat Pollard or Lonny Tripp would have to get mighty close before they recognized that face, he was thinking. Then it would be too late.

Twenty minutes later he was sitting in the Hawthorn Restaurant, across the street from the hotel. A waiter served the bowl of chilli he ordered right away, along with biscuits, coffee, and a dish of cherry cobbler. Renfro wolfed the chilli down in short order, then motioned to the waiter for a refill. "You're not the first man to ask for seconds since the boss hired that Mexican cook," the youngster said, heading for the kitchen with Kirb's empty bowl in his hand. Renfro emptied it more leisurely the second time and enjoyed the taste of the concoction even more. Seasoned to perfection, it was hot, but not too hot; and although many Texans scorned the idea of using any kind of beans or peas in a pot of chilli, the restaurant cook had added a generous amount of kidney beans, Kirb's favorite.

He sipped a third cup of coffee after he was done eating, getting to his feet only after it became obvious that his table would be needed to accommodate the many diners who were now arriving for the evening meal. He laid a dime beside his bowl for the waiter, then walked to the counter and paid for his supper. He smiled at the gray-haired lady who took his money, then walked through the doorway and out onto the boardwalk. He looked in both directions, then crossed the street.

Though the Salty Dog Saloon was owned by the Clancy Hotel and could be entered through a side door in the hotel lobby, it also had a false front of its own, with bat-wing doors that opened right off the street.

Moments after leaving the restaurant, Renfro shouldered his way through the bat wings and stepped aside quickly, waiting for his eyes to adjust. Though he could see a man standing behind the bar, he could make out little else, for the light was much dimmer here than in most saloons. "Ain't a thing in the world between you and the bar!" a man that Renfro assumed was the bartender said loudly. "Just keep walking straight ahead and you'll bump into it!"

Renfro stood in his tracks for a full minute. It was only after he could see the smiling fat man behind the bar plainly that he stepped forward. "I never was one to move before I could see where I was headed," Kirb said, seating himself on the corner stool. He pointed to the shelf behind the bartender. "Give me a bottle of the good stuff and two glasses," he said. "I'm expecting company pretty soon."

The man nodded, his smile remaining constant. He set the bottle on the bar and poured one of the glasses half full. He picked up the half eagle Renfro had laid on the counter, then hesitated. "Are you a hotel guest?" he asked. Not waiting for an answer, he hurried on to explain the reason behind the question. "I have to ask everybody that 'cause if you've got a room at the hotel, you get a ten-percent discount on this bottle."

Kirb nodded. "I rented a room for the night."

The man tapped the label with a forefinger. "That's a sixty-cent bottle," he said, "but you get it for fifty-four cents." He fished around in a drawer for a few moments, then laid Kirb's change on the bar. "Ain't seen you around before. You just passing through?"

Kirb nodded. "I'll probably be gone tomorrow," he said. He pushed his right hand across the counter. "I'm Bill Alexander, from up in Comanche County."

The barkeep grasped the hand. "My name's Joe Saxton," he said, "and I ain't never been more'n fifty miles from where I'm standing."

Renfro sipped at the liquor sparingly, then set the glass on the bar. "I never was one to drink whiskey by myself," he said. "Besides, the blacksmith's gonna join me in a little while, and I don't want to get too far ahead of him."

The barkeep raised his eyebrows. "Hank Macon?"

Renfro nodded.

Saxton chuckled loudly. "Hell, you don't have to worry about getting ahead of Hank Macon 'cause it ain't gonna happen. I've been working behind this plank for nine years, and I ain't seen nobody get ahead of him yet. That fellow can damn sure put it away, and I'll tell you right now, you ain't bought nowhere near enough whiskey to get him through the night."

Renfro chuckled softly, "I reckon I'll just have to buy some more then," he said. He wet his lips again, then sat quietly.

The bartender shuffled off to refill the glasses of two drinkers at the far end of the bar, then drew a mug of beer for himself. "I ain't got no doubt that this stuff right here's what keeps me so damn fat," he said, "but so far I ain't been able to give it up. I've tried pretty hard a few times too."

"I've never drunk enough of any kind of alcohol for it to turn into a habit," Kirb said. "I go for months at a time without even thinking of a drink."

The bartender nodded. "You'll be a lot better off if you stay that way too." He pointed to a group of tables and chairs across the room. "I guess you'll want to sit down over there somewhere when Hank gets here. Ain't gonna be nobody at none of them tables 'cause it's gonna be a slow night. They're all gonna be slow till another trail herd comes to town." He was quiet for a moment, then pointed over Kirb's shoulder. "Speak of the devil," he said.

Renfro turned to see that Hank Macon had just stepped through the doorway. Kirb slid off his stool, then picked up the bottle and both glasses. "Just pick out a table, Hank," he said. "I'll meet you there."

The two men were soon seated at a table along the south wall, with Renfro facing the front of the building. Macon inhaled half a glass of whiskey and licked his lips. "That black of yours is a mighty fine piece of horseflesh," he said. "He's wearing new iron now, and you ain't gonna have to worry about his feet for a while. I didn't pay no attention to the mule's hooves 'cause you said you'd done looked at 'em."

Renfro nodded. "I appreciate it all, Hank," he said. He picked up the bottle and topped off the liveryman's glass. "Drink up. When this one runs dry, we'll get another one."

They settled into meaningless conversation quickly. Macon drank two-thirds of the bottle's contents in less than an hour, never once commenting on the fact that Renfro had nursed the same drink for most of that time. Kirb filled their glasses once more, then walked to the bar and bought more whiskey. He set the new bottle on the table and reseated himself. "You told me earlier that two men from Comanche spent a week in the local jail for starting a brawl, Hank. Would you happen to know their names?"

"Oh, lemme see," the big man grunted. He took another swallow of whiskey, then set the glass down noisily. "Hey, Joe!" he called across the room to the bartender.

"Do you remember the names of them two jokers who started the fight in here back in January?"

"Ain't likely to forget 'em," Saxton answered. "I signed a complaint against 'em, but it didn't do no damn good. Didn't neither one of 'em have the money to pay for the stuff they broke up so the judge sentenced 'em to a week in jail. The redhead said his name was Pollard, and the other one claimed to be Lonny Tripp."

Renfro sat digesting the bartender's words in disbelief. The murdering sons of bitches had not even changed their names. Were they really that brave or just that stupid. Kirb preferred to believe the latter, for brave men did not go around raping and murdering women. He spoke to Macon again. "I'd like to have a talk with Marshal Dewberry, Hank. Do you think that's possible at this time of day?"

The big man shrugged. "Maybe so, maybe not," he answered. "Only way I know to find out is to walk up to his office and see if he's there. Even if he ain't, I reckon his deputy could tell you where to find him. His office is a block north in that little green municiple building. The building sits off by itself on the right-hand side of the street."

Renfro was already on his feet. "If you run out of whiskey, just order another bottle on me," he said. "I'm gonna have a talk with the marshal." He picked his hat up from a nearby chair, then left the building quickly.

Even as Renfro disappeared through the doorway, Hank Macon picked up the bottle and the glasses and walked to the bar. He took a seat on a stool and poured himself another drink, then spoke to the bartender: "I've got a feeling that I've been talking to a dangerous man, Joe. He just looks like bad news to me, and he seemed to take a mighty strong interest in Pollard and Tripp. He's gone right now to talk to Marshal Dewberry about 'em.'"

"I decided the minute he walked through that door that he wasn't nobody to mess around with," the bartender said. "From the looks of him, he could whup his weight in wildcats, and I'll betcha he can get that damn Colt in his hand quicker'n you can bat an eye." He took a sip of his beer. "Yessir, the man who tries to give that fellow any shit is gonna be making a bad mistake."

When Renfro stepped out of the saloon, he headed north at a fast walk. After walking only a short distance, he could make out the forms of two horses standing at the lawman's hitching rail for it was not yet fully dark.

The marshal's office was clearly marked, and a lantern hanging above the door lit up the sign. Kirb twisted the knob and stepped into the well-lit room. A young deputy who had been sitting behind an oversized desk was on his feet quickly. "Howdy," he said. "Is there something I can do for you?"

"I'm looking for Marshal Dewberry," Kirb said. "I need to have a talk with him."

The deputy nodded, and turned to face the back room. Cupping his hands around his mouth, he called loudly, "Marshal, there's a man out here who says he needs to talk to you!"

A tall, hatless man with thinning brown hair and a gray mustache stepped into the room. He appeared to be about forty years old. "Good evening," he said, offering a handshake.

Deliberately neglecting to introduce himself, Kirb shook the lawman's hand. "I'm just passing through your town, Marshal," he said, "but I've been talking with Joe Saxton and Hank Macon." He took one of the dodgers from his pocket and handed it over. "I just thought you might want to read this."

The marshal seated himself on the corner of the desk. He read the document and handed it back, then folded his arms and let out an audible sigh. "They came right through this town," he said, sounding as if he was talking to himself. "The sons of bitches were wanted for murder, and I turned 'em outta jail and let 'em ride right outta this town. The town of Lockhart even had to pay the bill for their horses down at the livery stable 'cause neither one of them had the money to do it." He shook his head a few times, then added, "The law plainly says that if you lock a man up, you've gotta take care of his horse, you know."

"No," Kirb said, "I didn't know that. It sounds like a sensible law to me though."

"Sure, it makes sense," Dewberry said. "I ain't complaining about the law, but knowing that I let two wanted men walk outta my jail just pisses me off."

Renfro shook his head. "I don't think they were wanted men at the time you had 'em, Marshal. They had already committed the crime, but Sheriff Miller was still in the middle of his investigation. It took him about a month to come up with enough evidence to get murder warrants for 'em."

The lawman nodded. "Dead-or-alive warrants, no less." He sat quietly for a few moments, then asked, "Have you got a stake in the manhunt other than the reward?"

Kirb was slow to answer. He stood looking at the toes of his boots for several seconds, then said, "The woman they killed was my wife."

The deputy dropped into his chair noisily, and the marshal emitted another sigh. "I'm real sorry," Dewberry said, with the deputy echoing his boss. A long pause that eventually became uncomfortable followed, with the marshal finally breaking the silence. "The third man on that dodger," he said, "the one named Wally Stovall. What about him?"

"I killed him a few days ago," Renfro answered matter-of-factly.

The marshal clamped his lips together and nodded slowly, looking as though he had expected to hear that particular answer. "You figure to do the same thing to his buddies, I suppose."

"Yes," Renfro answered firmly.

The lawman nodded. "I see," he said. "You haven't told me why you decided to come by here and tell me all of this."

"I figured that some time during the week they spent in your jail, you might have learned where they were going, and I was hoping you'd pass that information on to me."

The lawman got to his feet and walked to the window, then returned to the desk. "I don't know that I can help you one bit, young fellow, but I can tell you what they told the judge before he sentenced 'em. Pollard said he was gonna be working on the Star Ranch down at Pleasanton. Tripp said he'd try to get 'em to put him on too, but if they didn't have nothing for him, he'd move on west till he found work.

"Now they told the judge all of that before they knew that he was fixing to lock their asses up for a week, so they might have both been lying through their teeth. Tripp told the judge that even if he himself didn't get hired at the Star, he had no doubt that Pollard would. He said Pollard was the owner's cousin."

"That's the way I heard it," Renfro said. "I'd been told all of that stuff before, but hearing it again helps my feelings. I'll be checking out the Star Ranch in the very near future." He offered a parting handshake. "Good night to you, sir, and I won't take up any more of your time." He nodded to the deputy, then disappeared through the doorway.

He returned to the Salty Dog to find the liveryman sitting at the bar. "Did you find Marshal Dewberry?" Macon asked.

Renfron nodded. "He was in his office."

Macon shoved Kirb's empty glass down the bar, attempting to refill it from the bottle. "You've got some catching up to do," he said.

Renfro shook his head, and put his hand over the glass. "No more for me, Hank, I've got some sleeping to do." He counted out fifty-four cents and laid it on the bar, then spoke to the bartender. "Give this gentleman another bottle on me, Joe." Then he turned and headed for the hotel lobby. "I'll see you early in the morning, Hank," he said over his shoulder.

24

Named for Don Francisco Flores de Abrego, an early Mexican rancher who'd established his spread six miles to the northwest in 1832, the town of Floresville was founded in 1833 on land donated by the Flores family. Though the original homesteaders had devoted the land almost entirely to the raising of beef cattle, the next generation discovered that it would produce crops in abundance, and that it was particularly suited to the growing of cotton and peanuts.

Although those facts had hardly created a land rush, the town nonetheless held its own and eventually became a marketing point for watermelons, flax, cotton, and peanuts, as well as both beef and dairy cattle. Slowly but steadily, the small town had continued to prosper since the day of its inception.

Kirb Renfro rode into Floresville an hour before dark. He had left Lockhart three days before and had been spending long days in the saddle ever since. He had skirted

San Antonio well to the east and, adding credence to the old saw that it was a small world, met a man in the middle of the road who had been one of his schoolmates back in Tennessee.

Renfro had just topped a hill a few miles south of Seguin when he came face-to-face with Tate Lonnergan, a man whom he had known for most of his life. Because the two had been classmates all through school and had talked with each other several times since, Renfro recognized Lonnergan instantly. He sat his saddle smiling for a moment, then kneed his mount forward. "Tate Lonnergan!" he said loudly, pointing his finger, "I'd know you anywhere!"

The man pulled up and sat with his arms folded across his chest. "I wish I could say the same," he said, "but somehow I can't seem to place you." He stared at Renfro for a few moments, then asked, "Are you . . . you wouldn't be Kirb Renfro, would you?"

Kirb jumped to the ground. "I sure would," he said, offering a handshake. "I don't guess I'd have thought of you in a hundred years, Tate."

Lonnergan dismounted and pumped Renfro's hand a few times. "I haven't thought of you lately either," he said. He smiled, then added jokingly, "Ain't none of us Tipton County boys thought much of you since you made off with Ellie Mae Clemons." He stood quietly for a few moments, then asked, "How's the little lady doing these days anyway?"

"She's fine," Renfro answered. "She's probably a whole lot better off than most folks."

They led their animals out of the road to let a freight wagon pass, then seated themselves on the high side of the ditch bank. "I'd have ridden right on by you if you hadn't stopped me, Kirb," Lonnergan said. "That damn beard's done took you over, old buddy, and I never would have recognized you if you hadn't started talking. Ain't no way in the world to tell who's hiding behind a thicket like that." He paused for a moment, then added, "Ain't that damn thing hot?"

Kirb nodded. "It's hot, all right, and summer's coming on mighty fast. I'll be shaving it off before long."

"I'd sure think so," Lonnergan said. "I don't think I could ever grow one myself. I can't go no more'n two or three days without shaving before all the damn itching sends me hunting a razor."

Kirb nodded. "Mine itches too," he said.

They talked of old times for another hour. Lonnergan said that he had been in Texas for about six months. He was employed on a small ranch a few miles northeast of Seguin and had been on the road today only because his boss had sent him on an errand. "I'm mighty glad he sent me too," Lonnergan said, patting Renfro on the back. "Otherwise, I never would have known you'd moved to Texas."

Kirb explained that he himself was on a business trip, and gave no further details. He informed Lonnergan that he had bought a small spread of his own and gave him directions to the Circle R. "I should be back home in a month or so," he said, "and if you ever feel the urge, I'd sure appreciate a visit from you. Come up and stay as long as you want to." They shook hands once more, then remounted and went their separate ways.

Renfro paid close attention to the Floresville Hotel as he rode past, deciding immediately that he would spend the night there. Painted green and white, the two-story establishment looked as if it had been built yesterday. Red drapes were drawn open on a long, plate glass window, and Kirb could even see the clerk sitting behind his desk.

He made note of a pool hall and several watering holes as he continued on down the street. When he reached the livery stable, he tied his animals out front and walked to the office. When no one answered his knock, he walked into the barn and down the hallway. "Anybody here?" he asked. Getting no answer, he continued on past the stables till he reached the corral. The liveryman stood just inside the pole enclosure working on a leaky water trough. "Howdy," Kirb said. "Pardon me for just walking on in, but I didn't know what else to do. I've got a saddler and a pack animal that I'd like to leave with you."

"I'll be right with you," the man said. He dropped his hammer in the empty trough, then stepped through the gate. "I appreciate you stopping in, young fellow, and I don't mind telling you that I need the business." At least six feet tall and as skinny as a rail, he appeared to be in his late forties and wore no hat on his bald head. "You're the only real customer I've had all day," he added. "Everybody else just wanted something for nothing." He pointed toward the front of the building. "Let's go see about your livestock."

Moments later, the liveryman untied Renfro's animals and led them through the wide doorway. "They're probably a little tired," he said, "but otherwise, they appear to be in good shape." He ran his hand along the saddler's back all the way from its withers to its rump, then backed off a few steps. "That's the best-looking horse I've seen in at least a month. Is he anywhere near as good as he looks?"

"Yes, sir," Kirb answered, unsheathing his rifle and throwing his saddlebags across his shoulder. "He's exactly like he looks."

With no further comment, the hostler stripped the saddle and tied the horse to a post, then turned his attention to the mule and the packsaddle. "You gonna carry any of them packs with you, or do you want me to just lock up the whole works?"

Renfro smiled. "Just lock up the whole works," he said. "I'll be staying at the Floresville Hotel, if they've got a vacant room."

The skinny man chuckled. "A vacant room, you say? Hell, that hotel ain't been full since it was built, and it probably ain't never gonna be. The only times it ever did any business to speak of, was when a herd of cattle came through on its way to the Chisholm Trail. Most of the feeder trails have moved farther north now, though, and about the only business the hotel gets is from travelers like you. All these people you see walking up and down the streets live here, and they sure ain't likely to be renting no hotel room." He chuckled again, adding, "Yes, sir, I'd be willing to bet that six bits'll get you any room in the house."

A few minutes later, Kirb stepped into the hotel lobby, his Henry cradled in the crook of his arm and his saddle-bags draped over his shoulder. "I need a room for the night," he said to the young man sitting behind the counter. "I'd prefer an upstairs room with windows."

The youngster got to his feet. "You've certainly come to the right place, sir." He dropped a pencil on the register, then laid a key on the counter. "Just sign your name and give me seventy-five cents. Your room number is two-twenty."

Renfro signed his borrowed name in the book, then picked up his key and climbed the staircase. Moments later, he stepped inside the room and locked the door, then laid his rifle and his saddlebags on the bed. He raised windows on two sides of the room, then stood beside one of them looking at the activity below. He had an excellent view of the comings and goings on the street, and could even make out most of the sidewalk traffic on the north side of the hotel.

He watched for a while, then crossed the room and lit the coal-oil lamp for daylight was fading fast. He bathed himself as best he could in the wash pan, then took a seat in the chair. Even after his face was dry, he continued to fluff his beard with the towel till all of the moisture was gone. The cleaner and drier the beard, the less it itched.

It was full dark when he walked from the hotel. He ate supper at a restaurant on the opposite corner, then recrossed the street and headed for the pool hall he had noticed as he rode into town. He had always enjoyed watching men who played the game well, even though he himself was not a player. He had knocked the balls around the table on several occasions over the years, but he'd never played against a good shooter. Most of the good ones played the game for money, and he was not even in their category. With that in mind, he pushed the door to the pool hall open and stepped inside.

"Come in!" a deep voice said loudly. The speaker stood behind a tall bar that had no stools, and several men were standing there drinking. Of less than average height, the bartender was both wide and thick, and appeared to be about thirty years old. He sipped at a beer and wiped his brown mustache with the back of his hand, then spoke again, softer this time. "Welcome to Rooster's. The first beer's always on the house."

Renfro smiled and bellied up to the bar. "What if one beer's all I want?" he asked.

The man drew a mug of the foamy brew and set it at Kirb's elbow. "Well, I reckon, by gosh, it's still on the house." He thrust his right hand across the bar. "I'm Rooster Cline, and I don't remember seeing you before. Just passing through?"

Renfro shook the hand. "The name's Bill Alexander," he said. "I just stopped off to get some rest, and I expect to be gone tomorrow."

"Well, drink up," Cline said, pointing to Renfro's mug. "If a man puts away enough of that stuff, I'd almost guarantee that he's gonna rest awhile."

Kirb chuckled, and took a sip of the beer. "I can believe that," he said. When the bartender left to serve some of the other drinkers, Renfro turned to face the opposite side of the building, his beer mug in his hand and his back leaning against the bar. Three pool tables were located on the other side of the room, and two games were in progress at the moment. Unable to get a clear view of the action from where he stood, Renfro walked across the room and seated himself on a bench that ran along the wall beside one of the tables. "If it's all right with you fellows, I'll just sit here and watch the game," he said to one of the players. "If that bothers either of you, just say so and I'll move."

Both men shook their heads to indicate his presence was welcome. "Don't bother us none," a freckle-faced man said. "Get yourself a cue and challenge the winner if you want to. We're only playing for a buck a game."

"Only a buck a game," Kirb repeated to himself. A full day's wages for most men. He shook his head. "No, thank you," he said. "I don't play well enough to bet a penny, much less a dollar." The man shrugged, then chalked his cue and continued with the game.

Returning to the bar twice for refills of his beer mug, Kirb spent the next hour on the bench watching the pool players. It appeared to him that the freckle-faced man was making the most difficult shots, but the fact that he was usually the one who had to cough up a dollar made it obvious that he was losing most of the games. Renfro left the bench fully convinced that he himself would never be able to play the game as well as either of the contestants.

He returned to the bar to find that all the other drinkers had departed, and Rooster Cline was sitting on a stool behind the bar. He refilled Kirb's empty mug. "Bill Alexander, huh?" he asked. "Never heard that name before, but I reckon that don't mean nothing." His lips spread in a toothy grin. "You in the cattle business, or is it none of my business?

Kirb was slow to answer. He took a sip of his brew, then set the mug down noiselessly. "I've got a little spread up in Comanche County," he said finally, "and I'm hoping to eventually get into the cattle business. That's a mighty slow process unless a man's got a lot more money than I have."

Cline nodded. "By God, you're right about that," he said. "With all the money men moving into Texas and buying up everything they can get their hands on, the price of real estate has shot sky-high. I heard just the other day that a fellow from Florida named Dixie Rice paid nearly ten dollars an acre for twelve sections of land right here in this county. Now with rich sons of bitches like him coming out here and throwing that kind of money around, what the hell is a poor fellow gonna do?"

Renfro shook his head. "A man without a little money is gonna have to be mighty lucky," he said.

"That's the damn truth," Cline said, drawing himself another beer. "It's done reached the point where skinny-assed brood cows sell for ten dollars apiece."

Kirb nodded. "I know," he said. "I've already bought ten head of 'em at that price. I couldn't bring myself to sit around and wait, though, 'cause I sure don't think they're gonna get any cheaper."

"Hell, no, they won't," Cline said. "Not as long as the buyers at the Kansas railheads have got some money." He took another sip, then wiped his mouth on his apron.

"Even though they hafta pay the ranchers ten bucks a head for steers, a lot of men are making fortunes trailing 'em north. From what I hear, they can just about name their price once they get 'em to the railroad. I heard that one rich son of a bitch cleared more'n seventy thousand dollars off of one herd."

Renfro stared at the bar for several seconds. "That's an awful lot of money," he said finally, "but I don't doubt it. According to my own figures, it can certainly be done."

The bartender nodded, then left to serve a new customer at the far end of the bar. When the man returned to his stool a few moments later, Kirb changed the subject. "How far is it down to Pleasanton, Rooster?"

"About twenty miles," Cline answered. "That road out front goes to it damn near as straight as the crow flies."

"Would you happen to be acquainted with a man down there named Hanson Bray?"

The barkeep chuckled. "I reckon I know him about as well as he's gonna let somebody like me know him. He owns the Star Ranch, and he's one of the rich men I was talking about a few minutes ago. He's done made a killing trailing cattle to Kansas, and he's still at it. I've been told that he's sending three more herds up this year."

Renfro drank the last of his beer, then allowed the bartender to refill it. "I'm not actually interested in Hanson Bray," he said, "but I would like to meet up with one of his cousins who might be working for him. The man's name is Pat Pollard, and one of his friends up north suggested that I look him up."

The barkeep's eyes showed instant recognition. "Pat Pollard?" he asked. "Hell, I know Pat Pollard. He's been in here twice this year that I know of. Last time was about three weeks ago." He pointed across the room. "He had a squabble with a fellow over there at that table about the color of his damned hair. Pollard's got all that bright, red hair, you know, but he's real sensitive about it. Of course, the man at the table didn't have no way of knowing that, so during the course of their conversation he called Pollard 'Red.' Pollard beat him up pretty bad before I could get over there to break it up. I ordered Pollard off of the premises and barred him from coming back for a month. That month'll be up next Tuesday."

Renfro sat digesting the information quietly. "Did Pollard have a man named Lonny Tripp with him?"

Cline shook his head. "Not the last time. Tripp was with him when he came through here back in the winter though. Three weeks ago I asked Pollard about Tripp, and he told me that they had to split up in order to find work. Pollard said he himself was working on the Star Ranch, and that Tripp went to work for Cotton Tomlin's outfit down on the Frio River. The CT ain't nowhere near as big as the Star, but everybody who knows Tomlin speaks highly of him. I've never met the man myself, so I can't say nothing good or bad about him."

"You say the CT Ranch is on the Frio River," Renfro said, chuckling softly. "According to my map, the Frio's pretty long. Could you draw me a little better picture?"

"The CT's easy to find," Cline answered. "I never have been on it, but I've passed the road that leads to it lots of times. It's located up in the northern part of McMullen County." He took a sip of his beer, then pointed. "When you leave here you travel due south for about fifty miles, then you'll come to where the Atascosa, the Nueces, and the Frio all come together. The people who live around there call the area Three Rivers. Once you get there, all you gotta do is head west along the Frio till you come to the CT. That'll be some pretty rough traveling now 'cause the river runs right through a bunch of steep canyons." He paused for a moment, then asked, "Is Lonny Tripp a friend of yours too?"

Renfro shook his head. "Not exactly," he said. "Some people who know him just asked me to look him up."

"Well, Pollard said he was working on the CT, and you can't miss the ranch if you go the way I told you. Want me to draw you a map?"

Kirb shook his head. "That won't be necessary. I probably won't even go down there, but if I do, I can remember your directions easy enough." He set his mug on the bar, then pulled his watch out of his pocket. "Time flies when you're talking with somebody you like," he said. "I've enjoyed the conversation, but it's way past my bedtime. I'll make it a point to stop in to see you if I'm ever back this way again." He walked through the doorway and headed for his hotel room. He must get a good night's sleep, for Cline had said that the conjunction of the three rivers was a fifty-mile ride.

25

Renfro bought food supplies at a general store shortly after sunup next day, then rode out of Floresville. He would not be going all the way to Three Rivers. He had studied his map last night and again this morning, and had decided to take a different route to the Frio than the one suggested by Rooster Cline. The map showed that by traveling southwest, he could easily reach the Atascosa River before nightfall, and another day's ride in the same direction would bring him to the Frio west of the steep canyons Cline had described. He kneed the big black to a ground-eating trot and held the same pace for more than an hour.

At midmorning, when he came to a fork in the road and read on the sign that a right-hand turn led to Pleasanton, he turned left, taking a little-used road to the south. The sign had given no indication as to where the old road actually went, but he decided to stay with it as long as it led in the general direction he wanted to go. If it began to snake around toward the east, he would simply abandon it and head cross-country. According to his reckoning, he was no more than fifteen miles from the Atascosa River right now, and he had already decided to spend the night there.

He rode at a fast walk for the remainder of the morning and most of the afternoon, and cross-country travel never became necessary. Though the old road was completely barren of traffic nowadays, and had more than one rotting bridge that the packmule refused to walk across, it generally stayed with its course, and he followed it all the way to the Atascosa.

As he came in sight of the river, a glance at his watch told him it was four o'clock. After watering his animals, he forded in water that was less than a foot deep, then headed for a grove of pecan trees that grew along the west bank. Even as he rode he kept an eye out for anything that would burn, for he could easily see that the area was a popular campsite. Making a mental note to walk back and get some of the dead grass he was passing, he rode into the trees and dismounted.

Once he had selected a place to build his fire, he stripped the saddle and the packsaddle, then pitched his bedroll toward some leafy bushes a short distance away. He dried the backs of both the saddler and the mule with his saddle blanket, then led them fifty yards up the slope, for no grass grew beneath the canopies of the trees.

He had scarcely picketed them and begun to walk back toward his campsite, when a covered wagon drawn by four large mules appeared at the ford. The driver halted the big animals in midstream and allowed them to drink, then pecked their rumps with a long switch he held in his hand. As they leaned into their collars to pull the vehicle up the sloping bank on the opposite side, the fact that they were straining every muscle was obvious. The wagon was not only loaded, but loaded with something very heavy.

Kirb watched for a moment, then went about hunting fuel for a campfire.

As he continued to gather dead grass, bark, and as many dead limbs as he could find, the wagon left the road and headed north along the riverbank, coming to a halt about twenty yards south of his campsite. Obviously intending to spend the night, a middle-aged man and a boy who appeared to be ten or twelve years old jumped to the ground and began to unhitch the team.

Even though Kirb was busy building a fire, he continued to watch the newcomers out of the corner of his eye. The youngster had no doubt done it all before, for he had two of the animals unharnessed and was already leading them up the slope, when his father laid the hames and the collar of the last mule on the ground. That done, the man began to look around for firewood.

By the time the boy had picketed all four of the animals, his father had found fuel and was in the process of kindling a fire. Seemingly without being told, the young man picked up their empty coffeepot and headed for the river. When he returned, he poured a handful of grounds in the pot and set it on the fire. After watching the boy's movements at closer range, Kirb decided that he was neither ten nor twelve. He was probably no more than nine years old.

Renfro emptied his canteens into to his own coffeepot and set it on the fire, then walked to the river and filled his cooking pot with water. He had bought a half-dozen eggs at the general store, and he intended to boil them all. Not only would he be eliminating the chance of breakage, but a boiled egg could be peeled and eaten anytime, even while on the move.

Half an hour later, he was enjoying a supper of tinned fish, German sausage, and cheese. He also had a large tomato, which he salted and began to eat, peel and all.

Tomatoes had been one of his favorite foods as long as he could remember and had been a year-round staple in the household where he had grown up. When the plants ceased to produce in late fall, his mother had simply turned to the cellar and the dozens of jars she had put up during the growing season. Kirb had been taught in school that tomatoes originated in Mexico almost three hundred years ago. Now he raised the hand holding the half-eaten tomato and waved it toward the Mexican border. "Gracias," he said softly.

He was sitting beside the dying campfire eating oatmeal cookies and sipping coffee, when the other two campers paid him a visit. "Howdy," the man said, while the kid stood slightly behind him nodding courteously. "Me and the boy's just about run outta grub. I was wondering if you've got something to eat that you'd sell."

"Nope," Renfro said, shaking his head. Already reaching for his pocketknife, he added, "I've got a few things I'll let you have for nothing." He halved the roll of German sausage with the man, then cut off a good-sized slab of cheese. "Plenty of soda crackers there, and you can help yourselves to that bag of cookies. Have you got enough coffee?"

The man nodded. "Got more'n we can drink," he said. "My name's Clint Barnes, and this is my son, Hansel. We appreciate you sharing with us, and we'll certainly be packing more food on the next run." He pointed to his wagon. "Got her loaded down with twenty-four sacks of cement. As soon as we deliver it to the buyer over in Broken Arrow, we've got to turn right around and go back to Floresville after another load. All together, we've got ninety-six sacks to deliver."

Kirb nodded. "Broken Arrow is a new one on me," he said. "Is that a town? Where is it located?"

"It's about halfway across Atascosa County, and I

reckon you could call it a town, all right. It's got a bank, a hotel, several stores, a blacksmith shop, a livery stable, and a few saloons, so I'm pretty sure everybody living there calls it a town. Old Wink Davis is the man we're hauling the cement for. He's gonna dam up the lower end of Wolf Creek Canyon and build himself a lake."

Renfro nodded. He sat quietly for a moment, then asked, "Do you know where the CT Ranch is?"

"Sure do," the man answered quickly. "It's about twenty miles directly south of Broken Arrow in northern McMullen County. The Frio River splits the ranch wide open, so you'll actually be on CT property before you ever get to the river."

Kirb nodded again. "Do you know Cotton Tomlin?"

"Yep," Barnes answered, then began to chuckle. "People started calling him Cotton back when he had some hair. His head's about as slick as a billiard ball, nowadays. I reckon he must be about as honest as they come 'cause I've heard it said that the bank'll lend him money with no more'n a handshake for collateral." He paused for a few moments, then added, "No, sir, I ain't never heard nobody say a bad word about Cotton Tomlin." He paused again, then asked, "Why are you asking about him? You thinking about hitting him up for a job?"

"I reckon it has crossed my mind," Kirb answered. "A fellow up north told me what a fine fellow he was and said that the CT was a small spread. I don't like working on big ranches. Everything's too impersonal."

"I know what you mean," Barnes said. "I don't think it would be that way on the CT though, 'cause the outfit ain't all that big. I doubt that Tomlin runs more'n a thousand head year round."

"Do you have any idea how many men he keeps on the payroll?"

"I ain't got no way of knowing, but I suppose it would

depend on what time of the year you're talking about. Right now, I'd say he's got ten or twelve men, but in the wintertime he probably cuts back to five or six."

Kirb nodded and pointed up the hill. "Does that road there lead to Broken Arrow?"

"Straight to it," Barnes answered. "It's a little smoother going from here on too. Once you get to Broken Arrow, you're gonna have to travel cross-country to the CT Ranch 'cause there ain't no road, at least not till after you cross the Frio. A pretty good road runs east and west along the south side of the river, and there're several roads leading off of it that'll carry you on to ranch headquarters. There're plenty of signs, so you can't get lost. All you gotta do is keep traveling due south out of Broken Arrow for twenty miles or so, then you'll find yourself right in the middle of Cotton Tomlin's spread."

"Thank you, Mr. Barnes," Kirb said, "and I appreciate the information."

Seeming to take his cue from the tone of finality in Renfro's voice, Barnes turned to his son, saying, "Let's get back to the fire and eat this stuff before our coffee gets cold, Hansel." He nodded his thanks to Kirb again, then led the way back to his campsite.

Renfro extinguished his fire, then ate another handful of cookies and drank the last of his coffee. He sat on the riverbank thinking and trying to spot a fish in the murky water till sunset, then walked up the slope to check on his saddler and his packmule. He pulled up the picket pins and moved both animals to new grass, then walked back to his camp. Once the night had turned as black as pitch, he spread his bedroll in the bushes and stretched out, a loaded weapon within easy reach of either hand. Using a folded blanket for a pillow, he was asleep quickly.

After washing three boiled eggs and several slices of

German sausage down with strong coffee next morning, Kirb mounted the black and took the slack out of the packmule's lead rope. As he rode by Barnes's wagon, neither the man nor his son, both of whom were rolled up in blankets under the vehicle, showed any sign of life. Moving as quietly as possible, he took to the road and soon disappeared over the hill.

As Barnes had said, the road was in much better condition west of the river, and although that fact was not nearly as important to a man on horseback as it was to someone riding in a wagon, Kirb nontheless appreciated the smoother surface. In most places the road was wide enough that freight wagons could pass each other with ease, and the two wooden bridges he had crossed so far had been in excellent shape.

He expected to be in Broken Arrow by midafternoon, for Barnes had said the distance was only eighteen miles. Once there, he would look the town over, then make his decision as to what to do next.

Shortly before noon, he halted at a roadside spring long enough to water his animals and wolf down the last of his sausage and eggs, then took to the road again. He traveled steadily, and at three o'clock in the afternoon, pulled up at a sign announcing the town limits of Broken Arrow and boasting a population of 396.

He sat his saddle looking up the wide street for quite some time, for he had a good view of the entire business area. On the east end of town and about twenty yards from where he sat was the livery stable and the blacksmith shop. The town proper began about thirty yards west of the stable. Taking notice of the fact that the livery was the only building in town that was taller than a single story, Kirb kneed the black to the barn's open doorway.

"Get down and rest yourself, young fellow," a

bearded, middle-aged man said as he stepped from the office. "You and that horse both look like you've done about enough for one day."

Renfro unsheathed his rifle and laid his saddlebags across his shoulder, then stepped out of the saddle. "Give 'em both a good feed of oats," he said, handing over the reins. He jerked his thumb toward the commercial district. "Which side of the street is the hotel on?"

The hostler, already in the process of stripping the saddle from the black, spat a stream of tobacco juice between his boots. "There ain't no hotel in this town, young fellow. Never has been." He laid the saddle across a sawhorse, then continued to talk. "There is a place where a man can lay his head though." He pointed up the street. "Bulah Bain runs a boardinghouse at the west end of town, and she'll rent you a room for a night or a month. I never have stayed there myself, but her husband asked me to tell men passing through that she'll put 'em up and feed 'em like a king for a buck a day. I reckon that's pretty reasonable."

Renfro nodded. "Seems reasonable to me," he said. "A fellow told me last night that Broken Arrow had a hotel, but it sounds like he was mistaken."

The man shook his head. "I've had this stable for more'n ten years, and if there was a hotel in this town I'd certainly know about it. That fellow you talked to was either full of shit or he thought Bulah's Boardinghouse was one. I imagine that's the straight of it right there; he thought her place was a hotel."

Kirb nodded. "Probably," he said. "Anyway, I'll go see if she can put me up. I'll trust you to take good care of my animals till I need 'em again."

"I'll treat 'em the same way I treat my own," the hostler said.

Walking west on the plank sidewalk, a barbershop

was the first business he came to. Thinking how nice it would be to get a shave and put an end to the incessant itching, he scratched his face and walked on by hurriedly. In the middle of the block, with a vacant lot on each side, he walked past the town marshal's office. Even without the sign out front, the rusty iron bars on the rear windows were enough to identify the building as the local hoosegow. Pausing long enough to read the sign, Kirb made a mental note of the fact that the marshal's name was Clem Farrell, then walked on up the street.

There was no sign in front of Bulah's, but one was hardly needed. With several men sitting on its long porch waiting for suppertime, the house was easy enough to spot. Painted white and trimmed in green, the large building appeared to have at least a dozen rooms and had no doubt once been the dwelling of a well-to-do family. Renfro stepped into the yard and asked of no one in particular. "Is this the boardinghouse?"

An old-timer with a white beard leaned over the rail and nodded. "This it it, my boy," he said. "Good beds and the best damn vittles this side of New Orleans."

"Just talk to Bulah," a younger man said. "Her office is the first door on the right-hand side of the hall. I believe I heard her in there a minute ago."

"Thank you," Kirb said, then stepped up on the porch. When he knocked on the lady's door a few moments later, he was invited in. "My goodness!" she said, as he stepped into the room. She stood up behind her desk and pointed to the Colt in his holster and the Henry in his hand. "Is it really necessary for a man to tote around an arsenal? Why in the world do you need so many guns?"

He offered her the broadest smile he could muster. "Most of the time I don't need 'em, ma'am," he said softly. "But when I do, I've got 'em."

She stared at the desk for a moment, then raised her eyes. "Do you need a room?"

"Yes, ma'am, and I ain't too particular. Anything beats sleeping out yonder with the rattlers."

She was an attractive woman despite the fact that she was at least fifty years old and forty pounds overweight. A hint of a smile appeared at one corner of her mouth as she took a key from the desk drawer. "My rooms are all the same, sir, and they're all good." She handed him the key. "Take one-eleven, it's right down the hall on your left. I guess you know that my name's Bulah. What's yours?"

"I'm Bill Alexander." He took two steps toward the door, then halted and turned halfway around. "I've already heard about your cooking," he said. "What time do we eat supper?"

She chuckled. "Six o'clock," she said. "You won't sleep through it; the bell rings loud enough to wake the dead."

He nodded, then headed down the hall to his room.

26

When the supper bell rang, Renfro leaned his rifle in the corner and walked down the hall to the dining room. Six men were already seated at the table, and as far as Kirb could tell, none of them was armed. All of which drew attention to the Colt buckled around his own hip. The hostess, who was standing between the table and the stove, was the only one to comment. "You even wear that thing to eat?" she asked.

Kirb smiled. "Yes, ma'am," he said. "Even though I try to be a nice fellow, there are at least two men in the world who don't like me." He pulled out a chair and seated himself, then added, "I never know when I'll meet one of 'em."

A man sitting midway along the table chuckled, then pointed to the different dishes of food. "Soon as you make up your mind what you want to start with, just reach and get it," he said. "Ain't none of us too good about handing things."

Kirb nodded. He leaned over the table and filled his plate from the various bowls and platters, then buttered a couple of biscuits and reseated himself. Bulah Bain stood at his elbow with a cup of steaming coffee. "Sugar over there if you want it," she said, pointing to a small, white bowl. She stood quietly for a moment, then spoke to the men as a group. "Eat up, everybody. If you need anything else, it's all over there on the stove." That said, she disappeared down the hall.

Most of the men sat working their way through the meal quietly. Renfro had already finished off two pieces of chicken and was busy with a slab of beefsteak, when the man beside him suddenly became talkative. "I reckon you must've just come into town recently."

Kirb swallowed a mouthful of food, then nodded. "About three hours ago," he said.

"Figure to stay around for a while?" the man asked.

Kirb stared into his plate. "I haven't done any figuring about it one way or the other," he said after a time. "Seems like a nice place though."

"It is," the man said quickly. "Marshal Clem Farrell keeps it that way." He took another bite of food and another swig of his coffee, then continued. "The marshal ain't all that hard to get along with now, it's just that he don't put up with no nonsense outta nobody. He served notice on the riffraff a long time ago that their presence in this town would not be tolerated. He's big enough and tough enough to back up what he says too."

Renfro nodded, and said nothing else. He finished off his meal, then walked outside and seated himself in a cane-bottom chair on the east end of the porch. The man he had talked with at the table was not far behind. With fair complexion and a muscular build, he stood about five-ten and appeared to be in the neighborhood of forty years old. He pulled up a chair and offered a handshake. "My name's Bud Shingle," he said, "and I've been living here at Bulah's ever since my wife died, nearly three years ago."

Kirb accepted the hand and pumped it a few times. "I'm sorry about your wife," he said. "You don't look very old yourself, so she must have still been a young woman."

"Stella was thirty-five. She died during childbirth, her and the baby both." He stared down the hill toward town for a few moments, then added, "We'd been trying for fifteen years before she conceived, then it killed her. The baby never had no chance neither. Doctor said it died several days before Stella did."

Neither man spoke again for several minutes. "Do you work somewhere around here, Bud?" Kirb asked finally.

"Only when something pretty good comes along," Shingle answered. "Don't do nothing on a regular basis. I sold my place after my wife died, and the interest on the money pays my way here at the boardinghouse." He managed to muster a halfhearted smile. "I ain't getting ahead none, but at least I ain't going in the hole." He paused for a moment, then asked, "You looking for work?"

Kirb shook his head. "I haven't been looking too hard," he said. "Like you were saying about yourself, I don't think I'm going in the hole." He was thoughtful for a few moments, then asked, "Have you ever been down around the Frio River, Bud? Do you know where the CT Ranch is?"

Shingle nodded. "Yes, to both questions," he answered. "When you get to the Frio, you're already on the CT."

"That's what I heard," Kirb said. "I've chased a few cows myself, and a man told me that the CT was a mighty fine place to work. I wonder how hard it is to get a job down there?"

Shingle shook his head. "Probably about like it is

everywhere else. If they need you, they'll hire you. If they don't, they won't."

Renfro chuckled loudly. "That's a good answer to a dumb question, Bud."

The man appeared to blush. "I didn't mean to sound smart-alecky," he said, "but that's the only answer that came to mind. If you really want to know if they'll hire you though, you probably wouldn't even have to leave Broken Arrow to find out. Jim Benson's the foreman, and he's up here drinking in Hopp Ellis's Saloon just about every Saturday night. Fact is, most of the men on the CT payroll visit Hopp's place a few nights a month, especially on payday."

Kirb sat thinking for a moment. He remembered seeing Ellis's saloon a few doors east of the marshal's office. "Are you saying the CT hands ride all the way to Broken Arrow to do their drinking?"

Shingle chuckled. "I'm saying they don't have no other choice unless they want to ride a lot farther in some other direction. There ain't a single saloon in that whole county; ain't enough people down there to make one profitable. Most of the folks who do live there probably don't even drink liquor."

"So the CT hands all come riding up to Hopp Ellis's on the weekend, huh?"

Shingle nodded. "The ones who like to drink and party do. I stop in there for a little toddy every once in a while myself, and I ain't never been in there on a Saturday night when some of that bunch wasn't around. Jim Benson's easy to spot, even though he ain't very big. He's a wiry little fellow about five-seven, and most of the CT hands stick to him like glue. You won't have to ask nobody; you'll know Benson when you see him."

"I'll remember that," Kirb said. Noticing that the sun was rapidy sinking toward the treetops, he fished his watch out of his pocket to see that the time was a quarter to seven. Then he stretched his arms over his head and faked a yawn. "I'm gonna get on back to my room now, Bud. I've enjoyed talking with you, and I suppose I'll see you again in the morning."

"Good night," Shingle said. "I ain't gonna be far behind you."

Kirb walked to his room and seated himself on the edge of the bed. With his elbows on his knees and his chin resting on his thumbs, he sat taking stock of the things he had learned. He fully intended to walk down and look Hopp Ellis's place over, but he would wait till after Bud Shingle had left the front porch. Although he seemed like a very nice fellow, there was no logical reason for him to know about Renfro's comings and goings.

Kirb waited another fifteen minutes, then, as noiselessly as possible, walked back to the front door. Seeing that no one was on the porch now, he took the steps two at a time and moved out onto the street. He headed down the hill with his usual long strides and was out of sight of the boardinghouse in about one minute.

The sun was just dropping below the horizon as he walked past the marshal's office, and though there was still plenty of daylight left, a burning coal-oil lamp was already visible through the window. Watching people moving around inside the building, Kirb decided that a man might be on duty there twenty-four hours a day, at least on days when the marshal had prisoners in his jail.

He continued down the street without ever breaking his stride and was soon standing in front of Hopp Ellis's saloon. A quick inspection of the five horses tied at the two hitching rails revealed no CT brand. Nor was there any sign of the big sorrel that Oliver Blanding had described as Lonny Tripp's personal mount. Kirb shrugged, then pushed his way through the bat-wing doors.

A typical Texas watering hole, the establishment had a rectangular bar with a kitchen and eating area off to one side. Two billiard tables stood along the east wall, and farther back, in the center of the room and beyond, half a dozen poker tables were scattered about in complete disorder. No game was in progress at any of the tables at the moment.

Kirb walked around to the west side of the bar and took a stool beside a large post. He had to crane his neck to see the front door from this position, and anyone entering the building would be unable to see him at all. He could see all five of the men who owned those horses out front. Two were in the dining area eating, and the other three were sitting at the far end of the bar talking among themselves. None of the men bore the slightest resemblance of Lonny Tripp.

A tall, skinny bartender with a cigarette in his mouth suddenly appeared in front of Renfro. He wiped a wayward strand of stringy blond hair out of his eyes, then took two deep drags and extinguished the butt in an ashtray. "Can I get you something to drink?" he asked.

Kirb nodded. "A beer," he said.

The man delivered the brew without a word, then scooped up Renfro's coin and returned to the front of the bar, where he reseated himself on a thickly padded stool.

Kirb sipped lightly, for he had already set himself a limit of two beers. As it turned out, he would not even be drinking that many, for just as he set his mug back on the bar, the bat wings at the front of the building opened noisily. Renfro craned his neck so he could see around the post, then sat staring in disbelief. There, just inside the doorway, standing beside another man about his own size, was Lonny Tripp.

No doubt about it, Kirb was telling himself, he was now looking at the same man he had seen standing beside

Pat Pollard in front of the saloon in Comanche, the man who had brought Ellie to tears by staring at her, and the man who had eventually raped her and helped beat her to death.

As he continued to stare at Tripp, Kirb could feel the rage rising throughout his whole body. Then, remembering the advice he had been given by his friend Clay Summer, he forced himself to take another sip of the cold beer. "Don't take on either one of them bastards when your blood's pumping too fast," Summer had cautioned. "Just keep calm and take care of your business in a business manner. Otherwise, you're liable to get your ass killed."

As Tripp and his friend began to walk toward the bar, Kirb held his right hand between his legs flexing his fingers. He lifted the beer with his left hand and took a sip, then held the mug in front of his face as the two men took stools directly across the bar from him. Then, easing his right hand along his leg, he brought it to rest against the butt of his gun, for he and his quarry were now sitting face-to-face. Neither of the men gave him more than a brief glance however, then went about ordering their drinks.

Still holding the mug in front of his face, Kirb knew that when the bartender delivered the drinks he would momentarily block Tripp's view of the opposite side of the bar and, in essence, Renfro himself. The skinny man made the delivery a few moments later, and Renfro seized his chance. He slid off the stool and moved toward the front of the building casually, then circled around the front of the bar. Then, just as the bartender walked away, Kirb suddenly appeared behind the two drinkers. He patted Tripp's friend on the shoulder, then backed off. "You'd better move outta the way, fellow," he said sternly. "I've got some mighty serious business with your buddy."

The man suddenly stiffened, then eased himself off the stool backward. And though he wore a six-gun on his hip, he raised his hands above his shoulders very quickly. "I don't know who you are," he said, without turning his head, "but I sure ain't got no beef with you." He took three quick steps sideways. "Just leave me out of it."

With his feet spread apart and his body bent slightly forward, Renfro stood staring at Tripp's back. "Get off that stool and turn around, Tripp!" he said loudly.

Tripp set his drink down and slid off the stool, then slowly turned around to face him. "I ain't done nothing," he said.

Renfro ignored the man's statement, then made one of his own, making sure every man in the house heard it. "Listen up, everybody!" he began. "I don't know what name this man's using nowadays, but his real name is Lonny Tripp, and he's wanted in Comanche County for the rape and murder of a young housewife!" Then he lowered his voice and spoke to the wanted man again. "That woman was my wife, Tripp, and I'm here to settle up."

Tripp stood looking like a trapped animal for a moment, then made his play. The two men reached for their weapons at exactly the same time. Renfro knew instantly that his opponent's draw had matched his own, for even as he shot Tripp in the mouth, he could see the man's Colt spitting flame. It was only after Kirb heard the slug pass within an inch of his ear, that he knew Tripp had missed. Knowing how close he had come to dying, Renfro stood holding his gun in position for a quick follow-up shot. Tripp had already dropped his own weapon, however. He buckled at the knees and fell to the floor, his mouth open, and his sightless eyes staring at the ceiling.

Renfro stood looking from one of the saloon patrons to the other and did not reholster his weapon. "Would one of you men see if you can get the marshal down here?" he asked.

One of the drinkers at the end of the bar nodded, then slid off his stool and headed for the front door.

The man who had come into the building with Tripp stood looking at the corpse now. "He told all of us down at the ranch that his name was Tony Baxter," he said, then turned away shaking his head. He reclaimed his drink from the bar and emptied the glass in one gulp.

Though he had reholstered his Colt, Renfro was still standing in the aisle when Marshal Farrell pushed his way through the bat wings ten minutes later. He was a big man, maybe six-foot-four, and appeared to weigh about 250 pounds. He walked straight to Renfro, then pointed to the smaller man beside him. "Rufus tells me that you've killed a wanted man," he said. "Is that right?"

Kirb nodded. "Yes, sir," he said. Handing over one of the dodgers, he added, "He raped and killed my wife back in January."

The lawman leaned closer to the lamp and studied the document for a while, then thumped it with a forefinger. "I see that Sheriff Rudolph Miller is one of the men who signed this thing," he said. "I've known him for a long time, and I happen to know that he don't put his name on just anything." He pointed toward the corpse. "If Dolph says that jasper was guilty, you can just about take it to the bank."

Renfro nodded, and said nothing.

The marshal stood over the dead man and studied his facial features for a few moments. "He's got the looks to match one of the men on this dodger, all right," he said to Kirb. "You got any more proof that he's the man?"

Renfro shook his head, "No proof," he said, "but that's Lonny Tripp for sure. I didn't actually need to read that description 'cause I'd already seen him in person up in Comanche."

"Oh," the marshal said. He was quiet for a moment, then asked, "Did he put up a fight?"

"Yes, sir," Renfro said. "He came close to winning it too."

The lawman glanced from Kirb to the corpse a few times, then asked, "You gonna try to take the body all the way to Comanche in this kind of weather?"

"No, sir," Renfro answered. "I'll pay the undertaker to bury him right here, and I also intend to pay the bartender for the mess I made."

"You do that," the marshal said. "Give Sandy a coupla bucks for having to clean up the floor, and I reckon the burial's gonna cost about twenty dollars. You can just give that to me, and I'll pass it on to the undertaker."

Renfro laid two dollars on the bar, then handed the lawman a double eagle. "Could I get you to write me something saying that Tripp's no longer among the living, Marshal?" he asked.

"You ain't gonna need that. Just tell Sheriff Miller to get in touch with me if he needs anything more'n your word." He shoved the double eagle into his pocket, then left the building without looking back.

Renfro stood in his tracks till after the lawman passed through the bat wings. Then, walking sideways and watching every man in the room, he too disappeared through the doorway. When he stepped onto the board-walk he could see that the livery stable was still open. A burning lantern illuminated the open doorway, and he could see movement through the office window. He headed for the stable at a fast walk. He intended to re-trieve his animals and put some distance between himself and the town of Broken Arrow.

Twenty minutes later, he dismounted and tied up at

the boardinghouse. He walked down the hall and retrieved his rifle and his saddlebags, then stopped at Bulah's
office. When the lady answered his knock, he handed her
a dollar, then walked from the building without a word.
He mounted and continued west for a few hundred yards,
then circled the town and headed east. He should make it
back to the Atascosa River before daybreak.

27

★

Renfro reached the Atascosa River several hours before daybreak and set up camp and picketed his animals by the dim light of a quarter moon. He had the campground to himself this time and chose the same campsite he had used on his way to Broken Arrow. He made no effort to build a fire or even search for fuel but spread his bedroll in the same cluster of bushes. With his Henry and his Colt lying within inches of his right hand, he was asleep almost immediately, for he was a tired man.

When he opened his eyes again well after daybreak, the first thing he saw was the large mass of dark clouds hanging overhead. No doubt about it, he was thinking as he pulled on his boots, he must make other arrangements before everything he had got drenched. He got to his feet quickly and began to search for fuel. He soon had several clumps of dead grass and an armload of deadwood, all of which he placed on the ground beside some pecan saplings. He dragged his tarpaulin over and, within minutes, had it securely tied to four of the young trees about six feet above the ground. He deliberately tied the back side of the tarp a few inches lower so the rainwater would drain off quickly.

Then the thunder and lightning began, and the cloud-burst was not far behind. Renfro sat watching unconcern-edly as the water rolled off the lower edge of his tarp. He knew that the area needed the moisture, and the rain both-ered him not in the least. His bedroll, his pack, and his guns were all dry, and he had enough food on hand to last for several days. "Let it rain," he said aloud, then went about kindling a fire.

By the time he had eaten a breakfast of smoked ham, cheese, and crackers, and drunk his second cup of coffee, he was convinced that it was going to be wet for a while. The downpour was now over, and the light, steady drizzle that was treasured by farmers and ranchers had begun. He put on his slicker and tied the hood under his chin, then picked up his pot and his canteens and headed to the river for water.

When he returned, he dropped a few handfuls of kid-ney beans into the pot and set it in the fire, then went off in search of more fuel. The fact that it was wet meant little, for he would simply bank it around his fire and let the heat dry it out. When he had gathered several arm-loads of deadwood and piled it under the tarp, he turned his attention to his animals.

Both the saddler and the mule nickered when he ap-proached them, probably because they had eaten every-thing within reach and sensed that he might be about to move them to new grass. He did move them to better pickings, but not until he had first led them to the river for water. He staked the animals out on the best grass he could find, then walked back to his fire.

Though the beans were already simmering, he pushed

the pot farther up on the coals and added another stick
of wood to the fire. His breakfast this morning had been
far from the biggest meal he had ever eaten, and he knew
that he would be ready again as soon as the beans were.
He drank the last cup of coffee in his pot without bothering to reheat it, then dashed the grounds into the bushes.

Then, for the third time this morning, he went about
getting the water off the roof. Tied at the four corners as
the tarpaulin was, it soon sagged in the middle under the
weight of the rain. Starting on the uphill side, Renfro
spread his arms and pushed upward on the tarp, then
gradually made his way downhill, rolling the accumulated
pool of water off on the downhill side. The action had
been necessary twice during the heavy downpour, but now
that the torrent had turned into a drizzle, once every few
hours would be often enough.

He refilled his coffeepot at the river and returned to
the fire, then doffed his oilskin slicker and shook off the
water. It had come in handy, all right, for although his
pants were wet from the knees down, the waterproof gar-
ment had kept his head and the upper portion of his body
dry. He gave it a final shake, then folded it and laid it on
the ground beside his pack.

He spent the remainder of the day underneath the tarpaulin, even stretching out on his bedroll and dozing off
a few times. And though there were no more heavy down-
pours, the slow drizzle never let up for a moment. He ate
ham, beans, and crackers at midmorning, then again for
an early supper. As he sat sipping coffee an hour before
sunset, a familiar wagon came into view from the east.
Clint Barnes and his son, Hansel, sat on the seat. Barnes
drove the vehicle off the road and selected the same campsite he had used two nights ago. Both man and boy waved
to Renfro, then jumped to the ground and went about

their chores. He returned their greeting, then put on another pot of coffee.

He sat watching quietly till they had picketed their mules and walked back to their wagon, then he called out to them, "Building a cook fire ain't gonna be easy unless you've got some dry kindling in the wagon," he said. "I've got plenty of ham and beans here, if you want some."

"I reckon we've got plenty to eat this time," Barnes said. "The wife boxed us up a bunch of precooked stuff before we left home." He stood thoughtful for a moment, then added, "Now, if you've got plenty of hot coffee, I guess we could use a little of that."

"I'll have a new pot in about five minutes," Kirb said. "Just bring your cups and come on up anytime you're ready."

Kirb allowed the coffee to boil for about one minute, then pulled it off the fire. He had just poured a little cold water in the pot to settle the grounds, when Barnes and his son walked under the tarp, each of them holding a tin plate filled with beef and biscuits. "I see you didn't go down to the CT Ranch," Barnes said, "so you must've changed your mind."

Kirb nodded. "Thought I'd look around a little more," he said. The mere fact that Barnes had not mentioned it immediately told Renfro that, even though the man had spent the night in Broken Arrow, he had left this morning before word of the shooting in Hopp Ellis's watering hole circulated around town. Kirb smiled at the thought, then pointed to the coffeepot. "That thing's hot and it's full. You two drink all you want."

Both Barnes and his son filled their cups, then sat down on the ground. The man took a sip of his coffee, then spoke over a mouthful of food. "The wife saw to it that we ain't gonna be running outta food on this trip," he said, "but starting a fire of our own with wet kindling wouldna been no easy task. We sure appreciate this coffee." He took another sip, then added, "By the way, you never did tell us your name."

"I'm Bill Alexander."

"Well, thank you a lot, Mr. Alexander." He motioned to the tarp overhead. "It looks like you've sorta built yourself a little homestead. A man could live here all summer if he had to; wouldn't have no problems a-tall till cold weather set in. Now that north wind would cut him in two in the wintertime."

"You're right about that," Kirb said. He chuckled softly. "I don't expect to be here when it turns cold though."

"No," Barnes said. "Of course not."

The camp suddenly grew quiet, and darkness had already closed in by the time the visitors finished eating. Barnes handed his empty plate to his son, then spoke to the youngster. "You want another cup of coffee, Hansel?"

"Yes, sir," the boy answered, then helped himself to the pot.

Barnes turned to Renfro, saying, "I usually let him have two cups if he wants 'em, but I'm scared any more'n that'll stunt his growth. I don't know how true it is, but I've heard that if a boy drinks too much coffee while he's growing up, it'll knock three or four inches off of how tall he turns out to be. You ever heard anybody say that, Mr. Alexander?"

Kirb shook his head. "Not that I remember," he said. He poured his own cup about half full of coffee, then changed the subject. "I guess you're headed back to Floresville for another load of cement, huh?"

Barnes nodded. "Going back for another one. If it keeps on raining, we'll probably have to wrap the sacks with oilskin. The wagon don't leak, but a whole lot of moisture in the air sometimes plays hell with cement."

"I would imagine," Renfro said. He took a sip of coffee, then sat quietly for a few minutes. "Do you know very much about the Star Ranch, Clint?" he asked finally.

Barnes smiled. "I ain't never been out there, but I certainly know about it," he said. "Everybody in this county over six years old knows about the Star Ranch. You trying to find out something in particular?"

Kirb shrugged. "It's just that I've been hearing about it a lot lately," he said, "and it got me to wondering. How big is the ranch? How many cattle do they run? What kind of fellow is Hanson Bray?"

"I don't rightly know how big it is," Barnes said, "and neither do I know how many cattle they run. It's an awful big spread, though, and you can bet your butt that they run more cows than you can shake a stick at. I'd say the figure runs into the thousands 'cause I know for sure that they send two or three trail herds north to the rails every year. It's grown into such a big operation that folks around here don't call it the Star Ranch anymore. Even the newspapers have started calling it the Bray Cattle Company.

"Now, I never saw Hanson Bray but one time; shook hands with him one day when I was up in Pleasanton on a bridge-building job. He seemed like a nice enough fellow, but he was mighty closemouthed. Didn't say more'n three words to me and even looked over my shoulder all the time he was shaking my hand. At the time, I figured it was just 'cause he was such a busy man, but I've heard since that he ain't got much to say to nobody. So I really can't tell you what kind of fellow he is. I've been hearing his name about half of my life though, and I ain't never heard nothing bad about him."

Renfro sat for a few moments digesting the information, then spoke again. "I don't know exactly where the ranch is," he said. "What's the best way to get there from here?"

Barnes pointed north. "Everything north of Pleasanton and west of the river is the Star Ranch, so all you gotta do is ride in that direction about six miles. Don't cross the river, now, just ride up the west bank. You'll run into a little road about a mile up yonder, and it'll take you right into Pleasanton. Like I said, anywhere you go north of town and west of the river, you're gonna be on Bray's property."

Renfro nodded. "Thank you, Clint. I suppose I might be having a talk with Mr. Bray sooner or later." He pointed to the pile of deadwood and kindling. "Take some of that with you so you'll be able to start a fire in the morning. I've got more than I need anyway."

"We appreciate it, Mr. Alexander," Barnes said. "You're a thoughtful man." He picked up several sticks of wood while Hansel gathered an armload of bark and dead grass, then they headed for their wagon.

Renfro smothered his fire in its own ashes. When he lay down on his bedroll the only sounds he could hear were those of tree frogs and the light rain falling on his canvas roof. Though his eyes were a long time in closing, he finally got a good night's sleep.

When he awoke next morning the rain had let up for the moment, and Clint Barnes and his son were preparing breakfast beside their wagon. Hansel had no doubt brought their livestock in at daybreak, for all four of the mules were tied to wagon wheels and waiting to be harnessed.

Kirb pulled on his boots and rolled the water off the sagging tarp once again, then walked up the slope and moved his animals to new grass. He would not lead them to the river just yet, for he seriously doubted that either of them would drink. Eating the wet grass all night had probably supplied them with as much water as they needed for the time being.

As Kirb returned to his camp, Barnes straightened up from his cook fire and waved. Renfro nodded a greeting of his own, then bent over and stepped under his canvas roof. Moments later, he set about kindling a fire. He would eat more ham and beans for breakfast, and wash it down with coffee left over from last night.

Half an hour later, he sat eating and watching the Barnes's harness and hitch up the four-mule team. Paying close attention to young Hansel's actions, Renfro was reminded of his own early days on a Tennessee farm. The boy knew exactly what he was doing, and there was no wasted motion whatever. As was the case with Kirb Renfro, Hansel Barnes had been taught well. Working as a team, father and son did the job and climbed to the wagon seat in less than ten minutes. Both waved good-bye to Renfro; then the vehicle took to the road and forded the river.

The rain ceased as the morning wore on, and the sun occasionally peeked out from behind the clouds for a few minutes. In late afternoon, Kirb ate the last of his beans and washed up his cooking and eating utensils. Deciding that the rain was gone for good, he took down the tarpaulin and returned it to his pack. Then he watered his animals and led them into camp, for he had suddenly decided to spend the coming night in Pleasanton.

Though he believed that his heavy beard might fool Pollard at a distance, Renfro was doubtful that the same would be true up close. Although neither Tripp nor Stovall had been able to recognize him, deceiving Pollard would be another matter entirely. The day the two men fought in Comanche they had at times been close enough to smell each other's breath, and Pollard had no doubt looked Kirb over well. It was highly possible that, beard or no beard, the man would recognize him instantly. The odds were simply too great to chance it, Renfro had decided. He would ride into Pleasanton well after dark, then move about the town like a thief in the night.

Kirb wiped the backs of his animals dry with a dirty shirt, then saddled the black and buckled the packsaddle on the mule. He glanced at his watch to see that it was five o'clock, then mounted and headed upriver. Knowing that there were at least three hours of daylight left, he held the saddler to a slow walk. The fact that he would reach Pleasanton long before dark might work to his advantage, he was thinking, for it would give him a chance to sit back and look the town over from a distance.

A mile from his campsite, he came to the road Clint Barnes had described. Coming in from the west and making a sharp turn to the north just before reaching the river, the deep-rutted trail had obviously been around for a very long time, and no doubt led straight to Pleasanton. Kirb guided the black onto the grass between the ruts, then continued on his way.

Two hours later, with the sun hanging in the treetops to the west, he left the road at the top of a rise and pulled up between two large oaks. Pleasanton lay about a quarter mile down the slope, and from this position he had a good view of the settlement. Knowing that he would stay where he was till nightfall, he sat his saddle gazing toward town and trying to decipher the lay of things.

One thing he noticed right away was that, unlike other towns, most of which gradually fell off to a bunch of widely scattered buildings on all sides, Pleasanton ended where it ended, looking somewhat like something that had been chopped off in the middle. The boardwalk played out at the last building, and the livery barn and corral appeared to be about forty yards east of there.

Although his well-rested saddler was anxious to be on the move and kept prancing and slinging his head, the next hour passed quickly for Kirb, for he had also had plenty of rest. As the sun disappeared and darkness closed in, he took a drink from one of his canteens, then kneed the black onto the road again. Continuing at a walking gait, he approached the livery stable from the rear, then rode around the side of the building and through its lighted doorway. Failing to see an attendant, he cupped his hands and called down the long row of stalls. "Anybody home?"

"I'll be there in a minute!" a deep voice shouted from somewhere near the corral. Kirb dismounted and stood waiting. Moments later, a fat, red-faced man who appeared to be in his late thirties walked down the hall. "I was just doing a few last-minute things back there at the corral," he said, wiping his hands on his pant legs. "Didn't think I was gonna have any more business today, so I was about ready to close up."

"I'm glad you didn't do it before I got here," Kirb said. He laid his saddlebags across his shoulder and unsheathed his rifle, then handed over the reins. "Grain 'em and hay 'em good, and I'd sure appreciate it if you'd lock my pack up in your office."

The man nodded, "Consider it done," he said. He unsaddled the black and laid the saddle across a wooden rack, then stood looking his customer over for a few moments, his eyes coming to rest on the holstered Colt hanging on Kirb's hip. "I open up about daylight every morning," he said finally, "but if you happen to need your animals in the middle of the night, just pound on that southwest wall till you get an answer. I sleep over there in the back of the office."

"Thank you," Renfro said, "I'll remember that." He

glanced through the open doorway and up the street, then turned back to the hostler. "How many hotels are in this town?" he asked.

"Two," the man answered quickly. "About all of the working men and ranch hands stay at the Stockman, and men of better means usually put up at the Ripley. They're right across the street from each other at the west end of town, so you can take your pick when you get there."

Renfro thanked the man, then left the building. Noticing that practically all of the lighted businesses and doorways were on the north side, he chose the south side of the street and headed west. After walking a little more than two blocks, he was standing in front of the Ripley Hotel.

Although one glance at the fancy establishment convinced him that he was about to pay an extravagant price for a night's lodging, he nonetheless stepped into the carpeted lobby. The hostler had said that the ranch hands stayed across the street, and Renfro was willing to pay whatever was necessary in order to avoid them. He walked to the counter, where he was greeted with a warm smile by a clerk who appeared to be scarcely out of his teens. "Good evening, sir," the young man said, "and thank you for choosing the Ripley. May I help you?"

Kirb nodded. "I'll take an upstairs room if you have one vacant," he said.

"Yes, sir," the clerk said. "Our rooms rent for two-fifty a night, three and a quarter if you want a bath."

Kirb laid $2.50 on the counter. "I'll think about the bath later," he said.

The clerk put the money in a drawer, then slid a key and an open book across the counter. "Here's your key, sir," he said. "Sign the register, please."

Renfro wrote Bill Alexander in the middle of the page, then dropped the key into his pocket and headed for the staircase. Moments later, he let himself into the fancy room and relocked the door.

28

Renfro raised the windows and tied back the curtains, then sat down on the edge of the bed, thinking. He had noticed two saloons between the livery stable and the hotel, both of them on the opposite side of the street. He had no doubt that his quarry patronized both places, and he would be keeping a close watch on their hitching rails for horses with a four-pointed star on their hips.

Unlike Stovall, and possibly Tripp, Pollard had probably not even attempted to change his name. Since he was working for his kin, and had become acquainted with no telling how many people in Pleasanton over the years, suddenly taking on a new name would have been next to impossible. Kirb sat shaking his head at the thought. Nope, he said to himself, a man who was already well known simply could not pull it off. Whether at work or at play, Pat Pollard would be using his true name.

With that fact in mind, Renfro was trying to figure out a way to spot the man before he himself was seen.

Although it was possible that Pollard would be slow to recognize him because of the heavy beard, Kirb was unwilling to bet his life on it. He must move about carefully and keep a sharp lookout, for he was playing a deadly game.

His first chore would be to establish the fact that his quarry was indeed in the vicinity, then he would devote as much time as was necessary to figuring out a way to make a meeting happen. Riding out to the Star Ranch was out of the question, as was discussing his mission with anyone who lived or worked there. "Take your time and don't rush into anything," Clay Summer had cautioned Kirb the morning he left home. "Just remember, the cards'll always start falling in your favor if you wait long enough." Renfro could wait. Though he wanted Pat Pollard badly, he could wait. He could wait till hell froze over.

He got to his feet and washed his face and hands in the wash pan, then dried his beard on the fluffy towel. He had noticed that the longer the thicket grew, the less it itched, and he had not been bothered by it much lately. He was hardly ready to put his razor aside permanently, however. The beard would be gone soon after the manhunt was over.

He slid his rifle and his saddlebags under the bed, then turned down the wick of the coal-oil lamp. A moment later, he stepped into the hall and locked his door from the outside, then headed for the stairway. The desk clerk was nowhere in sight when Kirb reached the lobby, which was just as well. Renfro wanted to have a talk with the young man but not just yet. He walked through the doorway and turned east when he hit the boardwalk.

Both of the saloons he had seen earlier were between the Ripley Hotel and the livery stable, on the opposite side of the street. Renfro stepped out of the light quickly, then moved under the awning of a hardware store. He stood watching the comings and goings at the Stockman Hotel for several minutes. When he saw nothing that held his interest, he began to walk east, staying close to the front of the dark buildings and avoiding the light that shone from some of the doorways across the street.

When he was directly across the street from the first saloon, he moved into the dark recess at the front of a clothing store. Knowing that he could not be seen from any direction, he stood watching the place for a while. Though he could not read the name of the establishment, it was by far the smallest of the two watering holes. There were five horses at its hitching rails, but he could read none of the brands. After a few minutes, when no one had left or entered the building, he moved on down the street.

The second saloon was much larger, and he counted nine horses. The place was identified by a wooden sign illuminated by two lanterns. NIGHT OWL SALOON it read in foot-high leters, then boasted that a man named Joe Don Strickland was the proprietor. As before, Renfro moved under an awning and stood watching. Ten minutes later, after having seen no activity whatever, he left the boardwalk and stepped into the street.

Careful to avoid the streaks of light shining through the windows and open doorways, he inspected the horses at the hitching rail quickly, then kept walking till he reached the rails at the smaller saloon. The same five an-imals were still there, and one, a small roan, had a four-point star on its hip. Kirb moved back to the south side of the street quickly. He eased into the dark recess in front of the clothing store again, then staked out the hitching rail. He might be here all night, he was thinking, but he was not going anywhere till he saw who claimed that roan.

He moved his Colt up and down in its holster a few

times, then leaned back against the door frame. He watched both saloons closely, and although several men walked or staggered from one building to the other during the next hour, no one approached the hitching rail.

A few minutes later, the bat-wing doors of the smaller saloon flew open. Kirb suddenly stiffened, then stood watching as a man who was six inches shorter and fifty pounds lighter than Pollard mounted the little roan and rode up the street at a slow walk. "Damn," Renfro said softly, then walked back to the hotel.

The desk clerk was back on his stool now. Renfro walked across the lobby and leaned against the counter. "I just went out for a walk," he said. "A fellow can't see much at night though."

The young man smiled. "You won't see much in the daytime either," he said, "because there's really nothing to see around here. It's kind of pretty out by the river, but otherwise this is just plain old ranching country."

"I like to look at ranching country," Kirb said, offering a smile of his own. "Do you have any idea how many ranches there are in this area?"

"Lord, no," the clerk said quickly. "There're a whole bunch of them though. I do know that the Bray Cattle Company is the biggest spread in Atascosa County, and it's located right here at Pleasanton. Their headquarters are probably no more than seven miles from here."

"Are you talking about the Star Ranch?" Kirb asked.

"Well, yes," the clerk said. "Not many folks call it that anymore though, and I doubt that Mr. Bray does. I know it don't appear on his stationery or his business card. When he throws a big party he usually does it right here at the Ripley, rents several rooms and feeds dozens of people in the restaurant. Of course, he just signs his name and goes his way, and the hotel bills him later. After his last party, the job of figuring up the cost and making out the bill fell to me, and I remember my boss telling me to send the statement to the Bray Cattle Company. After that, I just quit calling it the Star Ranch."

Kirb nodded. "I see," he said. He was quiet for a few moments, then asked, "Do you happen to know how many men Bray keeps on his payroll?"

"No," the young man answered. He chuckled loudly, then added, "I wouldn't have any idea, but I'd bet a dollar that Marshal Youngblood knows. He's the one who has to put their rowdy asses in jail just about every week."

"Rough bunch, huh?"

The clerk shrugged. "It could be that they just start thinking they're rough after they get a snootful," he said. "Rough or not, I believe most of them have a hard time holding their liquor." He paused for a few seconds, then continued, "I don't know any of them personally. When they need a hotel room they go to roost across the street, because it's a lot cheaper. It's the same with our restaurant, ranch hands simply cannot afford to eat here.

"I know they do raise hell in the saloons, though, especially the Night Owl. I've heard that Joe Don Strickland lets them get away with anything as long as they don't tear the place apart. Marshal Youngblood usually drags two or three of them off to jail every weekend for fighting. Got one man twice on the same day a while back. Youngblood wouldn't let him pay a fine the last time he got him; kept his ass in jail for nearly a week."

"Is he one of Bray's hands?" Kirb asked.

"Sure, he works for Bray, but that don't cut no ice with the old man. People say he wouldn't bail his own mother out of jail. I've heard it said that the ranch hands keep a special pot that they pay each other's fines out of. Maybe they take up a collection or something. Anyway, the man who laid in that hot jail over there for six days not only worked for Bray, he was kinfolks, but the old man never lifted a finger to get him out."

Renfro drummed his fingers on the counter. "Maybe Bray was trying to teach him a lesson," he said after a while.

The young man shook his head several times. "I don't know for sure that the old man could have done anything about it anyway, because Marshal Youngblood was the one who was teaching him a lesson. The marshal started having trouble with that man right after he showed up around here back in the winter. Big fellow, they say, must be about your size. He's got hair the color of a beet, but they say everybody who calls him Red gets punched in the mouth."

Renfro was thoughtful for a moment, then went fishing again. "Does he tell 'em what name he prefers to hear after he gets through beating 'em up?"

The clerk nodded. "Oh, yes," he said. "The local newspaper ran an article about it the week he was in jail. According to the paper, he announces his name and makes the man repeat it, then makes him spell it."

Kirb smiled. "His name must be hard to pronounce, then."

"Hell, no," the young man said. "His name is Pat Pollard. Anything hard about that?"

"No," Kirb answered, shaking his head. "I reckon it's about as simple as they get. I guess Pollard's been giving this town a wide berth since the marshal won't let him pay his way out of jail anymore."

"Guess again," the clerk said. "He goes in both of those saloons any old time he takes a notion, and I'll guarantee you that he'll be in the Night Owl this coming weekend. I haven't heard of him punching anybody lately, but he will. Marshal Youngblood says he's a natural-born bully."

Kirb stood quietly for a few moments, then changed the subject. "What time does the restaurant open in the morning?" he asked.

"Six o'clock," the clerk answered. "Six in the morning till nine at night."

"Are they pretty busy at breakfast?"

The clerk shook his head, smiling broadly. "They're never busy except when somebody like Mr. Bray throws a big party. The company built the restaurant for the convenience of the hotel patrons, and the food is simply too expensive for ordinary ranch hands."

Renfro liked what he was hearing. He had not really been concerned about how busy the eating establishment might be, and the fact that their prices were high enough to discourage ranch hands suited him just fine. The only ranch hand he wanted to see was Pat Pollard, and he himself would choose the time and the place. He stood quietly for a few moments longer, then spoke to the young man again. "I'm gonna call it a day," he said. "I've enjoyed the conversation and good night to you." He turned toward the staircase and took the steps two at a time.

He lay on his bed till late in the night, thinking of the things he had learned. He had especially been happy to hear that Hanson Bray was a righteous man who tolerated no wrongdoing, for he had been concerned that he might have to fight the whole Star Ranch crew. After listening to the clerk, he had begun to doubt that Pat Pollard had many friends among the ranch hands, and there was no question whatever about how the local marshal felt about him.

Renfro had no intention of talking with Marshal Youngblood until after he had located his quarry and taken care of business. One glance at the dodger would send the lawman out to the Star Ranch to arrest Pollard, and Kirb did not want him in jail; he wanted him in the graveyard. He had already decided that, once he came face to face with Pollard, the man would get exactly the same chance he had given Ellie.

The clerk had guaranteed Kirb that Pollard would be in the Night Owl during the coming weekend. Tomorrow would be Friday, so Renfro would start keeping an eye on both watering holes about noon. If he had no luck, he would increase his vigil on Saturday. Judging from the things he had been told, getting drunk on Saturday was almost a ritual with Pollard. Oliver Blanding had said as much, and so had the desk clerk downstairs.

Determined to make Pollard's next drunk his last, Kirb lay awake for a long time trying to figure out how the situation was likely to unfold, and what he could do to make sure the man did not get the upper hand. After a while he managed to push those thoughts out of his mind. He would do whatever he had to do when the time came and depend on his quick reflexes to see him through. He fluffed up his pillow and turned on his side, then drifted off into a sound sleep.

He awoke at daybreak, but made no effort to get out of bed. He lay with his arms under his head for almost an hour before swinging his legs over the side and slipping on his pants. He walked to the window and checked out the weather, then sat down and pulled on his boots. He washed his face and combed his hair with his fingers, then put on his hat and stepped out into the hall. Moments later, he was standing inside the front door of the hotel restaurant.

Though there were several vacant stools at the counter, he walked on by, for he believed that he would be too noticable there. He walked past a couple seated in the center of the room, then pulled out a table and sat down with his back to the wall. Expensively dressed and gray at the temples, the man at the nearby table nodded a greeting, which Kirb acknowledged. The woman, wearing a big hat and an abundance of paint and powder, smiled flirtatiously and lifted her hand. Renfro nodded, then accepted the bill of fare from the waiter standing beside him. "Bring me four scrambled eggs and whatever kind of meat you've got," he said without glancing at the menu.

The middle-aged man set a cup of steaming coffee at Renfro's elbow. "What kind of meat do you want, sir?"

Kirb offered a big smile. "You got pork sausage?"

"Yes, sir. It was made yesterday, and it's been on ice ever since."

Kirb nodded. "That sounds mighty good to me," he said. "Bring me a double order." The waiter nodded, then picked up the menu and headed for the kitchen.

Though the breakfast was by no means the quickest that Kirb had ever been served, it might have been the best. The sausage was seasoned to perfection, and the eggs were soft and fluffy. The two large, buttered biscuits were still hot, and the platter contained two slices of cheese and a scoop of grape jelly. By the time the waiter returned with another cup of coffee, Kirb had already sampled the food. "Give my compliments to the cook," he said. "He knows exactly how breakfast oughtta taste."

The waiter smiled. "Mrs. Whitehead does the cooking," he said. "She started the day the restaurant opened, and she's been bossing the kitchen ever since."

Kirb washed a mouthful of food down with coffee. "Well, they better keep letting her do it, 'cause eating just don't get no better than this."

The man stood quietly for a moment, then chuckled as he turned to leave. "I don't think she's worried about losing her job, sir," he said over his shoulder. "The White-head family owns the hotel and the restaurant both."

"I see," Kirb said, before he noticed that the waiter was already out of earshot.

After finishing off his meal and leaving a dime under his plate, Renfro was up from the table quickly. He paid for his food and stepped back into the hotel lobby, notic-ing that a man old enough to be his grandfather was now seated on the stool behind the counter. He nodded to the man and said nothing, then climbed the staircase and walked down the hallway to his room. Then, deciding that he would lie down on his bed and think for a while, he dozed off quickly and slept away the entire morning.

29

Shortly after noon, Renfro ate a piece of pie and drank a cup of coffee in the hotel restaurant, then stepped out on the boardwalk. He stood leaning against the building for a few moments, then crossed the street and retraced his footsteps of the night before. The first saloon had two horses at its hitching rail, but neither wore the Star brand. Nor did any of the six animals tied outside the Night Owl. It was simply too early in the day for ranch hands to be carousing. After inspecting the brands, which he could easily read from across the street, he walked on to the livery stable.

The red-faced liveryman was standing in the open-sided blacksmith shop, hammering on a red-hot horseshoe. Laying his hammer aside, he locked his tongs on the shoe and submerged it in a trough of water, creating a cloud of steam and a loud, hissing sound. Then he turned to face Renfro. "I reckon you've come after your animals," he said, "and you got here at the right time."

He pointed to the horseshoe lying on the bench cooling. "I ain't gonna use them things till tomorrow morning, but I thought I'd shape 'em and temper 'em while I had the time. That one there's the last of the set."

Kirb shook his head. "I don't need the animals yet," he said. "I just happened to be on this end of town and decided to stop by to see you. Don't let me interrupt anything."

The fat man chuckled, making his belly shake like a bowl of jelly. "I don't let nobody interrupt my work," he said, his voice sounding even deeper than Kirb remembered. "When I've got something to do, I just go ahead and do it. If a friend happens to be hanging around, he usually leaves after he gets tired of talking to himself."

Kirb smiled. "I would think so," he said, then followed the liveryman to his office. He accepted the cane-bottom chair he was offered, then seated himself just inside the door. "It looks to me like you've got a mighty good layout here," he said. "Does your business pick up on weekends," he asked.

The man nodded. "It picks up a whole bunch," he answered. "It looks like today's gonna be kinda slow for a Friday, but I'll be busier'n a cat covering up shit tomorrow. I ain't had a slow Saturday since I opened this place up five years ago."

"Does most of your business come from the ranch hands?"

The hostler was thoughtful for a moment. "Well, it comes from the ranches," he said finally, "but not necessarily from the ranch hands. The majority of them spend their money for liquor and leave their horses tied up at the hitching rails all day. It ain't unusual at all to see the same animals standing in front of the Dragon or the Night Owl till closing time on Saturday night."

"The Dragon," Kirb repeated. "Is that the name of the saloon just west of the Night Owl?"

"That's it," the liveryman said. "Somebody probably took their sign with 'em to build a fire."

"Might have," Kirb said. He sat quietly for a moment, then suddenly shoved his right hand toward the man, saying, "By the way, my name's Bill Alexander."

"I'm Bert Caldwell," the hostler said, gripping Kirb's hand firmly. "Pardon me for not telling you that before, but it's been my experience that most men ain't much interested in names."

"You might be right, Bert," Kirb said, "but I always like to know who I'm talking to."

"It's the same with me," Caldwell said, "but it pays not to ask questions in my business. I've learned that if a man don't tell me who he is, it usually means he don't want me to know." He fidgeted in his chair and crossed one leg over the other, then continued to talk. "Take that fellow, Pollard, who works out at Hanson Bray's spread. I'll bet you he's been in here twenty-five times, and he ain't told me what his name was to this day. Only way I ever did learn it was by reading it in the newspaper.

"Marshal Youngblood's locked him up several times, and kept him for nearly a week the last time. According to the paper, he likes to beat people up, and that's why the marshal's always keeping an eye on him. The day Pollard got out of jail and came in here after his horse, he acted like he was gonna jump on me when I mentioned the newspaper article to him. I don't want nothing else to do with that man, and I'll guarantee you that I'll keep my mouth shut when he's around."

"Sometimes it pays to keep quiet," Renfro said. "The less a man says, the fewer words he might have to eat." He stretched his arms over his head, then got to his feet.

"You say you kept Pollard's mount while he was in jail, Bert. Was it one of Hanson Bray's horses?"

Caldwell shook his head. "I ain't never seen him riding a horse with the Star brand," he said. "I guess he rides one of 'em when he's out there at work, but when he comes to town he's always on his personal mount, a big chestnut with a flying W on its hip. I don't know whose brand that is, but it sure don't belong to nobody around here."

Renfro nodded, and headed for the door. "I'm gonna walk around town a little more," he said. "I've enjoyed talking with you, and I'll see you again when I need my animals."

"All right," Caldwell said. "They'll be here, and they'll be well-rested and well-fed."

Just beyond the doorway, Renfro headed north and walked at a fast pace for a few moments, then turned into the alley behind the commercial buildings on the north side of the street. He not only wanted to avoid a face-to-face meeting with any of the men wandering up and down the street, he also wanted to know the lay of the land in back of the buildings, especially the area behind the two watering holes. Seeing no one in the alley, he walked west at a casual gait.

Even though all of the buildings looked different from the rear, identifying the saloons was a simple matter, for their outhouses standing across the alley were clearly marked. Renfro entered the two-seater bearing the "Night Owl" sign, to relieve himself. As he stood reading some of the disgusting stuff on the walls, he could not help wondering if Pat Pollard had written some of it. Maybe, he decided, for the man might very well be the type.

He closed the door and returned to the alley, then suddenly stopped in his tracks. Turning around slowly, he stood staring at the small building he had just left. Hell, that's it, he said to himself: the outhouse. How many times would a man have to relieve himself during an afternoon and night of drinking? Maybe a dozen times if he was a beer drinker, and at least half as many if he preferred liquor.

It took Kirb less than one second to reach his decision: he would not meet his quarry in the Night Owl after all, but behind it. Once he spotted Pollard's chestnut at the hitching rail, he would simply head for the alley behind the saloon and wait him out. And he had already decided where he would do his waiting. A few yards east of the Night Owl's back door were two stacks of firewood, each of them at least a dozen feet long and almost as tall as a man's head. Taking up a position between them would give him a clear view of both outhouses, and he himself would be completely out of sight when he moved back against the wall. No matter which one of the buildings Pollard decided to use, Renfro could simply step out and call his hand.

Kirb thought the matter over for only a moment, then nodded and walked on up the alley. At the end of the block, he rounded the corner and crossed the street, then entered the lobby of the Ripley Hotel. The young clerk was on duty once again, his lips spread wide with a commercial smile. Kirb nodded a greeting, then selected a magazine from a stack of reading material on the counter. He flipped the young man a dime, then headed for the stairway.

He stepped into his room and relocked the door, then walked to the bed and seated himself. He pulled off his boots and fluffed up his pillow, then lay down and began to look through the magazine. There, on the inside of the front cover, was an ad for a Zimmler spring wagon, the very same vehicle that Kirb had often dreamed of owning. Though he firmly believed that he would someday have such a wagon under his shed, he expected it to be a long time in coming, for the price was almost three hundred dollars.

He read several articles on the first few pages of the magazine, then allowed it to fall to the floor, for he was sound asleep. He awoke several times during the afternoon, but did not get up because he had no reason to. After one of his many naps, he picked the magazine up from the floor and read another page, then dozed off again.

When he finally came wide awake he knew that the day was almost gone. He stepped to the window and checked the position of the sun, then returned to the bed and pulled on his boots. The big orange ball was already sinking below the treetops, and would disappear within half an hour. He wanted to eat his supper at sunset, then be on the street again shortly after darkness closed in. He would wait until every store on the south side of the street had closed its doors, then he could move about in the darkness freely, just as he had done the night before.

He ate stuffed pork chops and applesauce in the hotel restaurant, then sat at the table sipping coffee till the night turned pitch dark outside. He left a dime for the waiter and paid the lady at the counter for his food, then walked through the hotel lobby and out onto the boardwalk. He stepped out of the glow of light in front of the hotel, then leaned back against the wall, where he stood looking up and down the street for the next ten minutes.

Finally, seeing no one moving about, he walked on down the boardwalk and renewed his vigil of the saloons from the same recess in which he had stood the night before. Standing in the dark shadows beneath the low-hanging awning, his concealment was complete, and he had no concern whatsoever about being seen by anyone coming from or going into either of the watering holes.

There were seven horses outside the Night Owl, and three tied in front of the Dragon. Two of the animals in front of the Night Owl were chestnuts, and Kirb's curiosity eventually got the best of him. When the moment arrived that he could see nothing moving anywhere in town, he stepped into the street and inspected the brand on every horse at both rails. Neither of the chestnuts wore the Flying W, nor were any of the others sporting a four-point star. Renfro rushed back to the boardwalk and disappeared into the recess, confident that he had been seen by no one.

He continued his vigil for more than two hours, but the only new patrons to visit either of the saloons had arrived on foot. None bore the slightest resemblance to his quarry. Though he was a patient man, he finally decided that continuing the surveillance was pointless, for it was obvious that the Star Ranch hands would not be coming to town tonight. Unable to see the face of his watch he had to guess at the time, but he believed the saloons would be closing in about an hour. Bray's bunch had probably put in a hard day, but according to the hotel clerk, they would certainly be in town tomorrow. Keeping to the shadows, he returned to his hotel room.

Because he had slept so much during the day, he lay in the dark room staring at the ceiling till long past midnight. A thousand thoughts had raced through his mind, and at the moment, he was thinking of the strange turn of events that had taken place over the past year. His beloved Ellie had lost her life to the savage whims of three drunken renegades, and he, Kirb Renfro, had gone on the warpath.

Had the senseless murder of his little partner turned his heart to stone? Maybe, he was thinking. He would probably kill his third man tomorrow, and he even expected to feel good about it afterward. He had felt no remorse whatsoever about hastening the demise of Tripp and Stovall, and he would feel no empathy for Pat Pollard, the man who had no doubt been the instigator of the whole ordeal.

And Kirb intended to accept the bounty that Comanche County had placed on the heads of the murderers, for he felt that Ellie would want him to. He would buy a big headstone for her grave, but most of the money would be spent for brood cows. He could now buy as many breeders as his small ranch would support, and he would eventually be sending a few hundred steers up the trail with the Lazy B herd every spring. He felt that Ellie would be watching it all, too, and he knew that she would be proud. He smiled at the thought, then turned to face the window. Moments later, he was sleeping soundly.

He was awake at daybreak, and a glance at his watch told him that it would be more than half an hour before the hotel restaurant would be open. He dressed himself and pulled on his boots, then stepped over to the table and washed his face and hands. He picked up the towel and stood in front of the mirror for a while drying his beard. "Just one more day," he said to his image. "Some time tomorrow I'll most likely be scraping off this brier patch."

He had breakfast in the hotel restaurant, then returned to his room, where he intended to remain till noon. He knew that both saloons opened for business at ten on Saturday, but doubted that any of the ranch hands would be in town till well after twelve o'clock. They had morning chores to do seven days a week, and the ride into town would take another two hours. He nodded at his thoughts, then reached for his magazine. He would stay right where he was for at least six hours, for he believed it might be as late as two o'clock in the afternoon before Pollard showed up at the Night Owl.

As had been the case the day before, he read a few pages in his magazine, then his eyes closed in sleep.

Even though he slept much of it away, the morning was nonetheless slow in passing. When he finally looked at his watch and saw that it was twelve o'clock, he washed the sleep from his eyes, then began to walk around the room exercising his arms and legs. He stood in front of the mirror practicing his fast draw for half an hour. Then, satisfied that the speed was still there, he combed his hair with his fingers and put on his hat.

When he stepped into the hall he had his Henry in the cradle of his arm and his saddlebags lying across his shoulder, for if he managed to find his quarry and take care of business, he never expected to see this hotel room again. He closed the door and left the key hanging in the lock, then walked down the stairway and crossed the lobby.

He stepped out on the boardwalk, then stood leaning against the building for a few moments. Wagons, buggies, and men on horseback were moving up and down the street, and there was a good deal of foot traffic on the sidewalks. Even from where he stood he could see that the hitching rails in front of the saloons had about as many horses as they could accommodate. There's only one way to find out, he said to himself, then crossed the street and headed for the watering holes at a fast walk.

All of the horses at the Dragon's rail wore brands that Kirb had never seen before, but when he reached the Night Owl, the first animal he saw was a big chestnut with a flying W burned into its hip. Knowing that he had at last found his man, Renfro began to walk even faster now. He turned north at the end of the block, then west when he reached the alley. Seeing no one, he kept walking till he reached the tall ricks of wood, then stepped in between them. He leaned his rifle against the wall of the building, then laid his saddlebags on the ground beside it.

His place of concealment could hardly have been better. If he stood near the front of the ricks he would be in
plain view of anyone going to or coming from either of
the outhouses, but if he moved back near the wall, he
could be seen from neither building. Trusting his ears to
tell him when someone left the rear door of either of the
saloons, he eased himself back against the wall.

His wait was not a long one. One man visited each of
the outhouses during the next few minutes, then the back
door of the Night Owl slammed again. Renfro waited
about three seconds, then moved closer to the front of the
ricks. He had no problem whatsoever recognizing Pat Pollard's back as the man walked across the alley. The gun-
belt buckled around his waist supported a Colt
Peacemaker, and the holster was tied to his right leg with
rawhide. He was probably uncomfortable at the moment,
and Kirb had no intention of giving him a chance to relieve himself. He stepped out into the alley and went into
a crouch. "Hello, Pollard!" he called loudly.

Halting in his tracks, Pollard turned around slowly.
"Who . . . wha . . ."

"My name's Renfro," Kirb interrupted. "I reckon I
don't have to tell you why I'm here." Without another
word he drew his Colt and shot the redhead in the mouth.
Though Kirb's big forty-five had killed the man instantly,
Pollard nonetheless managed to get off a shot of his own,
with the slug going into one of the ricks of firewood.
Dropping his gun between his boots, Pollard leaned forward for just a moment, then appeared to will himself to
fall on his back, his mouth open wide and his glassy eyes
staring into the bright sunshine.

Marshal Youngblood and his deputy had been inside
the Night Owl making their rounds when the shooting
occurred in the alley. The sound of gunshots brought the
two men through the back door quickly. A dark-haired

six-footer, who appeared to be about thirty-five years old, the marshal was followed by several other men who were no doubt Night Owl patrons. Youngblood took a quick look at the corpse, then picked up Pollard's Colt and sniffed the barrel. He tucked the weapon behind his waistband, then walked across the alley to Renfro. "I reckon y'all must've got off one shot apiece," he said. "Is that right?"

Kirb nodded. "Yes, sir," he said.

The lawman glanced at the body again, then looked Renfro squarely in the eye. "Did that scum try to run some kind of shit over you? Is that what brought all this on?"

"He did worse than that, Marshal," Renfro said, handing the lawman one of the dodgers. "He raped and murdered my wife."

Youngblood stood reading the handbill for a few moments, then folded it and shoved it into his pocket. He glanced at the body once more, then spoke to Renfro again. "The folks around here owe you a big debt of gratitude for getting rid of that no-good son of a bitch, so I reckon the town of Pleasanton'll stand the cost of his burial." He stood quietly for a moment, then pointed down the alley to the east. "I already know that you've got a saddler and a pack mule down there at the livery stable. I think the smartest thing you can do right now is to go get 'em and get the hell outta this town."

"Yes, sir," Renfro said quickly. He retrieved his rifle and his saddlebags, then headed east as fast as he could walk. Half an hour later, he led his animals through the wide doorway of the livery stable, then mounted and took the road out of town at a fast trot. He was eager to see his own cabin again, and he had lots of things to tell Ellie.